I0626524

YOU DID WHAT ?

by

Isabella Harron

Copyright © 2023 Isabella Harron
All rights reserved.

No part of this book may be reproduced in any form or by any electronic or mechanical means, including information storage and retrieval systems, without written permission from the author, except for the use of brief quotations in a book review.

This is a product of fiction, any similarities to persons, living or dead or actual events are purely coincidental.

CHAPTER One

Natalee ran her fingers through her short brown wavy hair. With only the mirror as her companion, she hesitated while considering what to wear. Spring had arrived, bringing with it warmer weather. A new light and airy dress captured her full attention when she lifted it higher. And yet light gray trousers with a peach chiffon sleeveless shirt and matching cardigan laid out on her bed caused Natalee to second guess her first choice. Admiring her long, toned, freshly shaved legs, she was pleased by the results of her exercise routine. Discouraged by her pale limbs this early in the season, she chose the trousers. Admiring her narrow waist and hips, she turned to look at her backside.

"At least it is still where it should be." With a giggle, Natalee focused on her breasts in the pale pink push-up bra. "Please just let the girls stay where they are for at least a few more years."

Fear of turning thirty-nine loomed ahead, bringing with it the fear of aging alone. Tilting her head, she applied silver hoops to her ears and a long necklace around her slender neck. She slipped on a thin silver bracelet to her narrow graceful wrist. Picking up her purse and locked the door when her cell phone rang. Seeing her daughter's name flash across the screen, Natalee hesitated as a third ring finished, and with reluctance, she answered the phone.

"Hello?"

"Hey, Mom, are you going to be home tonight?" Taking a deep breath as trepidation swept through her.

"No honey, I was just heading out to Uncle Leo and Aunt Mary's. They are having a cookout. Is everything okay at school?"

"Yes, just missing you a bit." Natalee laughed. Knowing her daughter Jenny as well as she did, it was not hard to guess where this conversation was heading.

"Really, on a Saturday night? No other plans."

"Well." Jenny dragged out the response with emphasis on the last letters. "Remember I told you about Jared, the hot senior?"

"Yes," Natalee remembered this boy of the month very well. She started the engine on the Jeep now that she realized it was not an emergency.

Natalee, who was all too used to her daughter's trouble with men, listened to the remainder of the story. "Well, after weeks of telling me we were going to have a nice date tonight, he backed out. It seems he and his friends were able to buy tickets to a car race." Natalee swallowed the bubbling laughter as she turned toward Leo and Mary's neighborhood.

Natalee replied. "Honey, is it a race that happens every weekend, or is it one of those every-once-in-a-while things that are so hard to get tickets to?"

"I guess, Mom. He kept saying it was one of those chance-of-a-lifetime things. Mom, why are men so into childish things?"

"Well, honey, men mature at a different rate than women. But more than that, it is the things that matter to them. Compared to women, value is what makes the difference. Be patient." Hearing her delayed response.

"Okay. How late will you be at Aunt Mary's?"

"Probably late. They have been gearing up for this one for a while."

"Don't you get tired of all the cop stories? It has to be boring."

She giggled, "Jen, these parties that Leo throws yearly give me most of the ideas I use in my books. It is free research; the more they drink, the more stories they tell. Last time I had to sneak off to the bathroom and take notes on my tablet to keep all of them straight. I already have a tablet ready to go."

"Okay, Mom, I was going to come home tonight for the weekend. But since you will be partying over there, I will wait."

Riddled with guilt for discouraging her daughter, Natalee added. "Hon. If you want to come home, come. I am sure everyone would love to see you. If you don't want to go to Leo's, I will meet you at home. Just text me, and I will make an excuse to leave early."

"Love you mom."

"Love you too."

An hour later, Natalee helped her best friend, Mary, bring the giant platters of food to the patio. Heaping bowls of potato salad, baked beans, and coleslaw lined the table. Ribs from the BBQ pit were stacked on a large wood cutting board near the bowls of several sauces. A large ceramic baking dish quickly added hot steaks to the group. Each year Natalee was amazed by the amount of food consumed by the officers at one of these parties. Hot dogs and hamburgers stayed warm, wrapped in foil, waiting patiently for the group of children to take a break from swimming in the large pool. Thankful, she had chosen the casual pants while she played with several children helping to retrieve pool toys thrown from the pool.

Taking the time to pour herself a glass of wine, Natalee neared the pool, reaching down to throw one last beach ball back into the water to waiting hands. Standing, she turned and noticed a stranger among her group of friends. Her attempt not to stare was futile. His dark brown hair and glistening olive skin intrigued her from across the yard while she struggled to discern the color of his eyes from her vantage point. Her breath hitched as her eyes traversed to the tee shirt that molded to his broad shoulders, pulling tight across his muscular chest and loose around his trim waist. Feeling like a voyeur, she lowered her eyes.

She murmured, "No beer belly hidden there." Natalee quickly averted her eyes from the bulge concealed by khaki cargo shorts. Bringing a finger to her lips, she ran her tongue across the surface before she bit slightly on the end of her nail. Her sigh reached her ears while she admired his bare feet in his leather flip-flops. The assessment of the prime example of the male species would not have been complete if she had averted her gaze away from his legs. Her focus moved towards his muscular calves. The sexy stranger turned slightly, giving her a view of his well-formed backside.

Her pulse quickened, and beads of sweat rolled down between her breasts. In slow motion, the sexy stranger turned, allowing her to focus on his front again. Heat filled her cheeks. Natalee returned her focus toward his face only to realize his eyes were dark brown and lasered in on her. She jumped from the heat of his intense gaze. Natalee turned,

5

shortening the distance between her and the food table, searching for an escape.

Keeping busy, Natalee cleared empty paper plates and placed them in the trash. Leo's voice interrupted her task. "Nat, I would like you to meet my new partner." Turning towards the voice, she felt the instant heat to her cheeks. Leo gestured to the man that she had groped five minutes earlier with her eyes.

"This is Joe Costas. He is the new detective at the department I told you about."

"Nice to meet you. I am Natalee Brennan. Welcome to town." Her hand slipped into his, feeling the sense of warmth from his long slender fingertips up her arm.

She felt a gentle squeeze. "Thank-you. It is nice to meet you also finally. Leo talks about you often, but he never told me. Do you have a husband on the force?"

Natalee froze. Her bottom lip quivered as she removed her hand from his. "No." A slight tremor in her voice.

Leo answered for her. "Nat here actually was an officer herself. She had been a detective for two years before she retired for a much more glamorous life. Her husband, Patrick, was my partner. He died in the line of duty ten years ago."

Joe felt regret for the personal question when he noticed Natalee's rosy cheeks pale. The second she ripped the warmth of her hand away from his, he silently cursed his overzealous curiosity. He had noticed Natalee from the moment he had arrived. Monitoring her every movement while she had graciously served the younger children in the group. He finally asked Leo to introduce them.

"Natalee, I apologize for bringing up the subject." The sincerity in his voice caused her to force a smile.

"It is okay, really. It still happens quite often." Distracted by her beauty, he tried to guess her age.

When Leo grimaced, Joe quickly added. "Do you mind, if I dare be nosy again, what is this glamorous new career of yours?"

She giggled as Leo interrupted, explained for her. "She writes crime novels which always include a good looking detective, and this new one that she is working on is based on me." Leo was quite proud of himself.

Nat shook her head. "Leo is my biggest fan. And yes Leo, Quinn is just like you, except I wrote out the beer belly. Is that okay?" Joe laughed, as his new partner attempted to suck in his gut with very little success.

He patted it and then relaxed, releasing his wide girth before he admitted, "Yes, that is fine. I better get back to the cooking." Natalee nodded as he walked away.

Joe shook his head as he laughed. "So, he isn't modest at all."

"Nope."

»»

As much as she enjoyed the attention of the young detective, Natalee searched for a way to slip away. Joe was busy talking about his last job and his reason for coming to Mobile, Alabama. She attempted to listen to him. Instead, she noticed Leo and Mary eavesdropping from across the yard.

With dawning recognition. "Joe, it was nice to meet you, but I am pretty sure you would enjoy talking with the guys more."

"Oh? Why is that?"

"I am pretty certain that Leo introduced us on purpose. I don't date, and my friends are relentless. I don't believe they have realized the age difference."

Joe recognized the challenge, taking the bait. "Why, how old do you think I am?" He asked with a glint in his eye. She could not help but stare into his deep brown eyes that she tried to ignore. The strong urge to move her lips slowly over his jawline was overwhelming.

"Mid-twenties?" She answered with the first thought that came to mind, pulling her from the fantasy.

"Wrong. I am thirty. And you are what, thirty-eight?"

Surprised. "How? Good guess. No, you knew?" She stumbled over her words.

Joe laughed before confessing, "Yes, I saw you when I first arrived. I have to admit that I asked Leo about you then. So, I technically cheated. So, should we at least sit and eat? Then they will stop talking about us?"

Hesitating briefly before she responds softly. "Yes."

Joe smiled, leaning in close. Feeling his intense stare, she heard his sharp intake of breath when her tongue ran over her top lip. Her rosy lips felt the heat from his gaze. Time froze. Still, Natalee could see his lips moving without sound.

"What? I didn't hear you." He asked.

"Yes. I said yes."

They carried their plates to the furthest picnic table. Natalee wished she would have made an excuse before they filled their plates. Listening to Joe talk about his warm relationship with his family left her lonely. Hearing about his closeness with his parents and two sisters had her missing her family. Pulling herself back from her thoughts, she focused on him instead. "Where are you in the lineup with your sisters?"

Hesitating, he responded softly. "The baby." Laughing, she smiled and lost herself briefly in his eyes.

She teased. "I could have sworn that I just heard you say you are the baby of the family." His eyes averted towards the table when he moved his plate to the side.

He replied under his breath. "Yes. Guilty as charged."

"Are your sisters married?"

"Yes, each has a child, and Alina, the oldest, is expecting her second."

"So, is your Mother content with the grandchildren she already has, or is she already looking for more?" He took the last bite of the food on his plate and finished his beer. Natalee could not help but wonder if he was working up the courage to say something.

"She is." He laughed as he admitted. "Yes, she tells me, why don't you meet a nice girl and give me some beautiful grand babies soon."

Natalee's heart sank to her stomach in a nauseous churn. Attempting to hold down a large amount of food she had just consumed, she listened. "She also was extremely irritated when I took this job and left Tarpon Springs, Florida. My parents own a seafood restaurant and a small fleet of fishing boats. My entire family is a part of the family business. Uncles, Aunts, cousins, my sisters, and their husbands. I come from a large Greek family that owns several businesses." He paused briefly to

8

monitor Natalee's reaction as he glimpsed a shadow of sadness before she shut it down and smiled.

"So why law enforcement? And why Mobile?"

"I am what my family calls a do-gooder, always looking out for others. I have wanted to be a police officer for as long as I remember." As he talked about his childhood and his dream to be a police officer from a young age, Natalee could easily imagine him as a child. With his dark good looks, she easily envisioned the swarm of girls that must have followed him through his teenage years.

Stretching slightly, she moved her empty plate off to the side, leaving her hand on the table. It wasn't easy to hear Joe speak about his relationship with his sisters and their husbands and not imagine what it would be like to be his girl.

Natalee allowed herself to fantasize. If she stood and walked around the table, tapping him on the shoulder. He would turn to face her. She would straddle his lap and wrap her arms around his neck. Her body craved the warmth as he pulled her close, crushing her to his chest. His fingers would walk down her back towards her bottom until she felt the evidence of his desire pressed against her.

Moisture built between her legs as she rotated her hips against the plastic chair. Natalee jumped when she felt Joe place his hand on top of hers, returning her to the present. Shifting in her seat, Natalee looked down at his hand on hers. Her eyes rose in slow motion, meeting his.

Hot desire coursed through her veins as she heard him murmur. "I left Tarpon Springs for a change. Mobile has more opportunities in a larger department to advance my career. Also, I am ready to have a new relationship."

Natalee tingled from his touch on her hand. With a twitch of her fingers under his and the slightest movements, their hands turned in unison.

"What about you? Are you looking for a relationship? More children? How old is your daughter?" The small circles he drew on her palm sent shivers down her spine.

Warmth filled her belly, replacing the nervous churn while her mind shouted inside her. "What are you doing? He is too young for you. You don't want more children. He is at a

9

different place in life than you." All the while, her heart warmed to his touch and sincerity.

Her response vibrated against her tongue. "Jenny will be twenty next month. She graduates from the University in December. I am done. I have been married and raised a family. I can't see myself going through that again." With slow reluctance, she pulled her hand back, placing it in her lap out of reach. She shivered at the lost connection. Looking around the yard, she noticed that some of the families with young children had left.

"I better help Mary with the clean-up." She stood and picked up their trash, then turned once again towards him. "Joe, I have enjoyed talking with you. You are an amazing man. You will meet someone wonderful. I don't know if I am reading more into this than intended, but if I am, then let me just say that I am not the right woman for you. We are at different places in our lives, but I do find your attention extremely flattering." Before she could take a step away from the table, Joe rose, reaching out, and touched her arm.

"Natalee, I am interested in you. I have been, since I first arrived here in town, listening to all of Leo's stories about you. Then seeing you tonight confirmed it. I don't see the age difference. Instead, I see a smart, beautiful, kind woman."

She reached up and placed her hand on his chest. "Oh, but you will." Turning away, she walked into the kitchen to help Mary.

CHAPTER TWO

Natalee gathered empty beer bottles and chip bowls as she walked toward the kitchen. Mary stood at the sink with a stack of platters and large bowls to wash. She announced. "I am here to help."

"No, you won't. You get back out there and visit with Joe." Mary pointed her soapy finger at Natalee.

"Mary, you do realize that he is thirty, never married, and wants children."

"Nat, you are thirty-eight, not eighty. Women at your age are having babies all the time. You have the body of a twenty-five-year-old. What are you afraid of?"

Natalee was deep in thought. Pouring herself another glass of wine, she sighed.

"Mary, it's not about the age. It is that I am finally doing what I want to do. Jenny is grown." They both laughed. "Okay, almost raised. Besides, I have my freedom. Why would I want to do it again, diapers, teething, and all-nighters? Ugh." Tears filled her eyes. "I am attracted to him. I wanted to pull him behind the garage and rip his shirt off." Mary broke out laughing.

"No, please don't go back there. Leo has junk piled up. You will end up breaking an ankle on the stack of bricks." Both women laughed, talking about sexual fantasies. Before long, the platters were washed and put away. She stared out the window towards the men sitting around the table playing cards. Natalee could not help but notice Joe standing nearby, watching the game and mainly speaking to herself.

"It is strange how comfortable we were. There was no awkward silence. We just talked." Mary wrapped her arms around her best friend.

"Honey, that instant connection doesn't come around easily. There is a reason why Leo wanted you two to meet." Natalee looked up in surprise.

"What?"

"Leo didn't want me to tell you this. Leo started talking about him from the first day on the job. The more he knew, the more certain Joe was the guy for you. He didn't want it to be a blind date, so he waited till the party to introduce you. And he wanted to see if Joe was attracted to you." Natalee scowled. "Nat." Mary held her hands.

"Nat, we love you. We don't want you to be alone. You deserve the very best. Leo would not introduce you two if he did not think this was right." Nodding.

"Nat. Forget the age thing. It is time to open your heart again. Your fear of getting hurt is preventing you from living." Tears welled in Natalee's eyes. Mary wiped her friend's tears away from her cheeks.

"Honey, you have had more loss in your short life than any woman should have. My prayer for you is that you never have to bury another loved one. Losing your parents was hard, and losing Patrick the next year was unbearable. If I could take away one ounce of your pain, I would. But Nat, it is time to move on. Go back out there and let whatever happens for once in your life. Trust the possibility of something good."

Natalee dried her hands on the towel. Looking back once more, she nodded and then headed out the door. She went towards Joe, sitting on a lawn chair near the poker table. Looking around, she noticed the officers had thinned out, leaving only a few at the poker table. Natalee could not help but admire him. His long legs crossed at the ankles while watching intently the game unfolding before him. Surprised to see him look up and smile, their eyes locked. Joe stood, not breaking their connection, taking a step in her direction when she heard her daughter Jenny's familiar voice. Natalee broke the spell, turning towards the sound along with every male in the yard. Her young, vivacious long blond-haired beauty of a daughter ran across the yard.

"Uncle Leo." Jenny allowed Leo to pull her into a hug.

"Jenny bear, how have you been? We miss you around here so much. Haven't seen you since the New Year." He crooned. Jenny let him turn her around and introduce her to some she knew and remembered and, more importantly, one that she did not. Natalee stayed where she stopped as her daughter ran up and hugged her mother.

»»

Frustrated at the interruption, Joe watched Natalee turned away from him, stopping to talk to Leo and a girl. It wasn't until Natalee hugged her that he realized it must be her daughter. Disappointed, holding onto the hope he could spend more time with Natalee. The age difference did not bother him, even when she had told him more children were not in her plan, nor did it deter him. She was refreshing and different. He could carry on a conversation with her, unlike the twenty-year-old somethings he had met in the past. Joe watched as the young woman kissed her cheek and called her Mom.

Joe could not help but be surprised by the sight of Natalee's daughter in a very short skirt with exposed long tan legs. A tight blouse revealed a great deal of cleavage for the family crowd. Her long blond hair flipped every time she turned her head until she stopped and stared at him.

Feeling self-conscious under her scrutiny Joe turned to pull a beer from the cooler. Drinking the cold liquid, he could not help but notice the two in a deep conversation for a few minutes. Seeing them together made him realize what Natalee had meant. Having a new understanding of her life as a single mother dashed the hope of Natalee reconsidering a date with him.

Joe checked his watch. He had given up spending more time with Natalee at the late hour when he heard a female voice mention leaving and going to a club. Joe continued to nurse his current drink. He didn't play cards and was entirely too old for the group headed to the club downtown. More time with Natalee was the only thing on his mind at this late hour. But since her daughter had arrived, he had been unsuccessful. He could not help but wonder if Natalee felt self-conscious in front of her daughter. Jenny was busy trying to get her mother to go to the club. He foolishly believed Natalee was about to say yes when he suddenly boasted.

"I'll go." Natalee appeared shocked and then shook her head. Telling Jenny to be safe, she said she would see her at home in the morning. She verified her daughter had her house key, and with that, she was gone. By the time Joe ran around the side of the house, all he could see was the tail lights of her SUV driving down the street.

Feeling like he had just lost his chance, he made a bigger mistake by going to the club.

"Joe, dance with me, please." Jenny pleaded. Reluctantly he let her pull him out on the dance floor.

It was now after one in the morning. "Jenny, I am going home. Let me drive you." For the past two hours, he had watched her drinking heavily and dancing with an endless amount of men in the club. Giving up on his plan of leaving

13

earlier as his concern for her safety overrode his desire for sleep. Jenny had been an endless source of information since her plan to meet her friends at the club fell through. He had heard about how many classes she had left at the university. With the college only a little over an hour from home, it appeared she did this often, coming home when she didn't have a date for the evening.

With her words slurred. "You don't understand. The boys in college are so immature. They drink most of the time. They don't like getting dressed up and having dinner at a restaurant. All they want to do is go to sports bars. I am ready for a serious relationship as soon as I graduate in December." Joe had tried to get her to leave for over an hour.

Growing increasingly irritated, he snarked, "Jenny, why are you in such a hurry? You finished high school early and are fast-track through to your degree. Aren't you going to miss this freedom when you are married and have a family?"

"No, I don't think so. I will be ready to advance my career, and I know my mother will be an amazing grandmother. She would gladly take care of my baby."

Thinking back to the long conversation between himself and Natalee earlier, he shook his head in disagreement. "I think that needs to be a conversation between you and your mother. You don't want to assume what she might want to do with her time."

Jenny seemed to consider his response only momentarily before she shook her head and announced. "No, my Mom will do anything I ask. Besides, she doesn't have a social life. She hasn't even dated since my dad died. She could care less about men. She spends all of her time caring for me and spending time with Aunt Mary."

I snatched the drink from her underage hand. "Come on, Jenny. I am driving you home." Joe was surprised by her sudden willingness to leave. Jenny followed him to the parking lot without argument. As Joe opened the truck door for her, she leaned into him, giving him a full view of her cleavage down her shirt. Ignoring the temptation, instead, he secured the safety belt. He was relieved when she told him Natalee's full address before she dozed off.

Pulling up in the drive, he placed the truck in park. He nudged Jenny, "We are here." She did not move. He closed the truck door softly, mindful of the neighbors and the late hour. Walking around to the passenger side, he could not help but admire the manicured lawn with landscaping lights dotting the different greenery. Opening the door, he pulled her from the truck, standing briefly before slumping down.

Joe quickly lifted her, placing her over his shoulder and grabbing her purse, fishing for the keys while he walked to the front door. Struggling to hold her bag and find the correct key for the door proved to be a challenge. Hoping there was no alarm, he inserted the key as the door opened.

Standing in front of him was Natalee. Joe drank at the sight of her in a tank top and pajama bottoms. Her face was scrubbed clean. He caught the scent of coconuts, sparking a vision of them on the beach, and flashed before his eyes.

He managed to say. "Sorry, I did not mean to wake you. She fell asleep while I drove. I got the address out of her, and that was it. Wasn't able to wake her when we got here." Nodding, Natalee led the way down the hall to the first bedroom on the right and opened the door. He laid Jenny on the bed. Natalee removed her heels, covering her daughter with a light blanket. Jenny began to snore before they left the room. Joe followed Natalee towards the front door. Hesitating, he reached for her. His fingers lightly touched her arm while desire coursed through his body.

The intimacy of the late hour and low light only added to the sounds of each breath she took, heightening his desire.

Joe spoke, his words soft, caressing her in the low light. "Natalee, I enjoyed talking to you tonight. I heard what you said. And I understand more now than I did a few hours ago." Natalee crossed her arms. His eyes wandered towards the soft swell of her breasts above her top. The words were lost while his fingers ached with the desire to trace a fingertip across the top of her soft mounds. His heart thumped wildly, sweat formed on his hands, and he attempted to stall. He wanted to touch her, hold her until dawn. He was not ready to go home. He just knew he did not wish this day to end.

He wanted to ask so many things, but he didn't. Instead, he said. "I would like to see you again."

She surprised him when she opened the door instead of acknowledging his confession, "Thank you for bringing her home safely. Goodnight, Mr. Costas." His head hung low as he returned to his truck while he wondered how this night had turned out so wrong.

»»»

Natalee hesitated as he took the steps down the walkway toward his truck. When she heard his engine start, she softly closed the door. She leaned her forehead against the smooth mahogany wood as tears filled her eyes and spilled down her cheeks.

CHAPTER THREE

Natalee enjoyed her run the following day, pushing the previous night's events from her mind. Returning home, she wondered how her daughter's car had made it home after the club, yet she was thankful at the same time.

"Well, at least I don't have to explain to the insurance company why it was stolen." Laughing, she opened the kitchen door, laying her earphones on the table. Pulling off her t-shirt and wiping the sweat from her brow, she walked down the hallway. Seeing Jenny sprawled across her bed, her wet hair and oversized t-shirt on, flooded her with relief that her only child was safe despite the drinking. The Mom in her was tempted to wake her and get her to eat.

The new Natalee refused to take the bait. Instead, she immersed herself in the heated spray of the shower. Natalee sat down at the kitchen table, notepad in hand, admiring the beautiful spring Sunday morning while she contemplated her day as she finished her omelet. Determined to keep her focus away from the previous night, she glanced at her cell phone and decided to call Mary.

"Good morning." Natalee chirped.

"Morning." The voice on the other end of the line was less enthused. Natalee giggled while she inquired. "So, did you get any sleep?"

Mary snorted. "Ha. It sounds like a bunch of grizzly bears hibernating for the winter over here. They finally ended the game around two. Then they all passed out. And just when I got comfortable in bed. The noise began. I am surprised that the neighbors did not call the police. Ha, ha." Mary laughed at her joke. Considering a good portion of the force was growling in her house. "They are everywhere. Two of them slept outside on my lawn chairs." Natalee covered a giggle with her napkin as she envisioned ten men, all over forty, most with beer bellies snoring loudly.

She gave Mary an escape. "Mare, how does a day of flea market shopping sound? Unless you are too tired."

"Ha, I will be ready in an hour. Come rescue me."

Exactly one hour later, Mary jumped in Natalee's SUV. "Thank you. The noise has gotten worse." They both chuckled as they headed to the outskirts of town. All the while, Mary was giving updates on the poker competition. It had appeared that the final hand of cards ended around two. All the guys were too drunk or tired to do anything more than hit the first flat surface they could find, falling asleep. Mary went on, explaining how she had found sleeping grizzly bears lying on every flat surface they could find. The spare bedroom, every couch, recliner, patio chair, and even the pool layout chairs were all taken. She did not even try to awaken them. This was the twice-a-year thing. They were staying up too late, eating and drinking too much. They would regret it in a couple of hours. Then the guys would start planning the next time.

"You know Natalee, out of all of our friends, you are the only one with half the chance to snag a good-looking guy like Joe. All we ask is that we can live vicariously through you."

Natalee snorted. "I will try to get one a little older without babies on his mind so that I can tell you all about it."

Mary grabbed her best friend's hand. "Sorry, we did that to you last night. I thought you two would hit it off."

Natalee forced her smile as she replied, "I know. We were good until it was obvious what he wanted. It is okay. You didn't do anything wrong."

Mary looked at her best friend. "But wait, I thought you were returning to talk to him after we finished the dishes?"

"I was. He was sitting near the poker table, watching the game. I don't think he is into cards. I walked towards him, and he stood up and smiled. Then the next thing I knew, Jenny was there, and soon after that, he went to the club with her." Natalee concentrated on driving for several minutes before she spoke again. "He brought Jenny home this morning. She had passed out, and he carried her inside to bed."

"Oh, Nat."

"It's okay. He was a gentleman."

"Did he say anything?"

"He did mention what I meant earlier about the age difference. And that he understood it better now. He also told me he wanted to spend more time with me." Natalee bit her lip and continued. "It was horrible. He was out at a club with my daughter. I mean, what was all that about? Bringing her home, he told me he wanted to spend more time with me after we left her room. Then he reached out, touching me, and some part of me could not help but respond. Even though I did everything, I could not let it show."

Mary gave her hand a reassuring squeeze. "Well, it is time to start shopping, and I do not mean flea market junk." They laughed for the last ten minutes until they pulled into the parking lot. A conversation about men was put on hold. Shopping was serious business—no time for joking.

When Natalee arrived home with her latest flea market finds, Jenny had left the house. Evidence of her messy daughter was everywhere, bedroom, bathroom, and kitchen. With mounting frustration, she spent the remainder of her afternoon straightening up the house before she settled down to write.

Sipping her tea, she stared at the blank screen on her laptop. Distracted by the spring storm, Natalee knew it was much easier to watch the wind and rain through the large window above her desk. She sighed as the words would not come once again. Her mind quickly drifted to Joe, recalling his voice, eyes, and mouth when he smiled—having spent too much time thinking about him since the previous night.

Natalee jumped when her phone rang, breaking her thoughts. "Hello."

"Nat. Do you have any plans for lunch tomorrow?" Her best friend's voice was easy to recognize without looking at the caller id.

"No, not really. Just trying to focus on writing. I think I have spring fever." Mary laughed.

"Well, meet me at the bistro at noon. Okay?"

"Okay."

"Gotta run. Do not back out on me."

Natalee sighed, "I won't." She returned her thoughts to writing. Forcing Joe from her mind, she was relieved when the words began to flow easily.

Stepping into her closet, Natalee chose a sleeveless navy dress and a pair of heeled sandals. Grabbing a wrap and her purse she drove downtown. Checking her watch, she had time to run into a new small dress boutique that she had been driving past for the past few months. Pulling into the parking lot near the restaurant, she walked down the block towards the small shop. Greeted by the clerk when she entered, Natalee assured her she was only looking, when a flash of red caught her eye. Gently picking up the red dress by the hanger she admired the scarlet halter style when her thoughts were interrupted. "It is a four, the only one we have. I think it would look amazing on you. Would you like to try it on?" Natalee could only nod, the more entranced with the piece of material, she became.

The silky material slid down her body while she gazed into the mirror. Holding the dress tightly to her bare breasts, she left the small dressing room giving the girl access to the hidden zipper. The halter neckline hooked firmly in place, she followed the clerk towards the large three-way mirror. Surprised by her own reflection that transformed before her eyes, admiring her shoulders exposed by the material, down to the long dip between the breasts. Her hips were accentuated by the slight flair of the skirt. Moving her left leg from the material, she revealed skin to her upper thigh.

Natalee smiled, her thoughts were interrupted. "You look amazing. This dress was made for you." Nodding in agreement. This was her dress. Without looking at the price she donned her clothes and handed the dress to the clerk. Without regret she chose her credit card paying the eight hundred dollars without a second thought. Walking towards the Bistro, Natalee felt a new sense of herself, as a woman. Not as wife, a daughter, a mother, a police officer, or even as a writer.

"I am thirty-eight years old, and for the first time in my life I feel like a real woman."

Natalee entered the crowded cafe a few minutes later, spotting Mary at a table for four on the patio. Waving, she made her way past small tables and a few waiters while carrying her dress in its protective covering.

Before Natalee could say hello, Mary bombarded her with questions. "What is that?" Smiling with a twinkle in her eye, Natalee responded. "Do you want to see?"

"Duh, yes, what did you buy?" Setting her purse on a chair next to Mary, Natalee gently pulled up the plastic to reveal the red scarlet dress.

"Oh, wow, Nat, that is gorgeous. I bet it looks amazing on you." For effect, Natalee opened the full skirt showing off the slit.

"That goes how high?" Natalee pointed to her thigh, then blushed. They laughed in unison as Natalee turned the dress, showing her the back. "I can't wait to see it on you." She grinned.

She began lowering the plastic to cover the dress when she heard, "Hi, Natalee." She jumped slightly at the sound of the voice she had been trying to forget.

"Hello." She said softly toward Joe before turning to hang her dress on the lattice behind Mary.

Leo pulled the chair out beside his wife and asked, "Mary, did you buy that red contraption?" Natalee was confident he had already realized it was hers.

Mary giggled. "You must be joking. I could never fit in that thing. No, that is Natalee's new sexy red dress." Natalee quickly buried her head in the menu while her best friend gave every detail, describing the dress. Natalee lifted the menu higher, covering her inflamed cheeks.

Lowering the menu when she heard, "So, when am I going to get to see you in that dress?" A shrug of the shoulders was the only response she could muster. Mary jumped when she received the soft kick under the table, taking the hint to change the subject. By the time the food arrived, Natalee could not keep up with the conversation or the issue. All she knew was the man in the chair next to her was too close as she felt his warmth. She smelled his essence and felt the pressure of his leg against hers. Her skin turned into a prickly overheated fire, fighting for air on the covered outdoor patio, even though Mary had just remarked on how the spring air felt cool.

Natalee did not feel cool—quite the opposite. The visions started once again, like the first night they met. He sat on the boat dock next to her this time, without a shirt. His feet were bare, toes rippling through the water with each movement of his legs, and his thigh tightened. His hand moved to her thigh, running his fingers toward the hem of her shorts. Two fingers pushed under the material reaching her lace panties. Natalee took a sharp intake of breath when his fingers caressed her center, causing a release of warm moisture.

"Nat, do you want dessert?" The voice asked.

"Yes." It came out more as a moan. The deep laughter next to her brought her out of her musings.

"What?" She looked at Joe, shifting slightly in his seat. A knowing grin crossed his face when he reached under the table and touched her thigh.

"Do you want dessert?" Natalee licked her lips and nodded. His hand shifted higher while he ordered a large chocolate cake from the server. The heat from his hand bore into her skin. Natalee went in her seat, fighting an overwhelming urge to touch his hand, sliding it farther north and forgoing all her doubts and fears while his touch blinded her.

"Do you want to share?" He growled close to her ear. His hot breath brushed her cheek, sending a shiver of goosebumps down her arm. Nodding.

She heard Mary giggle and then say. "Leo honey, walk me to the restroom, will you?"

Leo looked up in surprise. "Why? Woman, you know how to find it." Mary stood and twisted her husband's ear lobe to get his attention, moving her eyes to the two across the table.

"Oh, yes. I will, my dear. We will be right back. Don't steal my dessert."

Neither responded, instead staring intently into each other's eyes. Joe leaned in closer and whispered. "So, Natalee, what were you thinking about?"

Natalee stuttered over her words, "Well, well, umm." She replied. "Sorry, my mind drifts sometimes, I started a new book this week, and I had a new scene in mind." Joe gave her a knowing grin. The warmth from his hand on her thigh continued to sear into her skin. Still plagued with the increasingly overwhelming desire for him to move it a little higher caused an ache within her. The only thing kept her from moving his hand.

"Babies." Her brain fought against the desire in her body.

Mary and Leo returned, followed by chocolate cake. Joe forgot about tormenting her with his touch in favor of cake. Natalee laughed while she witnessed his weakness as he devoured most of the dessert they had planned to share.

Natalee had not heard from her daughter in over a week, yet she had managed to run into Leo and Joe on more than three occasions since lunch. It was usually while she and Mary were out and about. Twice it had been while they were shopping, once at the nursery for plants and today as they left the mall after buying underwear.

Holding the bag from a lingerie store with the name plastered across the side in large letters while Joe stood less than two feet away left Natalee extremely self-conscious. She shifted the bag behind her other packages to avoid Joe seeing the name on the bag. Thinking about the money she had just dropped on her new wardrobe was close to obscene. Mary was taking this living vicariously through Natalee with an overzealous energy.

Mary, with her over forty and three boys later the figure had struggled with her weight for nearly twenty years. She longed to fit in size eight again but gave it up as a hopeless cause.

Ensuring Natalee's tall, athletic frame was dressed for maximum effect had become her new passion. Natalee shook her head, and her short brown waves bounced while laughter filled the air at Mary's animated story to the detectives of some of the things they had seen in the mall until Leo kissed his wife. Joe began to step forward, then stopped himself. He ventured a quick wave goodbye.

Natalee was walking to her car when Mary yelled. "Hey, what about dinner tonight? Maybe Leo can fix you up. We can double. Wear the black set." Watching Mary waggle her eyebrows,

Natalee rolled her eyes as she replied. "Just let me know when and where." Getting into her SUV. Putting on her sunglasses. She decided to stop fighting and let her friends assist her dating life. It was as if all of them had conspired to pull out phone numbers for every available man over forty within a reasonable distance. Realizing it was easier to go along with it now.

A few hours later, after writing and returning a call to her editor. Natalee stepped from the shower. She was struck with the thought of how lonely an author's life could be. The hours spent in her little office, deep in thought about characters instead of picking up the phone and making plans with friends. If it wasn't for Mary or a few other friends, she could spend days alone and not speak to another soul other than her daughter, who decided to call once a week or when she needed something, especially money.

Sighing, Natalee fought her lack of energy for the date tonight. She would have preferred the boat for a sunset ride and to enjoy a beer. She prevented herself before his name entered her mind instead of the fitted sleeveless black dress and matching heels she wore. She admired her slender figure. Smiling at the thought of the matching black lace bra and thong panties underneath her dress left her feeling decadent.

"Maybe shopping for something new is worth it." She laughed out loud. She no longer cared how much she had spent today. Instead, she enjoyed the way the new clothes made her feel. Running a brush through her curls, she applied a touch of makeup and a few silver pieces of jewelry before she left the house.

When she entered the restaurant, Leo quickly introduced her to Brad, a thinning gray-haired man in a suit. His appearance suggested more of a sedentary lifestyle than she was accustomed to. Surprised to see this is who they came up with after a man like Joe. Natalee realized he was friendly with a pleasant sense of humor, which helped make the evening enjoyable. Shortly after finishing their meals, Brad left the table.

Mary hit her husband on the arm. "Tell her quickly before he comes back."

"Sorry, Nat," Leo confessed. "I planned to get Martin. A nice, recently divorced man I play golf with. But he was tied up in meetings today. When I called Mary to tell her, Joe overheard me and tried to get himself invited. I am sorry." Leo held both bear-sized paws up in the air in surrender. He admitted with a sheepish grin. "I still believe you and Joe would be good together, but I didn't want to push him on you, so I told Joe that we were double dating. I'm sorry, but Brad is the first one I could think of. He works at the bank." Natalee could not be mad at him. Leo was her big teddy bear brother, one she never had until she joined the force. He gave great hugs, knowing he would protect and care for her as his own family did.

She touched his hand. "It's okay. Brad is nice. He is probably not my type, but he is funny and sincere. I don't think there will be a second date. But I am having fun."

Brad returned to the table, ordered desserts, and, after dinner drinks when she heard, "Hello." Natalee recognized the voice before she looked up. She could not hear Leo's hushed tone toward his partner.

When she heard. "Hi, Natalee."

"Hello, Joe." She squelched a sharp intake of breath when she admired his dark hair and olive skin in a dark gray suit. *His tall, muscular frame wore that suit as if it was made for him.* When she noticed his companion Natalee was quick to force away the jealousy of seeing him with the tall blond as the couple settled at their table. She was relieved that her group had neared the end of their meal. The thought of a torturous hour with Joe at a table so near would prove unbearable. Unable to control herself, she glanced at his table, meeting his eyes in an instant.

Even though the date with Brad went well, Natalee declined the offer for a drink at the small bar down the street from the restaurant instead of going home. Thankful she had chosen to bring her car, she is now enjoying her drive home. Somehow, the thought of walking into an empty house saddened her more. Avoiding the inevitable for as long as possible, Natalee drove slowly through her older subdivision, admiring the manicured lawns in the evening light. Many of the houses backed up to water, and most homeowners took advantage of the easy access. Natalee was no exception, longing to be on the boat tonight instead of the restaurant she had just left. Pulling into her driveway, she turned off her car and pulled the key from the ignition. Reluctant to move, she stared at her ranch-styled home and large manicured front lawn.

"Strange, it never felt empty before. But now it does."

She had just locked her car when her phone rang. "Hey, Mare. Yes, I am okay. Yes, he looked like a model in that suit. How the heck does he afford tailor-made suits like that?" Mary's tirade response caused Natalee to rub her temple with her fingers as she listened to Mary continue. Bypassing the kitchen door, she chose the path toward the pool. Kicking off her shoes, she slid her dress up her thighs and eased down onto the edge of the shallow end. Half listening to her best friend, while she envisioned Joe swimming in her pool.

He swam toward her, pulling her into the water and lowering the zipper on the back of her dress. She raised her arms. The clothing was removed from her body, revealing her black lace bra and matching thong. Sighing, she forced herself from the fantasy to focus on the call. "Nat, are you listening to me? I am so mad at Leo for putting you in that position. I think he purposely let it slip to Joe where we were eating."

Suddenly very tired, Natalee replied. "Mary, it's okay. There is always a chance I will run into him. Seeing him doesn't make me want him more or even less. I have feelings for him. It is obvious. It just isn't right for either of us. There is no sense in pursuing a relationship with him."

Saying goodnight, she pressed the end of her cell.

Staring again at the water in the moonlight, Joe stood in the shallow end and pulled her close. Natalee wrapped her long legs around his waist. Pulling herself from the fantasy, she shook her head. "This is insane." Chastising herself for yet another fantasy. Standing up, she stepped from the pool and removed her dress. Laying it on the nearest chair, Natalee walked into the water. The cool temperature caused her to gasp in sharp contrast to the heat in her body. Wearing only her black lace bra and matching thong panties, she worried briefly whether the chlorine would fade the expensive underwear. While slicing through the water, she acknowledged the wasted effort required to walk into the house and put on a swimsuit. No, this was better, easier, and much quicker than the satisfaction she had longed for all day.

Natalee quickly warmed up in the water. By the time she finished her thirtieth lap. Her frustration had disappeared. Relaxing for the first time since the party, she swam toward the shallow end. She rose from the water. She realized she was not alone when her foot met the first step.

His form was recognizable, sitting in the deck chair. Even in the dim patio light, she noticed he had removed his tie and jacket. His dress shirt sleeves were now pushed up to his elbows. His hair was out of place as if he had run his fingers through it repeatedly. She stepped onto the patio.

"Hello, Lee." She heard him whisper. Natalee hissed a curse under her breath at her decision to swim in her underwear.

»»

The sea nymph walked toward him and the pair of Adirondack chairs that faced the pool and overlooked the water. *Mesmerizing.* His mouth was dry, his throat closed and his breaths entered and left his body in short gasps as his heart thumped wildly in his chest. The full moon reflected in the tiny droplets of water that dotted along her chest and arms across the dark scrap of material that only served to accentuate her breasts. His eyes traveled over her body and despite the low patio lighting, the full moon gave him enough light to take in the black lace bra and matching panties. Suddenly everything he had planned to say was lost, entirely tongue-tied as he struggled to speak.

Natalee broke the silence with a snarky retort. "Surprised to see you. Your date must not have lasted long." She clutched her dress and shoes to her chest.

When she began to shiver, Joe rose from the chair. He was quick to apologize. "Sorry, you must be cold. I didn't mean to interrupt you. I want to talk."

With a quick bob of her head, she retrieved her belongings and motioned toward the house. Joe followed. As they moved closer to the porch lights, his jaw dropped when he caught a glimpse of a scrap of black lace. His mind began to race. *Oh my God. How am I ever going to be able to forget that sight?* He desperately tried to recall what he had planned to say to her instead of focusing on her well-rounded bare bottom in front of him.

Natalee opened the door, leaving her purse and keys on the counter. "Make yourself at home. There is beer in the fridge. I will be right back."

»»

Natalee trembled as she walked into her room. Her first instinct was to throw on some clothes and rush out to hear what her uninvited visitor had to say. "He can wait." She instructed herself as she steeled her nerves. Stepping under the hot spray of the shower, she shampooed her hair and quickly rinsed her expensive underwear. As much as she longed to remain in the shower, she rushed through her routine. Deep breaths continued in and out as she counted each one to calm her nerves as she towel-dried her hair, combing it and putting on a tank top and pajama bottoms. Her confidence lasted down the hall until she spied Joe standing at the living room window next to the fireplace, looking out over the backyard and the water.

So, sexy. So, young. Not the right person for me. But I want him so much. The thoughts poured through her mind, lingering on the tip of her tongue. She could not remember having such instant attraction before.

"Sorry, it took me so long. I got colder than I thought swimming." Turning to face her, she admired his long, strong hands as he rubbed his hand over his face.

"No, it is me that should apologize. I did not mean to intrude. After seeing you at dinner, I realized there were some things I thought we should talk about." Natalee walked into the kitchen, pulling a beer from the refrigerator. Opening the top, she tossed the cap on the counter. Sitting down on the couch, she tucked her feet underneath her. Joe sat down on the couch next to her. Even though there was a cushion distance between them, she could still feel the heat from his nearness, just as she had at the Bistro during lunch the week before. Every time his knee would brush hers under the small table, it sent shivers up her spine. Since their first meeting, every nerve in her body reacted each time he was near.

Waiting to hear what he had to say, trying not to think about him taking his clothes off or seeing her naked backside.

Joe spoke softly and interrupted her thoughts. "I wanted you to know that when you first explained the age difference, I didn't quite believe it. I reacted badly to that, I know." He took a long drink from his beer bottle. "It really did not hit me until I was at the club with Jenny, trying to keep her from leaving with some strange man. These guys were all close to my age, just looking for action. And I then realized that there was a difference between them and me. All I wanted to do was keep her safe." Joe paused, allowing Natalee a chance to let his words sink in. Reaching for her hand, he covered it with his. "Natalee, you are right. There are differences in what I have done from the age of twenty to thirty. I have not been married, nor have I had a child. I also have not experienced the loss that you have. But I am not your average thirty-year-old. I am somewhere in between." Natalee let his words sink in. "Lee, I came to Mobile for a change. To have a better career, to find the right woman, and start a family. Now I realize that life doesn't always fit in a little box. I did not consider that I needed to fall in love first." His thumb drew small circles on her palm. "Every time I am around you, I feel different." He lowered his drink to the coffee table. He took both of her hands in his. "I like that feeling. And I realized that because of who you are and how I feel about you, I am open to other ideas for a future."

She shifted her body away from him.

He pleaded. "Can't we just forget the babies' conversation?" Joe murmured. "Instead, can't we just get to know each other and take a chance and see where it goes?"

Natalee slowly pulled her hands from his. Standing, she walked toward the window. Wiping a small tear from her cheek. "Sorry, Joe. It is already out there. I can't be why you don't have everything you deserve."

His jaw ticked as he rose from the couch to his full height. He evaporated the distance between them in a few steps until his breath felt warm on her forehead as he gently placed his arms around her, pulling her close.

"Just answer this. Am I wrong? Do you not feel it too?" Not waiting for an answer, he tipped her chin and softly kissed her lips. Natalee wrapped her arms around his neck. He invaded her senses, controlled her soul, and stole her breath until Natalee doubted where she began, and Joe ended. When reality sank in and splashed away at the cold, hard truth, her lips closed slowly as she stepped backward.

With a shaky voice, she replied. "No, you are not wrong. I feel it too." She witnessed the realization of the truth in the firm tilt of his full lips. "Joe, I still can't. It is not fair to you. I have had my chance at all those things you deserve."

"Lee, you can change your mind."

She shook her head. She placed the palm of her hand on his chest. "No, sorry, Joe, but I won't."

CHAPTER FOUR

Stepping from the shower, she ran a comb through her hair. Natalee wiped the steam off the mirror and stared at her reflection. Applying facial cream, she read over the name on the bottle. Sure, to wipe away wrinkles. You need to be right. It better help." Thoughts of Joe flitted through her mind. Weeks had passed since she had turned him down. e had kissed her cheek, turned, and left without another word. Natalee's fingers rested on her cheek; still, after the time had passed, she could feel his lips. Hypocrite should be her new middle name for as many times as Natalee had hung on Mary's every word hoping that someone mentioned Joe.

She had picked up her phone the very minute she had heard his truck leave her drive. Knowing her friends as well as she did, she expected them to take her eagerness for Joe's phone number as a sign and to continue encouraging the relationship. Instead, she placed her phone on its charger and tried to sleep. She spent the entire night in the rocking chair, staring into the night out of the large living room window.

She tried her best to get excited about tonight, even in the red dress. t was more revealing than anything else she owned. Mary's words fluttered through her mind. *f you got it to flaunt it.* Running her hands over her breasts down to her waist, Natalee felt half naked with very little on underneath. So here goes. am officially flaunting it tonight." She admired her reflection, pleased with the results of allowing her hair to dry naturally with only a trace amount of styling cream to tame her curls. Diamond studs at her ears and a simple silver etched bracelet on her slender wrist. With her matching red clutch purse, she adjusted her red high heels and reached the door as the bell rang.

"Natalee, you look amazing."

"Thank you." She smiled at her date. Garrett, you look very handsome tonight." The smile she gave him did not quite reach her eyes. Garrett opened the door of his Cadillac. As he walked around the front of the car, she struggled not to compare him to Joe. Garrett is just a little bit taller than Natalee, probably five-ten at most. With his distinguished salt and pepper gray hair and beard, he was fit and trim without the definition and stature of Joe. s a local business owner, he was well respected. Several of her friends attempted to ignite her dating life, and Garrett was everyone's top pick. After saying no the first three times, she finally agreed to a double date with Janie and Mark, longtime family friends. Listening to Garrett as he did most of the talking during the drive to dinner was a relief. When she foolishly believed she would stop thinking about Joe Costas, with each passing minute, it became painfully apparent that few men could compete with the effortless conversation she had had with the younger detective.

Walking into one of the nicest restaurants in town, Natalee was bombarded with memories. His was her second trip to this establishment. While Patrick was alive, their money had been extremely tight. They did not get the opportunity to splurge on many of the nicer things in life, but one time Natalee saved some money and surprised her husband for their anniversary. t was the last anniversary they had before he died. Shutting down the sad memory, she pushed it aside for later.

Surprisingly, Natalee had enjoyed herself through dinner, and Garrett had proved to be an attentive date. He found the food amazing and the company enjoyable. When the server cleared their plates, Garrett had just finished telling a story about his neighbors.

Janie spoke up first. How about if we go to the Jazz Club for some dancing?" The group agreed, and a short time later, they entered the club and chose a table. Garrett led Natalee to the dancefloor.

»»

The oversized doors loomed before him. The neon sign flickered as it struggled in the night. For weeks Joe had avoided social situations ever since the party. After declining invitations from more than a handful of his new coworkers, he finally broke down earlier and agreed. He had stayed at home or on his boat, avoiding crowds. When the call came in from Sergio, he was on his boat with his feet up, a cooler at his side, and a fresh beer. The two beers he had consumed made it easier to convince him to join the group. Joe entered and spotted the group. Most of his coworkers were part of a couple. The audible groan he made as he took a seat went unnoticed by the few at the table. The rest of his friends were on the dancefloor, along with more couples. Joe ordered a beer. Filled with longing, he lost himself in the music as couples twirled on the dance floor. The dancers moved past him.

Joe stopped, beer in mid-air, when he saw red. The red dress he had caught only a glimpse of was now on the body that haunted his dreams, but she was in the arms of another man. With a clenched jaw, he leaned forward in his chair, Joe's jaw clenched, and his fingers twitched against the sweaty bottle. He monitored their every move, and when they turned, Natalee's skirt shifted, showing her long bare leg up to her thigh. He stood abruptly and moved closer, mesmerized yet berating himself for the feelings he had failed to forget.

After having only known Natalee for a short while, all he wanted was to get to know her better. Jealous fur built inside of him as he watched her smile. The stranger pulled her close and then turned her once again. This time Joe's breath lodged in his throat when he spied the deep dip between the smooth swell of her breasts.

"This man is holding her and dancing. But she would not give me the time of day." Anger and hurt mounted as he focused only on the lady in red. He stormed toward the bar, giving him a better view of the dance floor. His brain screamed leave now. His heart did not listen. Instead, he finished the beer and ordered another beer and a whiskey shot. By the time Natalee and the mystery man had begun the next dance, Joe had ordered a third drink. Pushing away from the bar, he weaved as he moved closer, never taking his eyes from the girl of his dreams.

»»

The slow dance ended, and Garrett turned her one last time. Natalee stepped off the dance floor. Picking up her drink from their table and sipping it slowly, when over the rim of the glass, she caught a glimpse of Joe standing by the bar, staring right at her. Feeling his eyes bearing down on her in her red dress, she began to shiver with nervous energy. She could not avert her gaze. Time slowed as Natalee's heart plummeted after not seeing him since that night in her living room two weeks ago. Natalee could not help but notice how good he looked. His black tee shirt was pulled taut across his chest, jean-clad legs, and his traditional flip-flops. Natalee could smell him in her mind knowing all she would have to do was walk across the floor into his arms.

Frustration and self-doubt erupted, angry at him and herself. She knew how his arms felt. His kiss burned inside of her, making this so much harder.

"Doing what is right sure feels like hell." Not realizing that she had said the words out loud. Garrett leaned in. "Couldn't hear you."

"Oh, I will run over to the ladies' room."

"Okay."

Natalee finished her drink. Losing sight of Joe as she picked up her purse, she weaved through the crowd toward the bar, unsure of what was driving her toward him. Looking up and down the bar, then back to the dance floor, she turned toward the door in time to see it close with force. A sudden nauseous churning burned in the pit of her stomach, feeling as if she had just lost her last chance at happiness.

»»

Joe pushed away from the bar, avoiding the torturous act of watching her dance in the red dress. Tapping his friend Kevin on the shoulder, he handed over his truck keys. "I'm walking home. Can you drop off my truck when you leave?"

Kevin nodded. "Sure man. No problem. Are you safe to walk?"

"Yea, need to clear my head a bit." Joe stumbled from the bar. Thinking the walk would clear his head, realizing he had lost count of how many beers and shots of whiskey he had drank. Images of Natalee swam before his eyes. Looking up at the moon and stars took him back in time to the patio two weeks before, when he watched her swimming.

"Why did I have to go over there, I should have stayed on my date." In his drunken condition the details of that night flashed before his eyes. Now feeling remorse when he hurried his date through dinner, and asked for the check before she could order a dessert or second drink. He walked her to her car and made an excuse of getting back to work, all the while planning on driving to Natalee's house as fast as he dared.

Joe relived the feeling when he spied her car in the driveway, as he pulled in. He had knocked once on the kitchen door when he heard the splash. His memories flooded before his eyes. Gone was the city street and buildings. Gone were the cars out this late Saturday night. Instead, he was there in her backyard lured by the sound of a splash.

Now, he could not remember what had possessed him to walk into her yard and sit down in one of the chairs. As he had stared at the lonely chair next to him. He wondered, *"Who sits beside you Lee?"* Joe failed to remember why he had started thinking of her as Lee instead of Nat as most of their friends called her. It was his own private nickname. His fists clenched when she had stepped from the pool. The scrap of black lace material lured him closer. He had used his resolve, not to reach for her.

His brain fumbled halfway between the past and the present, as he stopped at the cross walk. Joe leaned against the post, amazed at the amount of traffic for the late hour. Crossing the street, he looked up at his building. "Oh, crap I forgot about the stairs." Entering into the older building, he recalled how he had liked the brick and steel structure from the first moment he had seen it on his first visit to Mobile. The stairs had been an increased plus. At the time, he had thought even after a hard day it would still be good exercise to have to take the stairs.

"Too bad I didn't think about having to climb them after a night of drinking." By the time he had reached the top of the second flight Joe contemplated laying down right there. Realizing that his neighbors would not be thrilled, he forced himself up the last two flights when he saw long bare legs. "Lee." Even in his alcohol induced state, he realized, this was not her when he saw the mini skirt came into view.

"Jenny whattt are youu doing here?" Surprised by his slurred words.

Her reply was soft compared to the sound of his fighting the lock on his door. "I just wanted to see you again. I thought you would have called after we went out that night."

Opening the door, he kicked off his shoes. "That was not a date. I don't want to see you. Goodnight little girll." Closing the door, Joe stumbled toward his bedroom taking off his clothes as he walked. Sitting down on the side of the bed fighting to free his foot from his blue jeans. Joe gave up the fight and crashed back onto the bed. His head had barely hit the pillow before he began to snore, unaware of his company.

»»

Jenny watched while he stumbled, closing his door without the force to engage the lock. She entered, then closed it firmly behind her, following him down the hall, removing her clothing while she moved silently on the wood floor.

Surprise registered across her face, unsure of her actions. Pushing her indecision aside, Jenny stepped closer, reaching out with one finger to trace his jawline, feeling the effects of several days without shaving. With more bravado, her fingers moved of their own volition, tracing his chest down to his well-developed abs. Her fingers moved toward the band of his boxer briefs, lingering before pulling them down to his knees. Pausing when he murmured in his sleep, she held her breath as she tried to make out the word he had said. Filled with desire for this man. "He is so sexy." She moaned. Jenny denied herself the urge to kiss him, fearing he would awaken. Instead, she used the slight touch of her nail over his shaft, surprised as his hard length enlarged. She continued her mission and felt bold while watching him grow harder under her touch. Bending down, Jenny took the length of him into her mouth. Joe shook his head from side to side. The more he moved, the harder she sucked. Joe continued to moan, shaking his head and yelling out. Without opening his eyes, he pushed at her head, grabbing her hair. Believing that he was awake enough to realize it was her, he did want her after all. When he pushed hard, she almost fell off the bed.

Slurring his words. "What are you doing in here? You not Lee." Jenny crawled over him, sliding her bare breasts along his torso. "No, Jenny, no. I don't want you."

"Sorry, Joe, but your little friend says differently." She said with a smile.

She slid deftly down onto him while he pushed harder to free himself. She hoped he was hard enough. The more he fought, surprising her, the more erect he became. She continued her mission, surprised that it did not take long before his body betrayed him, exploding into her. She screamed.

"Yes, oh yes."

»»

Moaning, he turned over in bed and opened his eyes with his underwear halfway down his thighs. Strange memories danced around his fogged brain.

"Too much alcohol. "This he could remember. Forcing himself slowly out of bed, he looked around his messy room with clothes scattered down the hallway. Stepping over bedsheets and the quilt on his way to the shower, Joe hoped the water would ease the pain in his head. He remained under the steamy spray in an attempt to erase the bad dreams that lingered in his mind. Choosing his workout clothes, he struggled against the overwhelming urge to climb back into bed. He could not help but feel there was something wrong. Joe pulled the remaining sheet from his bed and tossed it onto the pile on the floor. He planned to wash them later. He picked up his cell phone calling his friend Kevin for his truck keys.

Throughout his workout, he could not shake the feeling that something had gone wrong the previous night. Visions of Natalee dancing with a man other than himself in her red dress still frustrated him. Now this morning, without the alcohol to make things worse, realizing how jealous he had been seeing her in the arms of another man, he recognized that he cared for her more than any other woman he had ever met. Running faster, he was determined to force her from his mind.

"She won't even give us a chance. All I need is some time to get to know each other." "finishing his four-mile run near the bay, Joe stretched and walked to his truck. Unsure of himself, he had no plans. Before last night, his goal was to send Natalee flowers and ask her on a date. He was overwhelmed by the fact that he had never had to work this hard to get a woman to notice him. He mumbled as he opened his truck door.

" I haven't had problems getting a date since grade school. Hell, they used to ask me out." Feeling empowered, Joe decided it was time to return to his former glory days and just date.

"I will forget the damn serious stuff and just get laid." Joe stuttered over that word, sparking a horrible memory.

"It had to be a bad dream because of the alcohol." Changing his mind once again to wait and see what happens.

Three weeks later, Joe stepped off his boat, carrying the large cooler to the back of his truck. Stowing his gear, he started the engine letting the air cool down the inside of the large black truck. He had stopped feeling sorry for himself after the first week. He had spent another week dating as many willing females as he could find. Then the third week, he relaxed and enjoyed his days off work with friends.

Tired and relieved after having a good day out on the water with Leo and some other friends from work. Their day had begun at dawn, fishing the entire day. Pleased with his catch, the cleaned fish were ready for the freezer, and he prepared for a shower and a cold beer. Muttering as he closed the tailgate of his truck and sent a wave to his fishing party. "I only thought about Natalee five times." Laughing. "Well, that was a damn lie. Maybe more like five times an hour. Damn, Costas, you got it bad." Shaking his head while he drove towards his apartment.

Blaming Leo for bringing up the fact that Mary and Natalee were relaxing by Natalee's pool today, encouraging Joe's overactive imagination to wonder if her bikini looked anything like the black underwear, a vision that continued to haunt his dreams. Pulling into his parking lot, he checked his phone. He was disappointed to see several missed calls and not one from the one he wanted to hear from most. I got a few messages from Kevin wanting him to go out this evening. "Not again, buddy. I learned my lesson the last time I partied with you." The other three were from an unknown number. All three of them hung up as soon as the voicemail picked up. Deciding it must be telemarketers, he tossed his phone onto the seat. Carrying the cooler up the stairs, he had a strange feeling when he spied Jenny sitting on the stoop in front of his door.

"What do you want this time? When he said the words, an unpleasant sinking feeling overcame him. Opening his door, he chose to ignore his guest. He loaded the packaged fish into the freezer. Washing his hands, then grabbed a beer from the refrigerator. He was not surprised that Jenny had followed him into his apartment. Taking a long swig of his beer, he focused on wiping down the cooler. "Do you want a drink or something?"

"Water is fine."

Handing her a bottle, he sat down on the couch opposite her. "So, what do you want?" For the first time since he met Jenny, seeing her without makeup, he realized how extremely young she was. The shorts, sandals, and oversized tee shirt were quite different than the mini skirt, high heels, and low-cut blouse. Her pale face with deep dark circles was a stark difference from the heavy makeup she wore the first time they had met. Her lips parted in expectation. Joe remained clueless, with a look of confusion on his face.

"Oh, God. What did I do? You don't remember, do you?"

"Remember what? What the hell are you talking about? Spill it now. Before I get pissed."

Panic set in as she blurted. "I am pregnant, Joe."

"So, what the hell does that have to do with me?" Even as he said the words, images came flooding back, the very ones he had thought were a bad dream. Now he sat speechless. Taking a sip of her water.

Jenny began. "Do you remember that night I was here when you came home? I think you were drunk."

"Drunk, my ass. I had to walk home from the club because I was drunk. I don't remember much, but I recall telling you to leave."

Biting her lip, tears streamed down her cheeks. "I did not leave when you asked. I followed you into your bedroom."

"We didn't. There was no way. I was too drunk for that. What makes you think it is mine?"

"I, I haven't been with anyone in over six months. My boyfriend dumped me that night. That is why I came here."

"Are you trying to tell me that I managed to have sex with you as drunk as I was? I don't believe it. I would not have done that. You are too young. I would have never risked everything for that." He fought the images that flooded his memory. Suddenly he realized the truth. "Aren't you on protection?"

"No, I don't take the pill." Embarrassed, she continued. "And I, well, I initiated it." Joe stood, then started pacing around the room. "What the hell does that mean? You initiated it?"

Her tears increased the more he yelled. She cried in frustration, "I waited until you passed out, then stroked you to get you hard. I took you in my mouth, okay." Scared by the expression on his face. She blurted out the rest. "I climbed on top of you, and I, until you came." Joe threw the glass bottle across the room toward the brick fireplace. As glass exploded onto the wood floor, Joe feared his life had ended.

CHAPTER FIVE

Natalee enjoyed the first few days of June, admiring her tan in the mirror as she slipped on her sun dress, adding a pair of long silver earrings to her ears. She had finished her last book and sent it off the day before. She decided to take the remainder of the summer off from writing. Instead of making stories about people, she developed a new plan to make her own story. Taking some getaway trips with friends was the highlight of her summer plans. Grabbing her purse and keys, she walked through to the kitchen door when she heard the front door lock turn and she heard. "Mom." Trying not to feel disappointed, she glanced toward her watch. Turning around and walking back to the den, she saw her daughter. The surprise came when she saw Joe. With her heart in her stomach, as memories of when he last came to her house while she recalled everything he had said to her.

"Hey honey, what are you doing at home today?"

"I, um, well, we need to talk to you." Natalee moved toward the door, her eyes avoiding his hooded stare.

Responding in a rush. "Okay, well, I was just headed out to dinner. Can we talk later?" She said the words even though her gut insisted. It was a new conversation.

Dread filled her when Joe growled, "Natalee, it really cannot wait. Can we sit?"

With trepidation, she stammered. "Yes, sure." Opening her hand to the couches, she left her purse and keys on the buffet, moved towards the sofa, and then chose the chair. She could not help but notice Joe waiting for Jenny to sit on the couch closest to her Mother, then he sat on the opposite chair. Waiting patiently for her daughter to talk. Joe remained silent. The only movement you could see was a twitching of his cheek. He kept his hands clasped together with his forearms resting on his legs.

Finally, Jenny started the story. "Mom, first, I want to apologize for my behavior at Uncle Leo's party. I did not tell you, but I had gotten stood up earlier that day. And well, I was feeling pretty sorry for myself." Looking toward Joe. Natalee noticed a slight nod. Jenny continued. "I was immediately attracted to Joe, I tried hard to get his attention, but he was not interested. When we were at the club, I drank too much and made a fool of myself. Joe made it clear more than once at the club that the age difference and life experience were making the difference between us. I didn't listen. Even after he brought me home more like a big brother would have done, I had hoped he would change his mind and call me."

Jenny paused. Natalee recognized her daughter's ploy, attempting to avoid getting into trouble, a trick she learned when she was younger. She would pause, and Natalee was not falling for it, especially after missing her dinner date for this conversation.

Reminding her. "And." Natalee picked up her cell phone, sending a text apologizing for her late cancellation notice.

"Mom, are you listening?"

"Yes, Jenny, I just had to let my date know that I was not going to make our dinner date." Her voice emphasized the word date for Joe's benefit.

"Oh, Mom, I am sorry. I guess this could have waited." Looking at Joe shaking his head. He was confused as to why he was so determined for her daughter to tell this story. But she was beginning to feel that Jenny was learning a valuable lesson. Jenny continued. "So, I waited two weeks and no phone call. I had even stuck my number in his pocket at the club. I got tired of waiting." Jenny paused again. Natalee fumed inside. The thought that her daughter had continued to hit on the man she had spent the last month trying not to get involved with. The mere thought of Mother and Daughter interested in the same man was horrid. Jenny continued, interrupting Natalee's thoughts.

"I came home a night, but I didn't tell you. I went by his loft, but he was out. I had already found out he was not on duty that night. So, I checked out some of the clubs. I saw him in this Jazz club downtown. He was hitting the bar pretty heavily. It looked like he was mad about something in the way he was downing the drinks. Four, I think, in just a matter of minutes."

When she heard the word Jazz club, snatching Natalee's attention, jerking her head up. Their gaze held as they both remembered the night, He was there, seeing him by the bar, and then he was gone. Natalee looked away, avoiding his gaze, wiping a small tear from her cheek. Not noticing the moment between them, Jenny continued in a rush.

"Joe was drunk. I drove to his loft and waited. He saw me when he opened his door. He had told me he was not in the mood to see me. He also said I have already told you I am not interested. I didn't listen to him, Momma. I guess he thought I went out the door because he walked down his hallway, taking off his clothes. I should have left, but I didn't." Jenny paused. Tears formed in her eyes as she pleaded with her Mother.

"Momma, I am so sorry. I locked the door and went down the hall. I took off my clothes." Jenny paused, looking at her Mother. Natalee was fuming, standing up her hands went to her hips. Turning her back to her daughter, she walked to a large window. Staring out of the window towards the water as her heart broke into tiny pieces when she spoke. "That's enough. I don't want to hear anymore. I get it."

»»

Joe watched Natalee near the window, her focus on the water, as she had done that night, he confessed his feelings to her. All he wanted to do was stand and obliterate the distance between them in more ways than one and take her in his arms. Now, all hope that he one day would have had that right again was gone. Natalee turned and looked directly at her daughter.

Joe was the first to speak. "Jenny, you know you have to tell her everything. Now."

She nodded and again looked toward her mother. "Mom, I promised Joe I would tell you everything. He insisted I own up to my mistake." Natalee returned to her chair, gently picking up the cotton throw and covering her lap as her legs curled beneath. Jenny resumed her confession. "I followed him to the bedroom. He did not realize that I did not leave. He had laid down on his bed in his underwear. I was undressed. He fell asleep quickly. I pulled down his underwear and stroked him." Her embarrassment was evident to Joe, who right now lacked the compassion to care. "It was me, not him."

Tears filled her eyes, Jenny tried to stop there, but Joe spoke. "Continue."

"Okay, okay." Reluctantly she continued, between the sobs. "I climbed on top of him. He was already starting to get excited even though he told me he did not want to. I continued to try to excite him. He was so drunk he was starting to fall asleep." Jenny took a deep breath. Wiping her eyes. "I knew that he was drunk enough that he had no control." Jenny paused again.

With a sharp intake of breath, Natalee's eyes widened in horror. "Please continue."

Jenny responded quickly. "So, well, it did not take him long. I did not care that he wanted someone else. So, as soon as he was close to being hard, I took him inside of me. He caught his snap, then. I think he had been dreaming before because he kept saying this name. He tried to move me off. It seemed only to make him harder. The more we fought, the faster it happened. He said stop. I don't have protection." Pausing again, Jenny exploded in tears streaming down her cheeks.

"Jenny, Jenny, what did you say?" Natalee hissed at her daughter.

"Momma, I told him I was on the pill." Joe stood and went toward the window. He needed to distance himself from the situation for a few moments. He could not help but wish he was sitting on that large deck in the chair with Natalee sitting next to him. Looking past the pool to a boat dock with a nice boat and the Mobile River, he allowed his mind to wander about this beautiful place to raise a family with someone he loved. Turning around, he walked back to the two women in his life.

He almost had to laugh at the situation, feeling like such a fool to let this happen.

Natalee yelled, interrupting Joe's thoughts. "You Did What?" Natalee stood with her back stiff and her hands in tight fists at her sides. Joe realized Jenny had finally finished her confession.

Jenny repeated it. "Mom, I got pregnant on purpose. I knew it was the right time. I planned the whole thing. It helped that he had been drinking. Because I don't think he would have let me near him otherwise. Momma, it wasn't Joe's fault. He didn't even know it was me. I am so sorry, Mom. I messed up."

»»

Without saying a word, Natalee left the room. When she reached the refrigerator, she leaned against the cool stainless and took several calming breaths. When she felt she had regained control, she opened the door and carefully removed three drinks. Returning to the living room, she handed a beer to Joe and the water to her daughter. Jenny looked up in surprise. Natalee responded with anger.

"Well, I can only assume I was forced to hear your confession because you must be pregnant, and your plan succeeded. Since you told Joe and me first, I can also assume that you plan on carrying the baby to term. So, for those reasons, water only for you from now on." Natalee stomped to the kitchen, flicking off the cap of her drink and tossing it on the counter. She stormed out of the French doors to the deck. Looking past her gardens to the river, about the upgrades to the boat dock she had planned for the next month along with all of her other summer ideas. Now, all she could wonder was how much time and money this baby would take.

"Surely, if Jenny had considered abortion, she would not have told me." Panic ripped through her as her breaths became short bursts through the silence.

Her attempt at control was lost as her next thought pushed her over the edge. *"What if the next thing they would say was they were getting married?"* Blood quickly left her head, causing her brain to scramble. Her already labored breathing worsened, fear of the unknown, as she gripped the handrail with one hand while the other shakily brought the beer to her lips. Feeling relieved as she recognized the signs of her panic attack instead of much worse, continuing to calm herself when she heard the door open. Hearing his footsteps, Joe walked out onto the deck.

He was the first to speak. "It is nice here. I like your view."

"Thanks. Where is Jenny?"

"She is sick again. Says it happens every evening for her."

Natalee turned to face him. "What are your plans?" Natalee asked as she lowered herself into the patio chair to watch the sunset. She was not surprised when he took the chair next to her, and yet the irony of the situation was that there had never been a man to sit in that chair next to me to watch the sunset.

Sadness filled her as he broke the silence. "Thanks for the beer. I needed that." He sighed.

"Yea, me too." Joe looked at her.

"I wanted to tell you I am sorry about all of this. I never meant for any of this to happen." Taking another swig of his beer.

"I know. It doesn't sound like you had much say so in it."

He hesitated before he replied. "Yea, but if I had not let things get to me at the Jazz club, then I would not have been that drunk. And I am a man. I should have prevented it." Natalee stared into his eyes with longing, the same feeling she had avoided since their first meeting. Turning away, she focused on the river instead of the sadness in her heart. Sensing the tension, he changed the subject.

"So, this is the Mobile River? You have direct access to the bay."

"Yes, about an hour on the water will get you close to Dauphin Island."

"I love it there. I was there this weekend camping and fishing. I caught several nice ones." He smiled.

"I love doing that. Leo, Mary, and a group of us do that several times a year. It has always been one of my favorite things to do." They did what came naturally. They talked. Ever since their first meeting, talking came easy. Joe relaxed while

Natalee pushed her fears aside for the moment. Joe raised his bottle towards her. She clinked her bottle to his. An unspoken vow to get through this together passed between them.

Joe broke the stare by asking about her boat. "How long have you had the boat?" They talked about boats, the river, and spending time on the Island for the next thirty minutes.

Reality returned when Jenny stepped out onto the deck, admiring the potted flowers in the early evening light. "Mom, the flowers look nice this year."

"Thanks, honey." Jenny stood for several minutes as she looked over the water. "Dad loved it here, didn't he?"

With wistful reminiscence, she responded. "Yes, he had a vision for the yard."

Jenny sat down in the chair furthest from her Mother, almost alone.

"Mom, I don't remember. Did he ever get to enjoy it out here?"

"No, baby. He didn't. He worked so many overtime hours last year. I spent all my extra time out here making it nice. I bought these chairs two weeks before he died. He promised me, *One more month, babe, then I can relax*."

Natalee let the tear escape. Joe shifted in uncomfortable silence in the chair meant for Patrick. The same chair that each time he saw it, he had an overwhelming desire to sit in this chair, with her beside him for the rest of his life.

"Mom, I guess we need to finish talking." Natalee nodded, and standing, she wiped away another tear, picked up her empty bottle, reaching for Joe's. Her fingers brushed his as she picked up the bottle, interrupting his thoughts. Pulling him from his daydreaming, he looked up into her eyes, his brown eyes filled with soulful sadness.

Natalee announced. "I am hungry, is anyone else?" She was met with two heads nodding. "I will make dinner, and then we will talk. Is pasta okay?"

"Yes, Mom, is it okay if I lay down while you cook?"

"Yes, I will wake you when it is ready." Not hesitating to hear Joe's response. Instead, she walked into the kitchen, putting the beer bottles into the recycle bin.

Natalee opened the refrigerator, ignoring the aching feeling of dread inside her. Instead, she focused on making dinner. Cooking had always been her scapegoat, quickly drowned herself in the complex technique of a new recipe to divert her focus away from the problem at hand. Tonight was no exception. She tossed a green salad adding almond slivers and a vinaigrette, setting it aside to chill while the pasta boiled. Her thoughts were interrupted by the sound of the door.

Joe's voice sliced through the silence as he asked. "Is there anything I can do to help?"

"Yes, you could slice and butter the French bread for toasting." Saying the first thing that came to mind.

"Sorry, I had planned to help with dinner. The station called."

Curiosity got the better of Natalee as she asked. "Oh really, is everything okay?"

"Yes, a new lead on the case I have been working on. It's been cold for the last several weeks, and now something that looks promising."

"That's good." The awkward moment between them disappeared. With the slight mention of a case, they relaxed and enjoyed cooking side by side until dinner was ready. Natalee called Jenny to dinner while Joe set the table. Dinner finished with some pleasant conversation, avoiding the mention of the baby. Jenny managed to maintain an appetite after her significant bout of nausea and consumed two helpings.

Natalee had cleared the plates when her daughter asked, "Mom, do you have any dessert?"

"I do happen to have a caramel brownie with fudge sauce if either of you is interested." Joe's lifted his head in anticipation at the mention of chocolate, responding. "I could use a piece." Natalee smiled genuinely for the first time since they had walked through the door. Warming the caramel and fudge sauce, she served the brownies on three plates, each with a scoop of vanilla bean ice cream.

"Mom, you didn't know we were coming over tonight. When did you make the dessert? You would not make all of this for just yourself. You would worry that you would eat the entire pan."

Natalee confessed. "Yes, you are correct. I did not make this for me. I would have eaten the entire pan before you came home for your next visit. I had planned on inviting my date back here for dessert tonight."

"Well, that worked out well for us because now I get some too." Natalee sighed, pouring generous amounts of sauce over each serving.

»»

Joe wished he had not heard the last part of the conversation between Natalee and her daughter. The thought was that if he was not here right now, another man could have been eating this dessert with the woman he wanted. Sighing, he sat down at the head of the table with the two women in his life, taking a bite from the best dessert he had ever had, fighting the urge to moan. He made the mistake of staring into Natalee's hazel eyes, seeing a tiny bit of the chocolate sauce on her upper lip before she used her tongue to retrieve it.

Averting his focus away from her lips and tongue, Joe avoided looking at both women, choosing the dessert and accepting a second helping without delay when Natalee offered.

CHAPTER SIX

Jenny and Natalee left the doctor's office. The last week in June reared its ugly head, with steaming heat rising from the pavement while they walked to the car. Natalee held a prescription for prenatal vitamins, a payment schedule, a next appointment date, and a packet of the healthy mom-to-be information packet. The headache she had fought for the past two days threatened behind her eyes. Unlocking the passenger door, Jenny jumped in, reaching for the ac to turn it higher as Natalee started the car. A part of her wanted to ignore her daughter, make her return to school and stay there. The need to force her daughter to grow up and take responsibility was overwhelming. One part of her could justify those actions. On the other side, the mother in her knew that her only child was not ready. However, she had shown a horrible lack of maturity. She knew in her heart that if she were to push Jenny into taking responsibility, the baby would ultimately pay the price.

So, doing what most mothers would, she asked the age-old question. "Are you hungry?" When all she received for a response was a shrug, Natalee tried another question.

"We can stop and get something to eat on the way back to the house." Jenny looked down at her phone.

Responding quickly to a text, she finally spoke in audible tones. "No thank-you, Mom. I will grab something on the way back to school. I have so much studying to do."

"Okay then, I will get you back to your car." They rode in silence for the next ten minutes. Natalee noticed the many moods of her daughter. Jenny was prickly and moody, hungry most of the time. But now, she seemed almost happy. She could not escape the sickening feeling her daughter was once again up to something. Pulling into the driveway, Jenny quickly grabbed her overnight bag and a couple of water bottles from the refrigerator. After a quick kiss to her mother, she was off, backing down the driveway.

Natalee stood in the driveway and wondered how she would survive the next six months. Her plan to write for the afternoon dissipated beneath the frustration she felt. Instead, she changed into her black bikini to swim away for the day.

»»

Jenny turned towards the highway; she had promised to call Joe after the appointment to keep him informed. Taking a deep breath, she picked up the phone, pressed his number, and he answered on the second ring. Giving Joe a quick update on the doctor's visit, disappointment mounted when she sensed his impatience.

Before she ended the call, he asked. "When do you want to start looking for the baby bed?"

Surprised by his interest, she replied quietly. "Oh, my mom still has mine. It was a family heirloom. She said she would get it out of the attic on Saturday and take it to a restoration specialist to have it refinished." Joe responded by asking when she was coming back to town. "Oh, three weeks. I have finals this week. Then a few days off for the holiday the second semester starts. My next appointment is in one month." Hanging up with a quick goodbye. Her knuckles turned white as her grip tightened on the steering wheel. Even though he was polite and appeared to care, his voice didn't lie. The idea that Joe would fall in love with her while she was pregnant with their child was a ridiculous, childish fantasy. "Stupid." She muttered.

»»

Joe hung up and attempted to return his focus to his work. The late June heat was getting to him, and the entire town and crime were up. Teenagers were out of school for summer break and had entirely too much time on their hands. The minor vandalism and petty theft had him irritated. Joe rubbed his hands down his face in frustration. The constant feeling of being out of control was wearing him thin; he hated the sudden change his life had taken. Picking up his pen and looking over his notes, he tried not to think about Natalee and back on work.

His thoughts were interrupted by Leo. "Hey, is there anything going on between you and Natalee?" Joe dropped his pen, answering in a rush.

"Why, why do you ask?"

"Well, she told Mary that she was too busy this weekend to go to the beach house. This is a yearly thing she has never missed before. Also, getting her to answer the phone lately is hard lately, and she is cranking out the books. She already finished that one with me in it, and now she is halfway through the next one. From what Mary says, Natalee has been writing ten to twelve hours a day. For her to write without taking

49

breaks, it is usually when something bothers her. I can't help but wonder if you two hit it off and something messed that up. She is like a little sister to me. I would sure like to think that you would never do anything to hurt her. I introduced you two because I thought you were a stand-up guy."

Joe fidgeted with his pen. The urge to come clean and tell him everything that had happened. The belief that it wasn't just his story kept him from spilling his fears to his friend and partner. Leo continued. "And you have also been distracted and short-tempered for the past few weeks. You disappear when your phone rings."

Joe chose his response carefully. "I think that Natalee will tell you when she is ready. And for me, I'm trying to decide if I am even ready to figure out women." Leo left it at that but shook his head as he walked away. Joe expected more questions from his partner soon.

»»

Saturday morning, Natalee rose early, making her run longer than usual. With the fourth of July a few days away, several of her neighbors had parties planned. She watched from her kitchen window when several boats passed by. A sense of loss settled in. Lately, one of the only things that had kept her sane these past few weeks had been writing, even though she had given herself the summer to focus on new relationships for herself. But now, it was the only thing keeping her from crying in bed every day. Her world had become overly dark and dismal. She spoke softly. "A life without purpose is one in which you imagined a life where you had done something right and made a difference. Only to discover one day that you had been wrong. Instead of doing something right, you had made it much worse."

Fighting the tears, she began breakfast. Food had lost its taste. The summer sun had lost its sparkle, starting with such promise, now it only looked devastating. She honestly could not think of one thing to look forward to, deep in thought. She chopped vegetables for an omelet. A knock on the kitchen door prevented her from self-diagnosing her mental health. She turned to see Joe through the glass before he opened the door. She refused to focus on how good he looked in his tight gray t-shirt and khaki cargo shorts. Leather flip-flops topped it off, berating herself for noticing. *"He has such sexy toes."* Natalee tried to appear relaxed as she whispered. "Just great I am covered in sweat, and he comes over looking like a model. I don't have one ounce of makeup on. Ugh, who cares? I am going to be a grandmother at thirty-nine. No one cares what I look like." Giving herself a pep talk as she reluctantly said. "Good Morning." Natalee went back to breaking eggs in a bowl.

"How was your run?" She looked up in confusion. "Oh, Jenny mentioned that you run every day."

"It was a good long one. It helps with the stress." Joe nodded. She asked. "Would you like an omelet?"

"Sure, I could eat." Natalee started humming while she cooked, afraid to ask why he was visiting. It didn't take long before they sat at the kitchen table to an omelet and toast. "This is amazing. You are a wonderful cook."

She called him out on his compliment. "Ha, you just want to see what dessert I have made." Laughing, Joe clutched his chest, wounded. "Well, I am on call this weekend, so I could not go to the island, and Jenny mentioned you were getting the baby bed out of the attic today. I could bring it down for you." Natalee was in a world of conflict. A part of her wanted so badly to send him out of her house. The other part preferred to watch the tight shirt pull across his chest and arms as he used his hands to describe the enormous fish he had caught.

The t-shirt won her over.

That was the excuse she continued to tell herself when, an hour later, in the hot attic, she was sweating while she watched Joe bringing the baby bed and changing table along with several boxes down from the attic. She had to admit it would have been much more work for her than for him, as she failed to ignore how his muscles tightened in his legs as he backed down the ladder. Averting her gaze so that Joe did not notice, she had stared at his cargo shorts-covered backside, feeling as if life was imitating fiction, while she continued to ogle the father of her impending grandchild.

He placed the crib and changing table onto the driveway and brushed off the dust and cobwebs. Joe talked while Natalee was lost in memories of her daughter in the baby bed. Her thoughts were interrupted by him asking. "Jenny said you were taking it to a restoration specialist?"

"Yes, these have been in my family since the early thirties." He resisted asking if she was the first baby to sleep in it. Before he could finish his thought, she said.

"And no, I was not the first baby to use these."

"Who me? I would have never thought that you were that old."

Natalee tried to refuse Joe loading the baby bed and changing table in the back of his truck. His time and care covering them with old quilts and securing both with ropes gave her a chance to run back into the house. A short time later showered, wearing a pair of shorts, a flowing two-layer tank top, and tennis shoes. She ran her fingers through her hair and applied some tinted moisturizer and waterproof mascara. Picking up her blush, she stopped herself.

"Why am I trying? He is the father of my future grandbaby." Regretting the moment, she said the words out loud. Swallowing the pain, she grabbed her cross-body purse, sunglasses, and two cold water bottles. Locking the door behind her, she could hear the phone ringing inside. Noting the time, Natalee was confident it was Mary. Ignoring her and Leo had been burdensome. Not sure how she would be able to tell them yet. Pushing unpleasant thoughts aside, Natalee instead decided to focus on the day at hand. Joe jumped out of the truck bed when she walked up, wiping the sweat from his brow. Gladly accepting her bottle of water, she opened the passenger door.

She watched him walk around the front of the truck, getting in, closing his door, and fastening his belt when Natalee surprised him when she said. "Next week."

Starting the engine, he looked at her in confusion and asked. "Next week?"

"Sorry, I sometimes do that. Have a full conversation in my head and then blurt it out like you heard the whole thing."

Joe started to laugh. "I will have to remember that. I thought my hearing was going." Now Natalee laughed when he asked. "So, what is next week?"

"Yes, sorry, okay, the full conversation is. I heard the phone ring as I closed the kitchen door. I am betting that it was Mary. I cannot hold her and Leo off long without telling them the truth. They know me so well. They have to know something is up."

Joe nodded. "They do. Leo cornered me at work yesterday. He asked if we had something going on." " Joe sighed. "I hated lying to him."

"I did not want to tell Mary until I talked to you. I was concerned that when she tells Leo, he might give you trouble at work with him being your superior."

Joe nodded. "I worried about that also. Not so much a career problem but a friend problem. I can always go back to Florida. They would be glad to have me. Of course, with the baby, that would create a new problem." Joe drove in silence, following her directions. Once he said he had considered returning to Florida, the atmosphere changed in the truck'struck's cab. Joe tried to focus on enjoying the countryside. "This is pretty."

Relieved for a change in the subject, Natalee added. "It is even better in the fall. All of the colors, like something out of a magazine." Reminding Natalee of when Jenny was a baby. "I took some beautiful pictures up here of Jenny as a baby." " She struggled between her memories of a sweet baby Jenny had been to now. She continued. "I have such a hard time understanding what I did or did not do that led her to behave this way." Natalee wiped away a lone tear as it snaked down her cheek.

Natalee had not anticipated Joe reaching over and taking hold of her hand. She did not pull away, even though knowing she should. In the bizarre situation, while she knew one thing in her mind, she battled what was in her heart.

She whispered. "You know I tried to blame you." " Joe slowed, pulling into the parking lot. Reluctantly he released her hand and placed the truck in park, leaving the engine running. He released his seatbelt and turned to her.

He said the first words that came to mind. "For me, it would be easier if I had been able to take all the blame. And a part of me wanted to. I did not want you hurt by your daughter's actions. I know it hurts." Her eyes filled with and fat drops spilled over onto her cheeks. She had not cried since that night when she had to listen to the confession.

Using the pad of his finger, he gently wiped away her tears. "Lee, I am so sorry." She pinched her lips together. He continued. "I never meant to hurt you. I didn'tdidn't want you to know the truth. I admit it would have been hard if she had decided to abort the baby, especially because I want children desperately. But, I knew that if I never had the courage for you to know what happened, I would have to leave town. Because I would never be able to look you in the eyes again." Joe traced her hand with his finger. "This is an impossible situation. There is no easy way out where someone would not get hurt." He hesitated, then choked, "I know I shouldn'tshouldn't, but I wish it were us having the baby." The words left his lips. Joe held his breath, waiting for her response. Natalee's tear-filled eyes averted his gaze towards the crowd moving towards the flea market.

Longing filled her, overcome with an overwhelming desire for him to take her in his arms and kiss her. As bad as she wanted to go in that direction, that road was blocked for now. Changing the subject, she placed her hand on the door handle.

"We should go."

»»

They dropped off the baby bed and changing table with Frank and Julia, longtime friends of Natalee. Joe enjoyed listening to them talk about their furniture business they began when they needed extra money to buy their home. Having three boys, they began to rely on the extra income. Now the boys were grown and on their own. They retired early from their teaching positions, they committed to selling and restoring antiques, full time. Feeling inspired, Joe listened and watched them together while he yearned for a partner in his life. He had wished for a child, now with one on the way, but he was without a partner.

Some moments were happy, others remorseful because he felt happy. He pushed away the sadness choosing to focus on spending time with Natalee. Accepting with ease when she suggested they browse through the vendors before the drive back. He continued to worry if he had said too much when he confessed his feelings. Fully aware he was taking advantage of the situation, Joe allowed his hand to brush hers while they walked. He continued touching her whenever he got the chance. Studying her hands while she perused through a stack of old books, he longed to have the right to hold her hand.

Joe followed her from booth to booth, enjoying her excitement. Returning from a trip to the truck with her purchases, he glanced around the third row of vendors, certain it was the last place he had seen her. A momentary flash of fear coursed through him, he quickly searched each booth on the row.

Filled with relief when he noticed her bent down in awe over an antique rocking horse that had clearly seen better days. "Hey, there you are." She looked up, Joe was surprised to see her eyes filled with tears. Bending down next to her, placing his arm around her. "Babe, what is wrong?" She leaned her head onto his shoulder. "You want her?" Natalee gave a short nod. "Let's take her home then." Her eyes lifted to his. Joe gently brushed the tears from her cheeks. "But you do have to tell me why this little horse made you cry." Natalee nodded as she tried to interject when Joe pulled his wallet, paying. Walking away from the antique market without hesitation Natalee slowly placed her hand in the crook of his arm while he carried the purchase.

Feeling the loss of her touch when Natalee settled in the front seat while he loaded the horse. Waiting until they pulled out on the highway, he glanced toward her as asked. "Why did you cry?"

She responded without delay.

»»

"Back when Patrick and I got pregnant, we were so young and very poor. He had just completed the academy when we got

55

married. I was grocery shopping one day, and there was this little second-hand shop next to the store. They had a horse just like this one. I wanted it badly, but we could not afford it." Natalee wiped her tears. "I never told Patrick. He worried about money. After he made the force, he worked as much overtime as possible. When Jenny was two, I applied to the academy and was hired into the force. We worked opposite shifts until we could buy the house. I worked and continued my education in criminology. I had just finished my degree when I lost my parents in a car crash." Natalee paused. She watched the trees while they drove. She continued. "Not only did I lose my parents, but also our babysitter, Jenny, was only four at the time. Luckily the Captain worried about Jenny and us. His concern about keeping Jenny from ever being an orphan pulled some strings and fast-tracked me to Internal Affairs. I was home every night, meaning one less parent at risk for Jenny."

Joe reached over and squeezed her fingers. Natalee did not pull away as she continued her story finding strength from his touch. "Jenny was ten when Joe and Leo went to make an arrest, and he was killed. I retired a few months later, taking our pensions and investing as much as possible, living modestly, and focusing all my energy on my daughter. It was then that I started to write. It began more as therapy for me, giving me an outlet from the sadness. Before long, I had finished my first book. I was surprised as anyone when it sold. I had only sent it to the publisher on a dare from Mary."

Natalee wiped her tears with her free hand. Joe slipped his fingers through hers, holding tighter. Natalee stared towards their intertwined fingers. "Writing was the best option for me, giving me an income and the freedom to raise my daughter. I was proud of myself, and I thought Patrick would have been proud of the job I had done raising our daughter." Tears flowed down her cheeks when she said. "But now, what if I caused this? This behavior could have directly resulted from what I did or didn't do. Or was it, the fact that Patrick died when she was so young."

Lifting her hand to his lips, Natalee held her breath while Joe's lips moved softly to her fingers. Sending shivers down the back of her neck as the warmth spread through her body, burning low into her belly. A feeling crossed over her that she had not felt in quite a while.

Longing was the first thought to cross her mind.

CHAPTER SEVEN

Natalee hit delete again, then threw the pencil across her desk. Every word, every thought, and every idea that came from her mind through her fingers always ended up with the same main character. He was tall, with dark hair, olive skin, and chocolate eyes so dark that you wanted to melt into them. Every one of them, each character, talked like Joe and walked like Joe.

All she had to show for the past two days was four chapters of wasted time in her computer trash bin and a full notepad of unusable ideas. He crossed her mind at least every hour, no matter how hard she had tried not to think about him. "Ugh," Natalee banged her head on the desk and braced for the memories to bombard her again.

Natalee admitted having Joe with her at the flea market had been a good day. She felt like an average couple that day. The sun had been warm with a comfortable breeze, and occasionally his arm would brush hers, keeping her body on edge. She had tried blocking the words he had said before she opened the door of his truck. Avoiding thinking that he wished it was them together having a baby.

Shaking herself from memory, she stared at the blinking cursor on her laptop. Frustration mounted, she closed her computer, and her eyes instantly drifted towards the pool, allowing herself to revel in the memories. She had seen Joe on several occasions during July. He seemed to find a reason to stop by after work frequently. The second week of July, he found Natalee in the garage, painting the rocking horse. He expressed his genuine excitement at her progress and volunteered to help her paint. Without reservation, he had accepted her invitation for dinner, and a short time later, they were sitting on the deck watching the sunset while eating steaks and twice-baked potatoes.

On more than one occasion, she fought the urge to invite him on a sunset boat right but never found the courage. Instead, they talked until the moon was bright, and she walked with him out to the driveway. When Joe paused, turning as if he had something to say, he stopped himself, leaving her curious with questions and a sense of loss when he left. She found herself in the grocery store, wondering what his favorite foods were.

Before long, she found herself planning meals in case he happened to stop by.

After Jenny's last prenatal appointment, she had invented a reason to step away while her daughter called him and gave an update on the baby's progress. Sometimes it felt like she was living in two parallel worlds, one where her daughter had done this despicable thing and interrupted all three of their lives. The second was her and Joe, friends enjoying each other with the possibility of something more.

Natalee sighed. "The problem is I am walking a tightrope between the worlds. They are bound to collide." She fussed at herself. Laying her head in her hands. "Ugh."

August had begun, hot and humid, adding to her misery. Jenny was knee-deep in her last summer session at the university while Natalee's days passed slowly, feeling more alone than ever before. Her heart ached inside. She had lost weight. Recently she ran harder and longer than ever before. Usually, after her run and a quick breakfast, she wrote for hours, yet she was disappointed with herself for the results of hours wasted on lifeless words.

By the second week of August, after deleting everything she had written that morning, she finally chose to stop the torture, rewarding herself with a swim. Donning the new black bikini Mary had dared her to buy, she was mesmerized by the results.

"Ha. All of my misery has paid off." She laughed. Walking out to the pool, she dove in and began to swim. Pushing herself harder and faster, reaching her thirtieth lap eased her frustration. Slowing, she allowed herself to daydream, and finally, Joe's face was not the first thing she saw when she thought of a main character.

Swimming underwater, she surfaced to stand. A pleasant smile crossed her lips when she saw a pair of flip-flop-clad feet, tan legs, and cargo shorts. She knew who it was without looking up at the broad, muscular chest. Natalee took slow steps as water droplets rolled down her body in the afternoon sun. Feeling a power that she never knew she possessed, she felt his line of vision lower, caressing her breasts and heating them with each second. He stared. Time stood still, feeling the warmth spreading while his eyes moved from her flat-toned stomach to the curve of her hips covered with the small black material.

She heard the change in his breathing when he leaned forward in his chair. His excitement was apparent in the growing bulge that strained against the material of his shorts. Boldly, she strolled toward him without embarrassment, stopping before him. Surprise registered over his face when Natalee smiled, reached up to the nape of her neck, and untied the black bikini top, releasing the strings. Before he could drop his bottom jaw, she held the material to her breasts, reaching around his shoulder for the towel behind his back.

While his line of vision was firmly on the swell of her breasts, she said,

"Hello, Joe."

»»

"Hi, yourself." He responded in awe when she wrapped the towel around her, tucking it over her breasts.

The small black bikini top swung from her fingers as she asked, "What are you up to?"

Joe crossed his legs and then uncrossed them, leaning back in the chair as he confessed. "I thought I would come by and see how you were doing." Natalee ran her fingers through her hair, sitting in the chair next to him. She could not help but glance at her legs, wondering if she had shaved close enough this morning.

She asked. "Oh, you are off today?" Joe purposely looked at the water, trying to avoid the thought of her bare breasts under the towel.

"Yes, well, I used a couple of vacation days, so I am taking the boat to the island in the morning. I wondered if you wanted to go." Joe wondered if he had made the right decision asking. After seeing her in the knockout black bikini, he would love to spend the weekend on the island with her. He was just unsure how they would ever move from him being the one who got her daughter pregnant.

"Oh, wow, that would be fun, and I would love to be down there. But I am flying out in the morning for a book signing trip. My latest book is in stores today. Mary is going with me. I am planning on telling her about the baby on the trip." Joe nodded. He wished he had mentioned going to the island a couple of weeks ago. He could have arranged his time around her.

"Oh, yea. How do you think Mary will react?"

She laughed before responding. "Well, I plan to get her completely drunk, then spill the beans. It will soak in overnight; in the morning, she will remember bits and pieces and question me. Of course, I will be too busy to answer her questions, so she will hopefully pass them on to Leo while he is fishing with the boys. And most likely, he will have already had a few beers so it might soften the news. Hopefully, this does not affect you too badly at work." He couldn't contain his chuckle when he saw her smile. "Sorry, I can't make the island this weekend. But thank you for asking. Have you heard from Jenny?"

"Not really. All I got was a text from her telling me the next doctor's visit was next Thursday at three thirty. It's an ultrasound appointment. I will leave work for a bit to meet you two there." Biting her lip, he watched her gaze settle on her boat dock. Glancing down towards Natalee's pink painted toes as she wiggled them in the grass. She crossed and uncrossed her legs, something that he had noticed she did when she was nervous. He admired her long, toned legs with her beautiful golden tan. He had been so surprised by the black bikini. It was not something that he would have expected.

"So, Lee has a sexy side." He had taken to call her Lee in his thoughts. Natalee was long, and most of her friends automatically called her Nat. He liked Lee. It was his.

"I am sorry I interrupted your swim."

Absentmindedly she responded. "Oh, it was okay. I had been in for a while."

"How is the writing going?"

She hesitated, looking again towards the river. "Not so good. That is why I am procrastinating. This morning I ran twice my normal distance. Then came back, ate some breakfast, and worked in the garden. Straightened the house. Then finally, I sat down around one to write. And it was pure crap. So, by three, I was out here."

Joe laughed, teasing her. "You know the story is not going to happen if you keep putting it off."

Sighing, she smiled when she looked at him. "I know." Joe tried changing the subject. He knew too well about procrastinating. He was doing the same thing, except instead of trying to write a novel, his problem was getting the courage to tell her how he felt about her. Instead of telling her why he came to see her, he asked another question. "How long have you lived in this house?" His eyes were steady on the river, but he was very in tune with her body, set only a few feet from him. Feeling her presence so near to his hand resting on the arm of his chair, one slight move and he could hold her hand.

Turning to look at her now when she answered. "When Patrick and I were first married, we lived in a tiny studio apartment. It did not even have a bedroom. I was pregnant with Jenny when he had just finished the academy and started working. We knew we would never be able to make ends meet on one income, and well, both of us were determined for Jenny not to be raised by strangers. I went into the academy shortly after her first birthday." Natalee paused and looked at the river again. "Thankfully for my mother and Patrick's sister, we had child care covered. And the best part was she was with her cousins all day. I finished the academy and started as a beat cop. Patrick and I worked opposite shifts to spend the most time with Jenny. He worked overtime as much as he could, and I returned to school to get my degree in criminology." Laughing. She reached over and patted his hand. "I am so sorry, you asked a simple question, and here I am with my whole life story."

Joe looked at her smiling face. He tried not to acknowledge her hand being there. Scared that she would remove it too soon. "I like hearing about your life. Our life experiences shape us into who we are. Please go on." Nodding.

She then removed her hand. "Well, the plan was for me to get away from the street duties. With the degree, it became much easier for me to make a detective. Patrick liked the streets. He had not planned on making detective. In those days, he and Leo were partners. A year after I made detective, we bought this house. It was in sad shape in those days. We did most of the work ourselves. We moved in just in time to have Jenny's fifth birthday party here. We worked on the house every chance we got. He did get to enjoy the house, just not enough. He loved the pool and the boat dock. We took evening rides on weekends."

The memories were getting to her. She wiped a lone tear from her eye.

Joe responded. "I am so sorry I brought it up. It must still be hard. You must still miss him a lot."

"No, it's not a sadness, more of a wishing he would have had a chance to do everything he had wanted. And I can't help but wonder if Jenny would have turned out differently if he had been here."

"It sounds like you had a wonderful life with him."

She nodded. "We did."

Joe hated stating the obvious. "You know, you still have plenty of time to have any type of life you want."

Worried that he had gone too far. Natalee stared at the water when she answered softly. "I know. The main reason I waited so long to start dating was Jenny. I did not want to bring a string of men through her life when she was so young. I became so involved in her life and writing my books that I never realized I was missing out." She said wistfully. "Thank you for the invitation. I wish I could spend the weekend with you, rain check?"

"You've got it." Joe stood, reaching for her hand and pulling her close.

Reluctant to leave, he held her close. "I better go pack the boat. Have a good safe trip. Many signatures to you."

"I am sorry that I have not told you yet. I hope my telling Mary about Jenny and the baby does not create a bad situation for you at the station."

Joe did not say anything. He continued holding her hand, using his thumb to make tiny circles on her palm. "Well, I did want you to know because Leo will find out by the end of the weekend."

"Hmm. How bad of a beating do you think I will get?"

She giggled. "Oh, I am not worried about that. You won't have to worry about fighting back. Just run. With his beer belly, he will never be able to reach you."

Now it was Joe's turn to laugh. "It will be fine. If he really has too much of a problem with it, I will turn in my resignation and go back to Tarpon Springs." A sudden sense of dread bombarded Natalee. Joe saw it in her eyes. He felt it too. It was the first thing he thought of also. He did not want to leave, and not just for the baby.

Natalee responded. "Surely it won't come to that." She insisted.

He squeezed her hand. "I will do my best to keep that from happening." There he had it, the perfect chance to tell her how he felt. But he could not do it. The fear of sending her away was too great. "It would be too far from the baby." Her smile slid into a grim, flat line.

Natalee responded. "Oh, yes, that would not work for the baby."

Joe paused. "I should get out of your hair. I still need to pack the boat. I will miss you this weekend."

Natalee released a snort. "Somehow, I think you will keep busy. Plenty of college girls will be around, and you will not miss this old lady's company."

Joe longed to tell her no woman compared to her. Where she saw aging, he saw a beautiful mature woman with legs that go on forever. A woman who needed no makeup, who was beautiful no matter what she was wearing. He had so many things to tell her. But he could not find the courage.

Instead, he settled on. "I seriously doubt that." Looking her in the eye, he squeezed her hand tighter. "I would like to talk to you sometime when I get back." He squeezed her fingers tight once more before he released his hold.

She was surprised by the sudden seriousness of his tone. "Okay. I'll walk you out." Walking beside her, his arm brushed against hers during their slow walk toward his truck. Natalee tightened the towel around her body as Joe opened the truck door. Natalee gave him a wave and started to turn toward the house. Unexpectedly, Joe shortened the distance between them and pulled her into his arms, holding her close. The towel dropped slightly as her arms immediately went around his back. Joe could feel her bare damp breasts pressing against his chest. Kissing her forehead, he whispered.

"See you next week.' She responded with a nod against his neck.

CHAPTER EIGHT

Natalee rose early Friday morning. Having packed the night before excited about this book tour. Ready to get away from home for a change. The constant struggle with her feelings for Joe and dealing with her daughter and the baby. When Joe had left, after their last encounter she had such hope for the two of them. Only to walk into the house and face a group of photographs of her daughter. Memories flooded in, images of Jenny throughout her life. Met with the truth, her sweet little daughter in the photograph was the same person who had purposely had taken advantage of the situation with the man.

Natalee could not help but wonder if she would have not shot him down at Leo's party if Jenny would have focused on Joe the way that she did. "Or would she?" Now she wondered if Jenny would have still done what she had done.

Pushing the thoughts aside she locked the door and loaded her bag in the back of her SUV. Driving the few miles to pick up Mary. She had a copy of her schedule, airline tickets for them both. Her mind set on the details of their trip. Pulling up in Mary's driveway she immediately forgot her troubles and laugh as her best friend came running to the car with her pink and leopard print rolling suitcase, bright hot pink purse and matching sunglasses. Her short brunette hair styled with fluff and plenty of spray. Mary was obvious ready.

She screamed, "Big city, here we come."

Natalee met her at the trunk of the car. "I am so happy you are going with me. We will have a great time." Jumping into the car the two of them headed to the airport. Boarding the plane and an hour later, Natalee beamed on the outside but the inside knew she needed to tell her friend the truth, and it could not wait for a night of drinking. She decided the plane ride to New York was the perfect time. She waited for the plane to level out and the flight attendants passed out drinks. Picking up her cocktail she made a toast with Mary for a wonderful life. Thinking to herself it was time.

"Mar. Do you remember when you had asked me several times what was going on?"

Mary was distracted with her drink. "Yes."

"Well, uh I need to tell you something."

This caught Mary's attention. "Nat, what is it? You know you can tell me anything."

Mary managed to control her emotions throughout the entirety of the Natalee's truth.

Natalee was exhausted when she finished. Shushing Mary as she loudly said. "She did what!" "She really did." Natalee nodded.

"Yes, I am afraid so."

Then came the questions. Mary peppered her with them, one after another. "First, what about you and Joe? Second, what does Joe say about this? Third, does Jenny know about you and Joe?"

Natalee grabbed her friend's hand that was waving frantically in the air. "Okay, first. Remember at your party. I basically shot him down because of the age difference and the fact that we are in different stages of our lives. We have gotten closer through the past few months. We talked several times, he is a good guy." Natalee paused, confessing not only to Mary but also herself. "The night of the incident, Joe had been drinking. We were at the same Jazz club, it was the night I wore the red dress. When I left the dance floor he was already at the bar. I saw him take two drinks quickly. I started walking toward the bar, he was gone. All I saw was the door slamming shut."

Mary realized the torment that her best friend was going through.

"Nat, it is not your fault. Heck for that matter it really is not Joe's fault. I can guess that he thinks he could have stopped it because he is a man. But in fact, Jenny took advantage of him."

Natalee took a deep breath. She hated telling Mary all of this, she would never want anything to change the relationship Jenny has with her Aunt and Uncle. Mary reached over taking her hands.

Leaning close as the plane started the descent. "Leo and I love you and Jenny. There is nothing that could ever make that stop. We are family. Forever and Always." Natalee nodded as a few tears rolled down her cheeks. Mary reached up and swiped away the tears with a tissue. "No more tears, you hear me? We are two Alabama women loose in New York, bring on the alcohol." They both laughed as the plane's wheels touched the runway.

Any further conversation was on hold, while they exited the plane. Picking up their bags, and finding their car service. Spying her name, Natalee pointed to the driver in the suit holding a name card. Mary quickly focused on the sights of New York City as soon as the car headed down the highway. Natalee, once again looked over the itinerary, interrupted by her cell phone ringing. Natalee looked at the caller id and hesitated, feeling guilty, she answered.

"Hello, Hi honey. How is everything?" Mary waited expectantly. "Oh, everything is great. Yes, Aunt Mary is excited about being in New York. We are headed to the hotel now, then the signing is at six." Natalee listened intently as Jenny went on about school and being sick. Already focusing on her expanding waist. "Okay, Jen we are pulling up at the hotel now. We will be back Monday afternoon." Listening again. "Okay, babe. Yes, I will be at the appointment on Thursday. Okay, love you, talk to you soon. Bye." Hanging up the phone. Dropping her cell into her purse.

Mary announced, "Your face is going to freeze like that."

Natalee laughed. "You can tell, can't you?"

Nodding. "Yes, it is pretty obvious that she is causing you extreme amounts of stress. What can I do to help?" Natalee hugged her best friend as she wondered how often she told little white lies to get off the phone with her only child. *"Sad."* Mumbling, as they finally pulled into the hotel. Mary could not look at everything fast enough. A short time later they were checked in, unpacked, cleaned up and changed for a late lunch.

Getting into the elevator, Mary reached over pulling her friend close. Saying the words Natalee needed to hear the most. "Nat, I am here for you no matter what. We will figure all of this together." Hugging her back and kissing her cheek. In true Mary fashion. "Come, on let's go get an amazing fattening lunch and dessert. Then tonight we go drinking and dancing."

"Lets" Linking arms the two of them, went through the door to hail a cab.

It was nearly midnight by the time they returned to the hotel. Giggling like school girls as they carried their bottles of wine to their room. Mary and Natalee always shared a room when they traveled together. They loved to use this time for a slumber party, reminding them of their childhood. This time like many, gave Natalee what she needed most, unconditional love. Both changed into their sleepwear. Opening a bottle of wine, Mary poured them each a glass and asked the question that she held in all night.

"Tell me, where do you stand with Joe?" Tears filled Natalee's eyes as she envisioned his face before her eyes.

"Mary, I think I am in love with him." It was Mary's turn to feel choked up. "Oh, honey. I am so happy for you. Finally, you found someone else to love. But."

"You said it. But. A giant but." Taking a large sip. Natalee continued. "A couple of days ago, he came by the house. I was in the pool in my new black bikini."

Pausing, giving Mary a chance to absorb. "What? You are kidding. You didn't stay in the pool, did you?"

"No, silly, of course, I got out. He surprised me, though. I felt so naked in that thing. But I think he liked it because he smiled and stayed awhile."

"What did he want? Why did he come by?"

"I will tell you everything. Slow down a minute. He was planning on taking his boat to the island for the weekend. He asked me to go with him." Sighing. "He looked so sexy. How can any man look that good in a t-shirt?"

"Mm. Go on. Back to you getting out of the pool sexy, right, not clumsy."

"Thanks a lot. Well, I was not trying to be sexy, or I would have fallen. I just walked up the steps. He had his mouth open. I could feel him undressing me with his eyes. I wanted him to take me into his arms and crush my body to his." Natalee laughed at her herself, burying her face in her hands. Mumbling. "I have to tell you what I did. I still can't believe I did it."

Confused, Mary leaned forward. "Nat, what happened?"

Natalee raised her head, looking Mary in the eyes, and confessed. "So, I have been having these crazy fantasy dreams about him. I was all hot and bothered and had just relaxed when I looked up from the water, and there he was. I went nuts. That is my best defense, crazy nuts. I got out of the pool, walked slow so he could watch the water drip off my body, then I reached around him for the towel." She hesitated.

Mary shouted. "What, don't you stop on me now."

"Okay, I am telling you. So, I untied my top before him, put the towel around me, and pulled my top off." Natalee grimaced as Mary broke into a roaring laugh.

"What did he do?"

Natalee responded. "Well, he kept stumbling over his words and got excited down there. Then he kept shifting his legs." Natalee blushed. Mary laughed until she rolled on the floor. "Mary, it's not funny, and there is more."

Mary jumped onto her knees, sipping her wine with her elbows on the low table. "What else happened."

Natalee paused, then continued her story. "He said he had something to discuss when he returned and held my hand, pulling me close. I walked him to his truck, and he pulled me into a hug, and when I put my arms around him, my towel dropped slightly." Natalee grimaced, biting her lip. "And when he pulled back, I hurried to fix my towel and looked, and he had wet marks from my breasts on his shirt." Mary laughed so hard that she hurriedly ran to the little girl's room. Then coming back, she pulled another bottle of chilled wine from the cooler. Mary sat down on the couch, opening the new bottle, completely speechless, a trait Natalee had never seen in her best friend.

"Mary say something. What should I do?"

Mary looked at her best friend and filled her glass of wine before responding. "Nat, all are laughing aside. I think, just like I did at the party, you and Joe are meant to be together. Pushing all the Jenny stuff aside, I still believe this. You can protest as much as you want. But you love that boy, and I believe he loves you. If there were more passion between you two, you would spontaneously combust each time you are around each other."

Mary pulled Natalee into her arms. "Nat, honey, you must let go of your fear." Natalee pulled back and stared into her best friend's eyes, a question forming in her mind.

Before she could ask that question, Mary explained. "Nat, your fear of loss. This is not about Joe's age. It's not about Jenny's antics. It is about your fear of being left by someone you love, dying. You have a fear of loving again and losing them. That is why you don't want another child or fall in love again. Nat, your parents, and Patrick did not leave you because they wanted to. It was their time, sweetheart. It doesn't mean everyone you love will leave. Look, Leo and I are still around. And we always will." Mary was determined to lighten the mood. "So, let me see if I have this right. You have a major lust for a younger man your daughter just happened to take advantage of, and now she is having his baby. Right?" Natalee dropped her head into her hands in defeat. Mary giggled. "Hey, it is only a little obstacle, right?"

"Ha, ha." And with that, they changed the subject and went about enjoying their girl's weekend.

Monday morning dawned bright and early. The three days of book signings around the city were successful. Natalee left Mary asleep with her hangover this morning while she met with her agent and editor. Her book sales had increased, and now they were both pushing for her next one.

"I am working on it. It is moving a little slower than normal. But I am sure that it will pick up speed." She addressed them both, trying to get a little faith generated. With a wave, she left the office building. Catching a cab back to the hotel, she planned to meet Mary, have lunch then head to the airport. She enjoyed the city, it was a nice break from the everyday routine, but she could never live here full-time.

"Mary, are you awake?" Natalee yelled as she entered the hotel room. The bed was empty. A moment later, Mary came out of the bathroom fully dressed.

They were enjoying the sunny New York weather at a local outdoor cafe when Mary broached the subject halfway through their meal. "Nat. I think you should go for it with Joe." Surprised.

"Really?"

"Yes."

"You don't think that a tiny little thing like he is the father of my future grandchild might make things a bit awkward?"

"Well, it will make for a perfect party conversation." Shaking her head, they both laughed. Natalee chose to table the conversation of Joe and her desire to jump him every time she was around him from her mind and instead focus on her best friend.

CHAPTER NINE

Natalee returned home Monday evening, tired but happy. The book signing had given her a perfect chance to get away from all the stress of her everyday life and Joe. A strange feeling came over her as she walked into her kitchen, realizing her home had not felt this lonely since Patrick's death. Now since she had met Joe, every day was lonely. She missed his presence the few times he had been to the house, talking at the kitchen table or sitting outside on the patio.

She lost herself in thought while carrying her weekend bag down the hallway. Slowly opening the door to Jenny's room, the bright, cheery yellow paint she had painted when her daughter was five was now a soothing blue since she had gotten the wild inspiration to make a change. Her lips moved into a smile, recalling how she had begun painting, having not gotten far when she heard the knock on the kitchen door—surprised to see Joe walk in wearing faded shorts and a worn t-shirt with a bag of painting supplies in one hand and a six-pack of beer in the other. Remembering, it had turned out to be a fantastic day even though. She wished she had not enjoyed herself.

Wistfully she changed her thoughts to instead the list of things she needed for the baby's room. Interrupting her thoughts when she realized. "Enough of the procrastinating." Reminding herself that she needed to get unpacked and write. Her editor and agent would not wait for long. They expected a new release for the holidays on the book they believed she had already started. Natalee changed into linen pants and a tank top, drink in hand. She sat down at her desk. Instantly her eyes were drawn to her backyard and the lowering sun. Lingering for only a moment before her writing brain forced her back to her reality, the books that supported her would not write themselves. Opening her laptop, taking a sip of her wine, a deep breath, and one last look at the night sky, she was off into the fantasy land of her characters.

The words flowed, a book that had no beginning, end, or middle until last week. With no characters in mind, she realized New York had been precisely what she needed to get this book started. Stretching as she looked up from her computer, she was surprised to see it was just after midnight. Logging off the computer, she stretched as she stood. Picking up her cell phone, disappointed with no new texts or calls, she sadly walked to bed.

Natalee returned from New York with a renewed sense of wonder and unlimited possibilities for the future. Gone were the anxiety and hurt from the summer, spending too much time focusing on Joe. Now she allowed her memories and daydreams to happen, enjoying them and then letting go. After her run, she showered, dressed, and headed into town on Wednesday morning. She was treating herself to a spa morning, including the nails and waxing, something she had never taken the time nor spent the money on for hair removal.

Spending the weekend with Mary, she recognized how behind the times she was. As she entered the cafe for her lunch date, she felt exceptionally smooth. She giggled.

"Nat." Mary waved from a nearby table. "Nat, you look wonderful. Where have you been?"

"Oh, this?" She gently patted her new highlights and waved her pale pink manicured fingers. "Yes, I got a little trim and some fingers and toes attention." Lowering her voice to a whisper. "And a little waxing. You did not tell me how bad that hurt."

Mary grinned. "Oops. Forgot to tell you it hurt like hell. But it is so worth it later." Waggling her eyebrows. They handed the waitress their menus after they placed their orders. "So, any phone calls or unexpected visitors?"

"Sadly, no. I can't keep worrying about every little thing he says or does besides. I finally started my newest book. If I can make the November first deadline, I will be able to take the spring off and get to be a grandma." Natalee grimaced. "That sounds so weird, doesn't it?"

"Yes, it does. I would have never thought it would be something either of us would be going through now." Mary paused. She did not want to upset her best friend. "I am so sorry to say this. But with all three of ours in college and the money flying out of the window faster than me and Leo can earn it, I am so relieved it is you instead of me." Mary gritted her teeth with a wide smile. "Does that make me the worst friend in the world?"

Natalee grabbed her hand and squeezed. "Silly, don't think twice about it. No, it doesn't, because if it were you instead of me, I would be relieved too." Mary shook her head, laughing. The waitress delivered their cocktails and the appetizer. The main course quickly followed. After a few drinks, with their problems forgotten, the idea of dress shopping was the best.

An hour later, while in the dressing room with Mary steadily handing dresses through the curtain, she doubted her decision to spend money while a pleasant buzz still filled her head. She guessed this was much safer than driving home, realizing shopping would take up the much-needed few hours until the three cocktails wore off. Stepping from the dressing room in front of the large mirrors, she admitted the black sleeveless dress, which was molded to her body, pulling tight at the waist and stopping above the knee.

Natalee turned so Mary could see the back. "Oh my gosh, Nat, that looks amazing," Natalee asked. "Does it drop down too far?"

Mary insisted. "No, honey, it stops before the waist. You are good. It shows off your back, really sexy." After shopping at several boutiques in the area, their last stop was the ice cream and cupcake shop for a fantastic fat-filled dessert. Mary laughed, claiming she would pull out leftovers for Leo's dinner.

Saying their goodbyes with a hug, Natalee got into her car and started the engine. Her cell phone rang. "Hello."

"Natalee, hi, it's Charles."

It took her a minute to place the voice and name on a face. "Oh, hi, Charles. How have you been?" Natalee remembered him as tall and handsome when she met him at the charity dinner last month. If she remembered correctly, he was a recently divorced businessman.

He interrupted her musings. "Sorry if I am interrupting. I got your number from Kathy Stewart. I hope that is okay?" Natalee hesitated. "Sure, it is. How have you been?"

"Good, busy but good. I called because I have a charity fundraising dinner for the hospital. Would you like to go with me? It is quite a fancy affair. And I am sorry it is such late notice, it is tomorrow night. Doesn't give you much time to find something to wear."

Laughing nervously, she responded quickly, thinking about the new black dress. "It is okay. I just happened to buy something perfect to wear. What time?"

Charles sounded surprised. "Really, wow, that is great. Sorry for the late notice. The invitation got lost in the sea of other things on my desk."

"I promise it is okay. I am excited. What time?"

"I will pick you up at six."

"Charles, six is perfect. I will text you my address."

CHAPTER TEN

Natalee stared in the mirror. The black material glided down her body, molding to her tall, lithe frame. Glancing over her shoulder towards the plunging back, she enjoyed the look of seduction. Tonight was about taking around her life.

"Who am I kidding?" Feeling old and unwanted, she willed her reflection to change. Instead, she could only see a bird's eye view of herself in the doctor's office. Her lips trembled as she relived hours before when Joe stood beside her daughter while Jenny lay on the table. Joe had placed his hand next to Jenny's on her exposed belly as they felt the baby kick right after the doctor announced the baby was a boy.

Somehow, she survived the remainder of the appointment. Thankful that Jenny had brought her car, Natalee made an excuse and bolted toward the parking lot.

She raced from the doctor's office towards the marina. She sat on the bench and watched the boats for an hour arrive and depart until she could take a deep calm breath and safely drive home.

Now, taking a few moments, she looked out the window. This was her favorite time, the sun starting to show signs of promise of the cooler evening to come. Glancing at the clock, she expected her date, taking a sip of wine, then returning the glass to the counter. Natalee picked up her purse at the sound of an engine coming up her driveway. She walked toward the front door. Startled by the sound of the kitchen door opening as she looked over her shoulder in surprise. She heard Joe's voice when she thought she had locked the door. "Lee, it's me."

Turning, she took a few steps back to the kitchen.

Joe stood speechless, lips parted. "Oh, Natalee, you look beautiful."

Her body ached for him as she whispered. "Thank you."

Joe took several steps forward. "We need to talk." She bit her lip and fought back the tears. Opening her mouth to speak, only to be interrupted by the doorbell.

Natalee pointed to the door. "Sorry, I do not have the time. I have plans."

Turning, she walked toward the foyer. She stopped and looked back at Joe. Tears burned in her eyes. Plagued with indecision, she struggled to run into his arms. Instead, Natalee chose safe and turned to open the door.

In her happiest voice. "Hi Charles, don't you look handsome."

"Me? You are beautiful. And to think I only gave you a day's notice." Holding out his hand. "Shall we?"

Pulling the door closed, she flinched when it reopened. Natalee took the front step with Charles when she heard from behind her. "Lee, I need to talk to you."

She glanced over her shoulder. "Joe, it will just have to wait. Can you please lock up when you leave?" Smiling back at Charles, she offered him her hand.

»»

As they followed the front walk to the car, Joe stood in the doorway watching each step she took further away from him when he heard, "I am sorry, did I interrupt something? We still have time if it is something you need to take care of. Do you mind me asking who is he?"

"No, silly it is no big deal. He is the well I guess the term for it is my daughter's baby daddy. And with Jenny there is always some sort of drama going on. So, it will surely keep."

"Baby Daddy. I have heard that term. Doesn't anyone get married anymore and make commitments?"

Laughing. Natalee replied. "I guess not."

Joe fought the urge to slam the front door. "That's my girl." He growled toward the fading tail lights as they disappeared down the street. The image of his girl walking away with another man while anger burned behind his eyes. Realizing the source of his torment, in his heart, is that Natalee was his girl. What had tormented him for so long was the realization that Natalee was his girl. Closing and locking the front door as he saw the way she looked standing here a few moments ago, blond highlights framing her tan face. The form-fitting dress, he tried not to imagine what was under that black dress. Pulling himself from his mood, he entered the kitchen, searching for leftovers. Joe opened the refrigerator, taking out a beer.

Smiling that even though they were not a couple, she kept his favorite beer in her refrigerator. Joe took a drink from the cold beer, recalling a long night when she had been swimming in a black lace thong.

Frustration increased inside him as he hated himself more for remembering that night. Not sure what he should be doing, he could not help but feel that if he had arrived thirty minutes earlier, they would have been able to have a conversation before her date showed up. Jealousy pulsed through his veins.

He had been beating himself up for the past few hours since he was the idiot that laid his hand on Jenny's belly. It was pure impulse.

"No matter what the situation that caused it, it is still my baby in there, damn it." Drinking his beer while he stared out at their chairs. His mind transformed him back to that awful moment in the doctor's office just a few hours ago. He knew the very moment he looked up and witnessed the sadness on Natalee's face. He realized what she must have been thinking. Joe had immediately rushed from the doctor's office, following the retreating Natalee as she raced down the street. His calls and texts went unanswered. He had planned on driving straight to her house. Instead, he received information on the case that had consumed his time. That tip took up much of the afternoon, leaving him racing over here, only to see her go. And now, he had no idea how he would get her to believe the truth. He intended to remain at her house until she returned home from her date when his cell phone rang, again interrupting his life.

"Costas"

"Yes, what's the address?" Joe looked around the kitchen with longing. "Yes, on my way, sir." Pouring the last of the beer out into the sink. "Damn." Placing the bottle under the sink in the recycle bin. Checking the front door once more, then walking to the kitchen door, he turned to look at the house. The comfortable home that he imagined when he thought about happiness. The vision of Natalee cooking in the kitchen, sunset across the river glowing through the windows. Now it just seemed empty and lonely. Locking the kitchen door, Joe took his time crossing the drive to his truck.

"Nothing is going my way." By the time he buckled his seat belt, he had stopped feeling sorry for himself for the moment

»»

Natalee smiled and tried to have a good time, willing herself to enjoy the evening. She did feel beautiful in her dress and shoes. Charles turned out to be a pleasant, attentive date. She was sipping her glass of white wine while wishing she was drinking a beer on her patio, watching the sunset over the river. Her heart stung, imagining Joe in that chair next to her, pushing the thought away, instead focusing on the band playing. Watching the happy couples dancing only served to increase her loneliness while the time spent with Charles convinced her it was time to focus on her relationships.

Sitting her glass down on the table, she placed her hand in his leading him onto the dance floor. Several dances later, she was surprised when the band played the last song. Enjoying herself, the pep talk she gave herself had worked, and Natalee enjoyed her evening. The sense of dread was gone, and a new sense of possibilities was in place. Charles opened the car door.

Before she could sit in the low sports car, he pulled her close, kissing her. *"Pleasant, but no sparks."* She hated that her first instinct was to compare him to Joe. Natalee accepted the goodnight kiss.

She did enjoy the evening despite thinking about Joe every other minute. Forcing him from her mind as she took off her dress. Washing her face clean, she pulled her hair back in a headband. She applied her costly facial cream and sipped on a cup of hot tea Natalee ignored the overwhelming desire to climb into bed, choosing to write instead.

Opening her laptop, she stared at the screen. The words blurred in front of her eyes, reflecting on the many changes in her life since the party last week of April. After writing a few sentences, she looked through the window into the night. Memories from the past, some happy, some sad, passed before her. Now all she could wonder is.

"Will I ever be happy again?"

»»

After a long, frustrating day, Joe was overwhelmed by several cases. Stopping his busy day to take a break, he bought sandwiches from Leo's favorite food truck. Joe pulled into the parking lot, quickly calling Leo and asking him to meet him at the park across the street from the station. Knowing Leo enough to realize he was happier when he received bad news on a full stomach.   Joe waited until Leo was halfway into his sandwich before he brought up the difficult conversation.

"So, Leo, I have not had the chance to talk to you in a while." Joe paused, giving Leo a chance to respond.

"Um."

Joe took that as a sign to continue. "I wanted to apologize for the situation with Jenny. I know you and your wife are close to her and Natalee." Leo finished chewing the last bite of the sandwich, taking several fries and dragging them through the ketchup. Popping the fries into his mouth, he swallowed. Joe monitored the drop of ketchup on his partner's chin. Leo took a large tea drink, wiped his mouth on a napkin, and removed the ketchup.

"I do not hold it against you what happened with Jenny. Mary and I think that she set out to deceive you. We worry about Jenny. We have always loved her, but we think she is heading in the wrong direction." Leo paused and looked around the park. The sun filtered through the trees, giving them some much-needed shade. The first week of September was warm, even though fall was just around the corner. Leo continued. "But as bad as it was, what she did, I can't say we were completely surprised. It seems the shock factor has been her goal for several years now. I am not sure why. Natalee is the best mother around. And she tried hard with Jenny." Taking a drink of tea to force it down with the large lump in his throat. "I guess the only thing I can say is that Mary and I worry a lot about Natalee. And we both have the impression that something was brewing between you two." Leo hesitated to see Joe nod. "So, I can't help but wonder what might have been if this accident hadn't happened." Joe waited for the chance to tell Leo more.

It was time for him to confess his feelings, and he began. "I liked Natalee from the first moment I met her at your party. She shot me down at that party because of the age difference."

Leo was confused. "Age difference? You two aren't that far apart in age." Nodding. Joe responded. "I know, but to her, it was not so much age the number but experiences. That eight years difference is not a lot. But she views the fact that she has had a marriage, a child, and lost a spouse all as life experiences that I have not had. She told me that she was not interested in having another child the first night. Even though she is young enough to have another pregnancy." Leo listened patiently. Finally, understanding what had happened.

He had to ask. "So, she shot you down then."

Joe nodded. "Yes. I only went to the club that night because I hoped Natalee would go." Shaking his head. Joe continued. "Instead of dancing with Natalee like I wanted, I babysat Jenny. She got roaring drunk and tried leaving with some strange guy. I ended up taking her home, carrying her into the house, and putting her in bed. Natalee and I talked for a moment after that. It just made me want to get to know her more."

Leo interrupted before Joe could continue. "So, did Jenny hit on you at the bar?"

"Yes. I set her straight then. I told her it was not happening. I was seeing someone else. Well, at least I was hoping to see someone else."

Leo threw the bag in the trash clearly frustrated when he asked Joe, "Hey, did you happen to mention anything to her about the age difference?"

Joe hesitated, "Yes, I did. I pointed out the same thing that Natalee had for me. Watching Jenny's behavior made me realize even more what Natalee had meant when she told me that. The difference is that I am closer mentally to Natalee than I ever was to Jenny." Leo watched as Joe finished his lunch. Taking a long shot of hitting the trash can.

Leo hesitated and then mentioned. "I think that is why she sought you out. Jenny has been trying to become older than her age since she was a young teenager. You know something else?" Joe looked at his partner with a question forming on his lips when Leo answered. "You know, what Natalee said is partly correct, but in all truth, she's just scared. Natalee has a defensive wall up. Ten feet tall."

"Oh, great."

Standing up, they dropped their empty cups into the bin. Leo slapped Joe on the shoulder as they walked back across the street. Right before he opened the door to the station, Leo asked the most important question. "So, since you love Natalee, what will you do about it?"

"I guess I am going to learn how to scale a ten-foot wall."

"That's my boy." Slapping him on the back. Joe sighed, wondering how hard this was going to be.

»»

Natalee sipped her coffee in the early morning light. The foggy mist surrounded her, leaving her head cold and damp, pulling the hood of her sweatshirt over her hair, and tucking her legs underneath her on the blanket. Reaching out to touch the granite stone, she ran her fingers over Patrick's name as tears fell in twin rivers down her cheeks.

"Oh Pat, why did you have to leave me? We should be growing old together on that rickety swing by the boat dock." Sobs racked her body. She knew she should not blame him. He did not choose to die that day. He never wanted to leave her. He was her first love.

"I am so sorry that I have completely messed this life up. Jenny would have never done this if I had moved on and remarried. She would have had a semblance of a dad." Finishing the coffee, she set the cup down on the ground. Pulling herself into a ball, her hand rested on the stone. A cold reminder of all that was left of the man, who had promised never to leave her willingly.

Tears continued to fall while she cried herself to sleep in the early morning dawn. Lifting her head and through gritty and swollen eyes, the sun streamed around her. Natalee stretched, wiping the dried tears from her cheeks. Feeling the sun's heat, she pulled the sweatshirt over her head. Standing, she picked up the blanket and her empty cup. Leaning down, she whispered.

"Thank you, my love. Somehow, even from above, you know how to make me feel better. I hear you. It will all be okay in the end." Walking towards her car, she heard Patrick's voice all around her, sending her the strength she needed to live.

CHAPTER ELEVEN

Mary left a message for her friend Robyn while she raced across town to meet a client. Longtime friends of both Mary and Natalee, Robyn and her husband Roy had accompanied them to the beach house on several occasions.

"Robyn, its Mary. Hey, look Leo just told me he and Roy were planning a weekend fishing trip. I would like to take this chance to get Natalee away for the Labor Day weekend. A girl's trip, head down to the beach house, do a little drinking. I think under the circumstances that she needs to get away. So, hurry up and get back to me. I want to leave early in the morning. I have cleared my Friday schedule. Hope you can do the same. Bye." Mary hung up the phone glancing at the time on her dash.

Taking the last several miles to the house she was showing. Mentally planning what she needed to pack for the trip. "Wine and rum. Both very needed." She giggled.

>>»

When her phone rang, Natalee finished up in the garden, washing her hands. "Yes, Mary." Natalee listened as Mary excitedly announced her plan for the weekend. Natalee looked around at her pool and garden, longingly staring at the chair she would love to sit in all weekend. Realizing she had to stop hiding. Avoiding life was not going to help things get better.

"Okay, I am in. I will be ready. Six am? Sounds like a plan." Hanging up. Natalee smiled. Walking into the house and calling her neighbor, letting her know she would be out of town for the long weekend. Picking up her black bikini and packed it into her suitcase, remembering the first time Joe stood at the end of the pool.

Holding it close. A small part of her wished that he would walk through her kitchen door right now and profess his love to her and apologize for the crazy predicament they were in.

"What the heck am I doing? This will never happen. And how can I ever completely get it out of my mind that he was with my daughter?"

Packed and ready shortly before six, sitting at the kitchen table looking over a photo album of her life. Forty loomed ahead, and twenty seemed so close and yet so far away. Looking back over her life, Patrick washed the boat in his tank top and shorts. Happy and proud of the day he had brought it home.

"What would my life have been like if he had lived?" Wiping a small tear away. "Would we have had another child? Would Jenny be a more settled young woman?" Closing the photo book. Placing it back on the bookshelf where old memories were stored. Picking up her keys and taking her bags outside. Locking the door to her past, realizing it is time for her to move on and stop blaming Patrick's death for everything that has gone wrong with her life.

"Natalee." Hearing them yell through the open car windows, she responded.

"Gees guys, so loud this early in the morning." Mary jumped out, grabbed Natalee's bag, and threw it in her trunk.

"Let's roll." Robyn moved to the backseat, placing her sunglasses on her head.

"Girls trip." She yelled. Natalee could not help but smile as she watched the Friday morning rush hour traffic headed in the opposite direction. Driving towards the island brought on a liberating feeling. To let everything go, the obstetrician appointments, the late phone calls with typical pregnancy complaints only accentuated by her normally whiny daughter, and not to mention the Joe situation. Take the easy way out, leaving for four days of a fun weekend. After sending a quick text letting her daughter know she was heading out of town with Mary and Robyn. She purposely limited the information and then turned off her cell phone. Looking out the window, fighting the urge to turn it back on, realizing this was one of the hardest things she had ever done, speaking softly to herself.

"This is my time."

The next day Natalee lowered her sunglasses to the end of her nose. Adjusting her hat, looking out at the water watching Robyn and Mary attempt to paddle the double kayak into the waves. Robyn's blond hair falling loose from her pony tail as she tried to yell directions over her shoulder to Mary. Natalee laughed feeling relieved that she declined the chance to try kayaking in the ocean. Taking a sip from her tumbler, carefully concealing the mixed drinks they had with them on the beach. She yawned slightly while stretching on the sand rolling over and unhooking her bikini top.

The sun was a welcomed warmth on her back, ignoring the possibility of sunburn choosing instead to enjoy the moment. A short time later she awakened to Robyn and Mary laughing as they settled once again on the beach blanket.

"You missed it. We got whistled at by some hot young guys out there." Mary refilled her tumbler and settled back on the blanket to people watch.

Natalee swatted Mary's leg. "You two are a riot. I am glad y'all made it back to dry land safely. And those guys know beautiful women when they see them." Robyn topped off her drink from the large pitcher in the cooler. Natalee closed her eyes as her friends followed suit.

Natalee stood and stretched, walking into the water to cool off. Feeling tipsy from the lack of food and the continuous drinking, she sank into the gulf water allowing the waves to crash over her relieving the heat in her body. Walking back to the beach blanket.

Natalee reached down and gently shook her friends awake. "Okay guys, we need food." Mary and Robyn sat up, picking up the beach belongings and walked down the block to the cafe. After eating a large late lunch, the trio decided they had enough sun for the day it was time to make plans for the night. Natalee was the first in the shower, after shaving smooth and applying lotion to every inch of her body. She touched up her nail polish and styled her hair. Still wrapped in her towel, taking her time looking through her clothing she had brought with her.

Deciding on a black mini dress with spaghetti straps that crisscrossed from her shoulders to the middle of her back tying in a bow. A slight flair to the skirt showed off her tanned legs. Topping her look off with black high heeled sandals, the shiny pink polish of her toes peeking out, perfectly against the black straps. After the final touches to her makeup, she added large silver teardrop earrings with stones on the ends.

Hooking the back onto the earring, staring into the mirror a vision of Joe standing close to her with his hand on her shoulder, one finger trailing down her neck. Longing and sadness overcoming her, pushing the fantasy from her mind.

Picking up her small purse. "Girls, let's party."

Pulling into the crowded parking lot of the beach bar, a local hot spot for many years. The band, a crowd favorite for the past two seasons, playing many of the most popular songs with amazing accuracy. The band had just taken the stage and were playing their first song when the girls grabbed a table close to the dance floor. Mary ordered drinks while Natalee forced all sad thoughts aside and instead enjoyed being in the moment. After their first drink Mary and Robyn pulled her to the floor dancing. Natalee danced with several men ranging in ages anywhere from twenties to fifties, enjoying plenty of potential partners. Natalee felt relieved when the band took a break. After dancing every dance during the first half of their set, she welcomed the night air when she stepped out onto the deck.

Enjoying the sound of the waves and looking up at the stars when her thoughts were interrupted. "Hi, saw you inside. I am Trent."

Natalee shook his outstretched his hand. "Natalee, nice to meet you." They chatted for several minutes.

When the band began a new song, Trent placed his hand against her back and asked, "Shall we?"

"We shall." She responded with a smile. Letting him lead her back to the dance floor. Surrounded by their new friends drinking and dancing she enjoyed the rock music new and old with a little bit of country thrown in. The crowd quickly worked up when the drummer started a beat.

The guitar player joining in, the lead singer sang. *Ala-Freakin-Bama by Trace Adkins*. The crowd went wild. The new friends lifted Natalee and Robyn up onto the bar nearest the dance floor, dancing to the music.

#

Leo, Joe and Roy walked into the crowded bar, carrying their beers they moved closer to the action. A sea of heads moved on the dance floor, while the band belted out a new hit. With arms above their heads, the crowd sang out Ala-Freakin-Bama.

Joe shook his head laughing. "No one ever made a song this cool about Florida." They were enjoying watching the crowd, most were college age girls moving about the dance floor holding their attention. When Roy shook his head, and slapped Joe on the shoulder. Joe's eyes quickly followed the direction of Roy's pointing fingers to the bar closest to the band. He was in shock as he watched Natalee, his Natalee on the bar in high-heeled sandals, long bare legs and a black mini dress. Black lace panties tantalized him each time she moved, certain that every male around her saw the same thing as him, Joe clenched his fists in frustration. The straps down her bare back, made his fingers ache with the need to untie them. The front was not much better, dipping low between her breasts leading him to believe she was naked under that dress.

One part of him was mesmerized, while the other side wondered what in the hell she was thinking. He watched as Roy walked over to his wife Robyn as she danced. Surprised when he realized Roy was laughing, enjoying his wife's display. Joe didn't laugh, instead he saw red, watching as a younger man's hands reached up and stroked Natalee's legs while his lips moved. Seeing his girl laugh while she sang along, as she waggled her finger at the younger man. Joe stared in disbelief as his Natalee flirted, fury built inside of him. He shoved his way through the crowd trying to move closer to the bar.

The song came to an end and another began. Oblivious, Natalee recognized the next song, she bounced up and down on the bar. His mind was set on reaching his girl on top of the bar, nearing his destination in time to see the man with the grabby hands once again stroke her thigh. Joe pushed the man aside, anticipating when the younger man pushed back with a swinging fist.

Joe dodged with assured ease, recognizing his advantage of five inches of height and near thirty pounds compared to his opponent. Not taking into consideration his years of boxing experience. Joe grabbed the man throwing his arm behind his back. Yelling into his ear.

"You don't want to mess with me. That is my woman you are groping and I am not here alone." It did not take but a moment before the younger man held up his hands and backed away. When Joe looked up he realized that Natalee had witnessed the altercation.

Her mouth was opened, he heard her over the music. "Joe, what the heck are you doing here?" Not taking the time to talk, he grabbed her by the legs and threw her over his shoulder. Holding tight against her flailing, glaring at anyone who dared interrupt him. He caught sight of Leo only to see a huge smile on his face, laughing while his belly shook. Leo nodded as Joe mouthed "boat". Roy had finally convinced his wife to get down from the bar. Mary ran up, handing Natalee her purse, she stopped her flailing fists towards Joe's backside. Instead she held onto the pockets of his cargo shorts.

Mary smiled as she yelled. "It's about damn time."

CHAPTER TWELVE

Joe waited until they neared the street to lower Natalee. Their bodies molded together as he held her at eye level with her feet dangling above the ground. Mesmerized while staring into her eyes, he had nothing to say, the feel of her breasts crushed to his chest his body did the talking. Lowering his lips, he kissed the swell of one breast then the other. Her eyes softened as her lips parted, heat radiated from him into her. Joe heard her moan, just before he brought his lips to hers. Deepening the kiss, his fingers walked underneath her skirt, until he felt the lace panties that taunted him.

Abruptly ending their heated exchange he looked around toward the crowd going in and out of the club and slowly lowered her until her feet touched the ground.

Pleading softly, "Please, come to the boat with me."

Natalee did not hesitate, instead she bobbed her head with unbridled excitement. For the first time in a long time, she followed her heart. Holding hands while they walked the few short blocks to the marina. Fear of breaking the spell, kept them quiet while both feared interrupting whatever had happened between them. Under the marina lights Joe stopped them on the landing and pulled her close. Bending down, Joe slipped Natalee's high-heeled sandals off, handing them to her one by one. Trailing his fingers up her legs, until he found smooth skin under her skirt. Slipping his hands under the lace panties he squeezed her rounded bottom. He lifted her up to his waist, holding tight, carrying her onto the boat. Joe lowered his girl until her feet met the smooth surface of the deck.

Averting her gaze from his, Natalee focused instead on the small boat cabin. She tried to slow her ragged breaths. Unsure of the source of her anxiety, she swallowed hard. Waiting as Joe opened the small port hole windows allowing an air flow to cool the small cabin. He turned towards her, the lump in her throat threatened to swell. Her resolve melted, when he moved toward her placing his hands on her waist, and gazed deeply into her eyes talking low he said.

"Don't be scared, nervous or worry. Can tonight and the rest of the weekend be about us? Let the bad go away and just be us?" Natalee bit her bottom lip. He used the pad of his finger to gently apply pressure and lower her lip. Natalee released her inhibitions, taking his finger into her mouth, while enjoying the sounds of his obvious pleasure from her tongue.

"Mm." Natalee smiled around his finger. Joe moved his hand toward her neck while the other hand firmly pressed her hips to his. The object of his harden desire pressed against her. Arching her back, when she felt him pull the tie releasing her dress into a pool of material at her feet. Leaving her bare breasts illuminated by the moonlight that spilled through the small portholes of the boat. Joe eased down, sitting on the side of the bed. Softly touching her hips, he lowered the scrap of black lace down her thighs. Pulling her into his lap, she could feel the hard length of him pressing against her, while warmth spread from deep inside her belly.

Lifting her slightly, then lowering her on top of him, taking him deep inside, wrapping her legs firmly around his waist. Joe teased her breast with one hand while the other held firmly to rounded buttocks. His lips parted her own using his tongue to invade her mouth.

»»

Natalee stretched, feeling the arm beneath her head. Opening her eyes, she looked around the small boat cabin a smile came to her lips recalling the night before. With no regret, she could only thank fate and Mary for bringing her to the island and well the beach bar. Dancing on the bar was most likely not her finest moment. But after the way things had turned out, seeing Joe obvious so clearly filled with jealousy had changed things for the better. Looking at him now, sleeping peacefully with his hand possessively lying across her hips. Hearing his soft snores, realizing she could wake up like this every morning. Touching her lips to his, opening his mouth she deepened the kiss. Growling Joe rolled over on top of her.

"Good morning." He growled out.

"Good morning to you too." She smiled before he leaned down kissing her lips, down her jaw line to her neck. Moving further down to her bare breast, blowing his warm breath across the nipple, turning it into a taut bud.

"Mm." She moaned. His lips left her soft mound, her back arched mourning the loss of his hot moist lips. Soft moans, escaped her lips while her hips bucked in anticipation. Joe smiled against her silky skin, wetting the yearning bud with a swipe of his tongue. Grazing the pink bud with his teeth.

"Ooh." She yelled out. Joe laughed when he trailed butterfly kisses moved from the soft swell of her breast down to her abdomen. Her legs opened in anticipation, her fingers pressing against his head urging it lower.

"You aren't tired from last night?" He asked. Receiving a moan while his tongue traced lower to her moist center plunging deep.

"Oh no. I'm not tired. Oh gosh Joe. No." Lifting his head.

"No? You don't want me to?"

"No, I mean yes." Breathless. His tongue entered, rewarding him with a rivulet of moisture. Taking the small tight little bud in his lips sucking, feeling spasm after spasm while her fingers clutching his hair holding him tight. Moving his tongue, delving deep, he lifted her hips plunging deeper.

"Oh, oh Joe, please." Pulling his tongue.

"Yes Lee." She knew what he was doing. Teasing her into begging. He had tried this last night but he gave in as fast as she did. This morning on the other hand, he seemed to have much more control.

"Joe, please."

"Yes babe, what would you like?" He moved up her body, his tongue trailing up this time. Capturing an erect nipple between his teeth. She moaned. He could feel the moisture building as she rubbed her moist center over his muscled thigh yearning for her release.

"Ugh. Joe, you are going to make me ask for it, aren't you?" Arching her back, pushing her hips towards him, wet with anticipation.

"Yes, Lee. I want to know what you want."

"I want you Joe, I want you and only you inside of me now." Kissing her. Pushing inside of her, with more force than he intended.

"Yes, ma'am." Lifting her legs around his hips, she met him thrust for thrust. She urged him faster and deeper until Natalee yelled out.

"Oh, oh, oh my oh Joe." Surprised by her own voice, yelling his name. Joe plunged his tongue into her mouth capturing her moans to keep from alerting the neighbors. Pushing up onto his knees, he lifted her with him. Sweat dripped from their bodies in the small steamy cabin, he drove deeper and harder with each thrust.

Stimulating every nerve in her body, tremors ran down her spine. Tingling through her hair down to her toes as Natalee pushed further for a second release. With each thrust, she felt her body awaken from a deep sleep while her belly burned with desire. The stimulation increased even more then, the previous night. Their bodies welded together, her leg, his hips. her breasts, his palms.

"Grr." He moaned out, holding the flair of her hips saturating her with an explosion of himself. They fit. Their lips had found each other, as if they had always kissed. Their tongues mated in unity. Filling her completely, two missing pieces of a puzzle that now had found each other. Just when she thought, she was spent. Instead Natalee cried out as she exploded in spasms once again with him.

»»

Natalee grabbed one of Joe's t-shirts and pulled it over her head, barely covering her panties. "Scandalous." Realizing she had never done anything remotely this wild before. She was happy. "Happy." Saying the words to herself. Looking up on the landing watching as Joe boarded the boat with the bag of food.

After the last time, they had made love this morning they had both realized they needed food. Also as Natalee had pointed out it was rather hot in the cabin. Checking her cell phone while Joe pulled the croissants from the bag, along with coffee.

Natalee responded to the text. "Mary wants to know when we come up for air if we will come to the beach house for supper and spend some time with the old people."

Laughing. Joe leaned in to kiss her. "I guess we can spare some time. It is too hot down there as it is. Besides, we will have plenty of time back here tonight." Smiling.

She responded to the text. "Okay, I told Mary we would be there around one."

Joe glanced at his watch. "Oh, well we have two hours what shall we do." Picking up a croissant, he tore off a bite placing it in Natalee's mouth, she took his finger in her mouth with the bite of flaky pastry. Tracing his finger with her tongue.

"Um," Joe pulled his finger from her mouth, grabbing her he laid her down on the cushion.

An hour later Natalee finally convinced Joe they needed clothes and real food. Putting on her black dress, carrying her heels she grabbed Joe by the hand pulling him along the landing. Stopping to buy a pair of flip-flops and drinks at the marina store, holding hands while they walked towards the beach house.

Joe stopped every few blocks, pulling her into his arms for a kiss.

Taking the steps at the beach house they heard, "It is about time you two came up for air." Mary bellowed from the sliding door. With her hands full of platters of food, Mary motioned for the couple to join the party at the table.

»»

Natalee turned her baseball hat around backward and leaned against the captain's chair. Joe reveled in the feel of her arms wrapped around his shoulders, her breaths on his neck while he drove the boat. Pleased when she accepted his invitation to return to Mobile by water. He wanted to savor every moment with her taking their time, returning home. He knew it was selfish since Natalee had gone on the trip as a girl's weekend. He had changed it into a Joe and Natalee vacation. Mature enough to realize the difficulties they faced could return once they reached the dock. He held onto this moment, while the eyes that stared into his were filled with passion and not the torment from before. He felt her breath on his neck change into soft kisses, then the kisses changed, when her teeth grazed his neck. Her hands circled over his bare chest. He jumped when she flicked his small nipple.

Turning to look at her in surprise. "Lee, honey would you like me to anchor?" Natalee giggled, pinching his nipple. "Lee, again?" He watched as she playfully bit her bottom lip, nodding. Joe looked around, slowing the boat turning towards a small island out of the heavier boat traffic. Dropping the anchor and cutting the engine. Natalee released his chest from her fingertips and rushed into the cabin.

Stepping down the steps, he knew he would never tire of seeing his Natalee naked, lying on the bed ready for him. They both knew, there was still an hour left until they would reach her house. Somewhere in the conversation over the weekend when they were lying naked in bed, she had invited him to dock his boat at her place.

Excitement coursed through his veins at the mere thought after a hard day at work each day he could possibly come home to a life with her, like this. Happiness invaded his soul, these past two days. Even seeing her dancing on the bar, had turned into a great memory because it led to this moment as he said, "Hi babe,"

"Hi yourself. What took you so long." With the heavy breathing, the small cabin heated up rather quickly. Joe longed for a full night in her house, in her bed.

Still smiling, as he started the engine. Taking off slowly, as she sat in the seat with him. Sipping his beer with his arm around his girl, Natalee leaned back in the chair with her feet on the console. He rubbed her leg while they watched the sky turn to pink.

"Life is perfect now." Feeling amazingly happy. *"Love."* Was the word that came to mind when he looked at Lee.

Speaking over the sound of the boat engine, into her ear. "I love you."

Natalee pulled back looking, into his eyes, "Really?" Joe nodded slowly. "You sure?"

He nodded. "Listen woman, I am sure. I love you. You are it for me."

Squealing, Natalee grabbed him around the neck. "I love you too." Kissing him, she laid her head on his shoulder.

The problems at home were set aside, yet not forgotten.

»»

Natalee jumped out of the boat, tying off the rope across the dock from her own boat. The large fishing boat towered over her little cruiser. She did not mind. Instead, quite the opposite giving her a sense of belonging. Their bags, rested beside her feet, while she watched him close the little cabin, memories from the weekend warmed her insides. The sun had disappeared behind the horizon leaving in its wake a pink painted canvas, colors exploding light surrounding Joe as he walked towards her. Reluctant to have the weekend end, she easily stepped into his arms. Eagerly she gave him her lips, oblivious to the increased darkness surrounding them.

Stepping off the dock, onto the grassy lawn they walked hand in hand across the yard nearing the patio when Natalee dropped her bag without warning, wrapping her arms around his waist. Joe slowly lifted her up, eye to eye. Then, kissing her deeply. As he broke the kiss he whispered. "I meant what I said. I love you. You are it for me."

Tears welled in her eyes. "And I love you." She laughed.

"What is so funny." He countered.

Her smile was infectious. Shrugging her shoulders. "We are." Twirling her around, as she laughed more.

Joe growled. "So why are we so funny?"

Biting her lip as he lowered her feet to the ground. "Because, what do we do now?"

He softly kissed her forehead, then her nose. Staring into her eyes. Joe's response was soft and low. "We go to bed. Then in the morning we get up, have our day then we get to go to bed together again."

"Really?"

"Yes, and hopefully it is for the rest of our lives." Joe lifted Natalee again, kissing her deeply.

She wondered if he would lay her down in the grass right there or if they would make it to the bedroom this time. His tongue plunged inside her mouth. With her feet lifted off the ground he continued to kiss, when they were interrupted by screaming, "Mom. Mom. What are you doing?" Their passion came to an abrupt stop, Joe lowered Natalee's feet to the ground. The next few minutes, time swirled as tears filled her eyes. Feeling Joe pull back a step, Natalee immediately mourned the loss of his touch. "Mom, how could you." Jenny screamed at the top of her lungs.

Natalee picked up her bag, walking towards her daughter. "Jenny, we can go inside and talk about this. There is no need to yell." Not hearing a word her mother had said. Jenny continued her tirade. "He was mine, Mom, mine, you had no right, no right." She continued to yell, with tears streaming down her cheeks.

Joe interrupted. "Jenny, now wait a minute. I was never yours. We never were. It has always been your Mom." His voice softened when he added. "Since the first moment we met." Natalee's eyes met his, full of tears and regret as she turned away from him to follow her daughter.

CHAPTER THIRTEEN

Stepping from the shower, she pulled on her robe, tying the sash, she walked into her room. Picking up her cell phone once again, she noticed no return calls or texts from her daughter. In its place were ten missed calls and twenty unanswered texts from Joe, the man that only six hours earlier she had professed her love to him. Now at three in the morning instead of sleeping next to him and waking in the wee hours of the morning to see him off to work. She sat looking out the window from her chair next to the window with a head of wet tangled hair.

Too tired to comb the tangles out from the hours on the boat. Too tired to apply her expensive face lotion nor her body lotion to her sun-kissed arms and legs. Her bag sat unpacked with damp, wrinkled and sandy clothing. The bed, her bed that should now be their bed, remained made since before the weekend. With a blanket covering her legs as she stared out at the moonlit dock that only hours before she had felt alive with meaning and purpose. Now instead, she felt old, useless and unloved, even a bit used.

Her brain fought with her heart. "Why oh, why did you let him in. You got caught up in the island, the alcohol, somehow managing to forget the truth." Her daughter was having his baby, reminding herself of the real life she had managed to forget while on the island. Tears fell. The loneliness returned. Natalee cried herself to sleep in the chair.

Dried tears caked her sunburnt skin. Her mouth was dry as the desert. Loneliness surrounding her as gritty eyes opened out to a light pink sky. A beautiful peaceful morning. Wishing that she had not fallen asleep, as she had replayed the events of the previous night throughout her dreams. Natalee rose, dressing in her running clothes. The image of Joe's expression on his face as he stood several feet away from her as she had tried to reason with her daughter. Jenny had suddenly turned and ran to her car, holding her belly as she ran. Joe tried to talk to her as she slammed the car door.

Turning to Natalee, he had reached for her as he told her. "She will recover from this in time. We just have to give her a chance to grow up and realize the truth."

His heartbreak was apparent when instead of taking his outstretched hand Natalee told him. "I just need to figure this out. We can talk later." Her voice had been cold and distant. She knew it had hurt him. She could tell. But at that moment, she had nothing else to give.

»»

Joe stumbled into work the next morning. Four days worth of stubble dotted his jawline he had no reason to shave while on the island, now he just didn't care. With his hair, a mess from him running his fingers through it. He had not worked out this morning nor taken the normal time to pick out his wardrobe. He had been concerned with appearances over the past ten months on the job, trying to impress the top brass. Right at this moment he did not care one bit. He would give it all up, the nice apartment, the boat and the job for Natalee back and his baby.

Saying those words under his breath he realized where he had gone wrong in all of this. In his mind, he had seen Natalee and the situation with Jenny as two separate things. Seeing the hurt in Natalee's eyes when her daughter walked away, he finally realized the pain caused by a spouse, a lover or a friend did not begin to compare to the hurt one could possibly cause their parent. Finally, sometime in the middle of night, sitting on his patio watching the moon and remembering Natalee's face reflected with moonlight, he saw this situation from her point of view. He now understood the pain and anguish she had been going through.

"It all makes sense." Rubbing his face once again as he downed his third cup of coffee taking the stairs to the detective division office. If he had not just been off for five days he would have called in. But judging by the look on his bosses face he was pretty sure it was a good thing that he had gone against that idea.

"Morning." Smiling. Leo nodded then taking in Joe's appearance his concern quickly replaced the smile. Before Leo could inquire, he heard his name.

"Rivers, Costas, O'Neill, Martinez. Get your asses in here now." Joe set down his cup of coffee and walked into the Captain's office. He was quickly followed by Leo, Roy, and Carlos. "Don't bother sitting down, you won't be in here that long. While you ladies were out getting your tans on the holiday weekend that S.O.B. that raped that woman down in Chapel Hill Estates, struck again. This time he grabbed one off the jogging trail early Sunday morning on the opposite side of town near Sunset Place. I need you out on the street, figuring this one out. Brown and Lewis worked the case this weekend. Get the lists from them. No days off until this bastard is caught."

Panic gripped Joe pulling his phone from his pocket. Hitting speed dial for Natalee's cell number, he left a quick message. "Lee babe, I know things are bad right now. That can all wait. I need you to be careful. There was another rape Sunday morning, not far from your subdivision. Please run at home until we catch this guy. I love you." Pressing end. He quickly sent a text with the same message. Then worrying whether she was deleting everything from him he sent one to her email also.

Looking at Leo. "I need a favor. Can you please have Mary call Natalee and get her to not run on the roads until we catch this guy." Clearly confused. Before Leo could ask a question. Joe explained. "There was a problem when we got back last night with Jenny. Lee needs time to think."

Nodding, Leo pulled his cell phone and relayed the message to Mary. Promising she would get a hold of her immediately. Leo ended the call, placing the phone on the clip on his belt. Slapping his hand on Joe's back. "Come on, lets grab some more coffee and you can tell me all about it while we go get this bastard off the street."

Walking out to the car getting in, Joe buckled his belt. Roy and Carlos climbed into the car beside them. Driving out to the Sunset Place subdivision gave the two, ample time to talk.

97

Leo waited until they reached the first stop light when he asked. "You ready to talk about it?"

Nodding, Joe took a deep breath. "Well, after we left you guys at the marina we took our time going back. We stopped and ate. Talked and well." Hesitating. Joe had never been a kiss and tell type of guy. And he did not plan on starting now.

Leo nodded. "I understand. You two were happy. We all could tell. You both have been dancing around this all summer. Any fool could see you two belong together. That is why it broke me and Mary's heart to hear what Jenny had done." Joe waited. He didn't know if there was more to come. Leo continued. "Joe, I could not be prouder of everything that you have accomplished here at the force even if you were my own son. I want you to know, I have come to respect you as an officer, a detective and as a man. You are a stand-up guy. Me and Mary, we do not blame you in all of this. As much as it pains me to say this, we blame Jenny." Joe watched in surprise as Leo swiped a lone tear from his eye.

Leo had been his mentor this past ten months since coming to work at the force. He looked up to Leo, aspired to be as good as him. Hearing these words meant a lot.

"Thank you, Leo this has been by far the hardest thing I have ever gone through. And I have questioned myself with each step I take. Knowing that you believe in me, means a lot." Leo cleared his throat, turning down the air conditioning on the car.

"So, what happened when you got to Natalee's house?"

Joe briefly looked out the window before he answered. "Everything was perfect. We were happy. I told her I loved her and she was it for me. We had not talked about the baby. We were trying to figure us out. She told me she loved me." He paused to gage Leo's reaction. When he remained focused on the road. Joe continued. "We got our gear off the boat, walked onto the lawn. We were close to the patio. And Natalee stopped and we started kissing. The next thing I knew the light came on and Jenny is screaming at the top of her lungs asking Natalee what did she do, that I was hers."

Leo sighed. "Wow. That, I was not expecting."

Joe continued. "We both tried talking to Jenny. She would not listen. She drove off, speeding down the road. The look of horror on Lee's face. I knew then that we, us would have to wait. The pain she must have felt, it made me finally realize what she had been going through, all these months. I see now that losing me, a lover or even a spouse does not compare to losing a child."

Leo could relate. He knew that if he ever lost Mary he would be devastated and lost. But he could survive it, because they had built a life together. A child was different. It was all your hopes and dreams and love combined into one. There was no greater pain that could be inflicted than by ones' own child. They sat in silence for the last few minutes until they reached their destination.

An hour later after conducting a few more interviews and reviewing the scene looking for security cameras. Getting back into the car, they picked up the conversation where they had left off. Joe deep in thought, spoke first. "I can't help but wonder, if I have to choose between my unborn child and the woman I love, what am I going to do?"

CHAPTER FOURTEEN

Natalee came in from her run. The dreary cold January day would have most likely turned even the most avid runner off this morning. But to Natalee it was more of an escape than anything. Whether she was running or writing those were the only two times of a day where she felt that she had any control over her life. Her home, her life, were controlled by the actions of her daughter. Ever since the baby shower the house had been overrun with friends of Jenny's visiting. Baby gifts were everywhere. The baby's room was finally set up and all the layette washed and folded. She was well stocked with diapers and other baby necessities. Natalee was conflicted on her feelings. One part of the excitement of being a grandmother but at the same time she felt a huge restriction on her life.

Stepping into the kitchen, the warmth of the house hit her. Pulling off her sweatshirt and cap throwing them on to the table. Making a protein fruit shake using the blender. For once she was not afraid to awaken her daughter. Natalee had gotten used to living alone. She liked her independence, her routine. Now since Jenny had graduated from the University, she had brought home a different person than the one that had left home after high school. Gone was the fun loving, sweet positive girl that was ready to embrace life. This new person that only looked like her daughter was negative, cynical and convinced she was unlovable. The pregnancy only enhanced the person she had become the last two years of college. Natalee tried to talk to her. Instead Jenny seemed to focus on what she thought was the person she needed to be. Natalee had an uneasy feeling that if Jenny could somehow get the baby out, she would leave.

Sighing, Natalee despised how incredibly sorry for herself she felt and the direction her life had taken she poured over her troubles. Watching the blender spin, lost in thought wondering how her life had changed with one simple night at Leo and Mary's party.

The last few weeks since the holidays had been close to unbearable. This was not the way she would have imagined becoming a grandmother. Giving Jenny a beautiful wedding would have been first after really getting to know the boy. Nothing about her daughter had gone the way she had planned, from early graduation from high school to rushing through college Natalee felt that her only child was on a collision course with life, instead of gently enjoying everything that she had experienced.

Taking her protein shake with her to her bathroom she was not surprised to see Jenny still sleeping. Natalee focused on herself, taking a quick shower then sitting down at her computer. A short time later while she procrastinated at her desk and watched the icy rain hit the river, thankful she had taken the time to put the boat up in the garage for the winter. Turning on the radio instead of the music she usually enjoyed, the news gave increased coverage of the winter storm and icy road conditions.

Natalee opened her laptop and the words flowed easily. Surprisingly she was out of a slump once again, the last few chapters were completed. Saving and sending her latest file to her editor, she once again stared out the window while the computer was processing. Instantly Joe's face swam before her eyes, recalling the last time she had seen him. His eyes had been filled with sadness, she could not help but feel responsible. She had yet to tell him how she truly felt about him instead she kept imagining him with Jenny.

Since Labor Day weekend, their relationship was placed on hold. Natalee attempted to shut down the flood of memories without success. She thought back to the encounter with her daughter. Natalee finally accepted Joe's calls two days later, surprisingly it was him, that suggested they wait until the baby was born before they attempted to continue their relationship. Agreeing with him had been hard on Natalee, but she chose her daughter first. Jenny never mentioned that night again.

Natalee was caught in her own misery heightened by the gloomy weather. She stared mindlessly at her computer screen until she received the confirmation that the file had gone through when her cell phone rang. It took several rings before her groggy brain registered the sound of the ringing phone. "Hello."

"Oh, thank goodness you picked up. An accident."

"Mary, Mary what accident? You keep cutting out."

The three words that she never wanted to hear were the ones that broke through the static and noise. "Joe in accident."

Natalee's heart plummeted. "Where Mary, where is he?"

"St John's Hospital."

"I'm on my way." The connection was broken before Mary could respond. Natalee ran to her bedroom throwing on a sweat jacket over her long- sleeved t-shirt. Running her fingers through her hair, she walked into Jenny's room. "Jenny, I have to go to the hospital, a friend has been in an accident. I have my phone, call me if you need anything." Holding her breath at the same time not wanting her daughter to ask questions. Natalee had this overwhelming urge to be the one at the hospital, to see if he was okay. And to not have her pregnant daughter there reminding her of what had happened.

She needn't have worried, Jenny rolled over and pulled the blanket closer. "I will be fine. Go see whoever you want. Oh, and mom bring home some ice cream."

Natalee sighed as she responded. "Sure."

Natalee drove as slowly as possible while at the same time trying to hurry. Fear gripped her heart, she could not understand why she even cared. Her head told herself to turn around, go back home, write and enjoy her time. But her heart, willed her to drive, to the hospital, to Joe. Pulling into the crowded parking lot it appeared to be a sign of the day the rest of the population of Mobile, must be having. Stepping out of the car, she pulled up her hood of her winter jacket, stuffing her wallet and keys into her pocket, her cell phone in the other pocket. Locking her doors, she took off running to the emergency entrance hoping to avoid the patches of ice in her way.

Stepping into the overly crowded emergency room, she lowered her hood removing her winter jacket. Walking past the full waiting room to the information desk she attempted to wait patiently, watching as two emergency service members pushed a gurney past the double doors. Natalee had seen one ambulance pull out and now another pulled in during the short time that she had been there. Making her way up to the desk, willing herself to remain patient, waiting her turn to speak to the information attendant all the while her heart continued to scream inside.

Reaching the desk, she heard. "May I help you?"

"Yes Ma'am, I was told my." Hesitating for a moment, while she wondered what was Joe to her. The attendant was briefly distracted by the EMS bringing in the latest patient. The attendant hit a button and they were whisked back.

She returned her attention back to Natalee. "I am so sorry. Can you repeat the name?" Looking at her computer screen.

"Joe Costas, police officer."

"Oh, yes ma'am so sorry Mrs. Costas, they said to expect you. You can go right back, room four. It is to the right." Natalee nodded. The words caused her to stumble over her hurried steps as she made her way through the doors. Seeing two uniformed officers with Leo standing outside a curtained area. Gripped with fear, she came to an abrupt stop then proceeding at a slower pace. Flashbacks gripped her, memories of seeing Patrick in this same hospital after being shot. Reaching out for the wall, her world spun out of control.

Next thing she knew, she was wrapped tight in Leo's big arms. "I've got you Nat. You are safe. He's not Patrick."

Her head filled with fear as she fought with herself. *"Oh, why in the world did you fall for another police officer when you knew darn well something could happen."*

Leo interrupted her internal chant. Leo was always comfort for her. "I am so glad Mary got through to you. He has been asking for you."

"He is alive?" Natalee's jaw began to tremble and tears threatened welling in her eyes.

"Yes, silly girl. He's alive. Your man is one tough guy."

Leo showed her through the curtain.

Not prepared for what she saw the instant she walked through the curtain. Joe's beautiful face, now his left eye was swollen completely shut, covered in bruises, a myriad of colors extending towards his jaw. His bare chest was covered with wires and tubes. Looking above his head to the beeping monitor reminding her that unlike Patrick he is very much alive. One of his muscular arms that had held her tight, now was wrapped in ace wrap from fingers to shoulder. Looking at it held securely in a sling, fear of the unknown kept her from touching him. Slowly she reached out as her fingers lightly touched his uninjured hand. Bruises forming across his chest and down his side, his lower body covered only with a sheet.

Whispering softly, "I'm here Joe. I am here."

"Nat. The doctor wants to talk to you." Hearing Leo's voice from the other side of the curtain, she softly squeezed his hand, then moved through the opening. Natalee struggle to stay focused as the doctor explained this condition. Her world swirled before her eyes, hearing words that she could not begin to process.

"Broken ribs, collapsed lung, chest tube, fractured arm. Admitting the patient to the intensive care unit." Natalee's world spun out of control. Images of Patrick at this hospital, in this emergency room. And now Joe, fortunately no bullets pierced his body, but so near the same result. He was injured and in serious condition. She had spent the past four months of their lives pushing him away, trying to build an impossibly broken fence between her and her daughter. Instead she should have been with the man she loved, to stop blaming Joe for the incident that was beyond his control. It was Jenny that had done the wrong.

Tears streamed down her cheeks as she watched him on the stretcher being taken toward the elevator. A nurse was kind enough to give them directions to intensive care, explaining when she would be able to see him again. Natalee looked up to see Mary walking toward her in a rush. Feeling Mary's love as her arms circled around her. "Mare, I messed up so royally bad. I wasted the past months blaming him for the problems with Jenny. I pushed him away and now I may lose him forever."

"Shh honey. He is strong and healthy, he will be okay I know it."

"How did it happen?"

Leo pulled her close. "Nat. He was responding to a call. A domestic dispute involving a suspect that just happened to be the one we were watching for a string of driveway car-jackings. The suspect has been following women alone home from the shopping mall and robbing them in their driveway. There have been ten so far. We finally got a break on a description of the car and a partial license plate after watching this guy for the past two days. A 911 call came in about a domestic dispute from a neighbor. Joe had a hunch that he could take this opportunity to get the guy. He was driving, another car spun out of control on the ice and he swerved to miss it. He ended up tangled with a guard rail. The air bag did not deploy. So, he ended up with broken ribs and a collapsed lung. And well you saw the fractured arm." Leo reached for her as Natalee teared up biting her knuckle. "Nat. He is in good hands. He will be okay. I know it. Come on lets, get some coffee and head upstairs." Natalee nodded as she followed Leo and Mary to the cafeteria.

Natalee sipped coffee outside the intensive care unit. She had made the call to Jenny, letting her know the situation. Surprised by Jenny's lack of genuine concern without any desire to see him. Instead, she asked how long her mother expected to be gone, asking for a list of food for her cravings. Shaking her head as she again replayed the conversation in her head, muttering to herself as Mary walked up, she asked. "Talking to yourself again?"

"Sorry, it's Jenny. She went to so much trouble to try to get Joe's attention. Then she threw a damn fit when she saw us together. And now that he is lying in there. There." Natalee threw her hand in the direction of the ICU ward. "She put all of us through all of this mess. Bringing a baby into this world. It is so apparent that she was never in love with him. She didn't even like him. She was a predator. She wanted him and she went after him. How did I raise a child like that?" Tears filled her eyes, her jaw trembled and sobs ripped through her body. "Oh, Mary what if I screwed up and wasted time that I could have spent with him."

Mary pulled her best friend into her arms. Holding her tightly as she softly rubbed her back.

"He is going to be fine. And someday all of this, Jenny and all-of-her escapades will be a distant memory. And you will be happy once again with Joe."

Interrupted by the nurse approaching. "Mrs. Costas, you may go in now and sit with him." Natalee pulled from Mary's arms. Catching a glimpse of Mary's surprise registering across her face.

Natalee responded. "Thank you for always being there for me. And oh that, I have no idea why they call me that."

Mary nodded and went to sit down in the waiting room next to her husband. "Leo honey, do you know why by chance, the nurse would think that Natalee is Joe's wife?" Leo gulped loudly as he swallowed the mouthful of candy he was eating. "And why are you eating candy when you promised me you were sticking to your diet?"

"Okay, first I am sorry, but I am stress eating. I just hung up the phone with Joe's parents. I had to tell them about the accident. Joe's mother was gathering the family. She said they were driving and would be here tonight." Leo took another handful of candy, chewing slowly. "Also, you don't know this. But they do not know about the baby."

"What? He has not told them?" Leo shook his head. "Leo, how do you know he did not tell them?"

"He told me. Said he planned on telling them this week. He was going to let them think he had a one night stand with Jenny and she just told him she was pregnant."

"How in the hell is he going to explain dating her Mother then?" Shrugging his shoulders, Leo shook another mouthful of the chocolate candy, into his mouth. Chewing them dramatically as if he was talking when in all reality he was avoiding more questions. Mary slapped him on the arm. "Why didn't he tell them when he went home for those two days for the holidays?"

"He said he chickened out, said his Mother had arranged a blind date while he was there. He did tell his parents about Natalee."

Mary shook her head. "Wait, but why does the nurse think she is his wife."

Sheepishly, Leo whispered. "I might have told them that at the front desk to expect her she was on her way here. Then when the doc asked for next of kin I pointed to Natalee." Mary stood, and poured herself another cup of the sludge, they called coffee and sat down in the hard chair.

"So, honey. How are we going to explain that the hospital personnel think that Natalee is Mrs. Costas, when his mother the other Mrs. Costas shows up?"

Leo responded with a shrug. "I don't know babe, all this story telling and arranging lives is a chick thing. I am sure you and Natalee will figure it out. I have bigger fish to catch. The car jacker is still out there and more people are going to get hurt. I am burning daylight. I am heading back to work." Giving her a kiss on the head.

Mary nodded. "I will wait here and make sure Natalee is okay. I will give you updates on Joe's condition." Standing and wrapping her arms around her husbands' wide girth. "Please my love, stay safe I need you more than anything in this world."

»»

Walking outside into the freezing night air, Natalee glanced at her watch realizing it was not as late as it felt. She looked back up at the hospital wondering how she would survive more hours of waiting to learn of Joe's condition. She walked away from the building and the lights choosing to look up to the stars, taking a deep breath. The past eight hours she had been holding vigil in the waiting room or next to Joe's bed, creeping by with snail like procession. Mary had left briefly to pick them up some food for dinner, after she had tried convincing Natalee to head home. Opening her heart and admitting her fear of leaving, afraid something would happen to him while she was gone. Now thinking back to the past year and the changes that had taken place.

Setting her own personal fear of abandonment aside, as she instead focused on Joe and somehow him making it through this, for him to be here when his son arrives. Gone were the feelings of betrayal, the anger and the hurt towards not only her daughter but to Joe himself. Not realizing that deep down she did blame him.

"You are a man damn it. You could have stopped all of this and in the process, you mademe fall in love with you. No, you couldn't have left me alone like I asked. You had to keep coming by, just happened to run into me in town. Always where I was." Shaking her fist to the night's sky while tears rolled down her cheeks. "And you, stupid man, you kept at it, being all charming and sweet, just had to keep it all. You did it on purpose, you knew what you wanted even if I didn't. I did it I fell in love with you. And now you might leave me. Damn it Joe, you better not leave me. God, you don't want him yet. He is a royal pain in the ass, he never does anything anybody else wants. He is selfish, he will just cause more problems for you. And, and, you can't have him."

Tears burst down her cheeks as she yelled. "You already took Patrick. Please. Please don't take Joe." She gasped.

Collapsing, she felt the familiar burly arms wrap around her hugging her tight. "I've got you Nat. Joe is strong, he will make it through this. And all of the other stuff will just work out the way it is suppose too."

Natalee released the last of her tears while Leo held her tight. Turning in his arms. Standing on her tip toes she gave his cheek a kiss. "Thank you. You always show up at the right time."

Using the large pad of his fingers he stopped her tears. "Nat, he's not Patrick. You will have your happy ever after this time. I know it. But you have, to stop running from love babe. You can't let your fear of loss keep you from playing the game. Let yourself fall in love, be loved. Everything else will be what it is suppose too. Don't let the fear of loss keep you from enjoying the time you do get." Natalee nodded as he turned her, placing an arm around her shoulder, guiding her towards the glass sliding door.

She mustered. "Thank you for rescuing me."

"I had too. It's freezing out here, and well I had to rescue you. Someone had already called for security for a mental health alert. Seems some crazy woman outside was shaking her fists and yelling at God. I was concerned for your safety, you could have gotten attacked by this crazy woman." He laughed as they walked into the first floor of the hospital. Not sure how he had done it. But Leo in all his wisdom, had changed her from fearing all the bad in her current situation, instead to realizing how much more she did have. "Oh, and you probably need to hold off on all of this crazy shit until after tomorrow."

"Why what happens tomorrow?"

With concern written across her face as he explained. "Oh, you didn't know?" Natalee shook her head. "Joe's crazy family is coming. And babe they don't know about Jenny, the baby or you." Natalee threw her hands to her face shaking her head.

»»

Natalee shifted on the small waiting room couch. Opening her eyes, dry and gritty and swollen from hours of tears. She had sat patiently by Joe's bedside holding his hand each time they had allowed her into his little room. Then she would come back to the small waiting room and get back on the couch with Mary. Each time Mary would awaken and ask how he was doing. The night nurse had promised to wake her if there had been any changes in his condition. Now looking at the large clock on the wall she tried to focus her sleep deprived eyes, realizing it was just after five, she rose. Her body was stiff from the night. Natalee stretched, doing several yoga poses focusing on her breathing and stretching her body.

Fifteen minutes later she began, to feel human again. When she walked to the hallway she could see into the intensive care unit. She could not see Joe, but she felt relieved seeing the nurses relaxed. That meant to her, he was not in danger. Natalee headed toward the vending machine a short distance down the hall. Looking at the choices, realizing they needed real food sometime today instead of more junk. Deciding to wait for the cafeteria to open in an hour instead of pouring more sugar into her body, that would only sicken her later. Hoping they would let her in to see Joe early, she stepped up to the door. "Mrs. Costas, would you like to see him?"

With hope in her voice she asked, "May I? I know it's not time yet."

"It's okay come on."

"Thank-you and please call me Natalee." The nurse smiled and gave her an update on his improvement over the night. Lost in translation, Natalee took her word for the improvement. Noticing that his color had improved far from the pale gray. It was not his normal, but she could feel joy at the improvement. Natalee sat by his side holding his hand, talking to him.

Telling him everything that she should have said months ago. "Joe, babe, I should have never walked away from you that night. It was Jenny that was wrong. I had nothing to be ashamed for. I am so sorry. Please come back to me. We have so much time to make up for. I, I love you Joe." Natalee gently kissed his cheek, then went to wake Mary.

Tapping Mary awake, she stretched as she rose from the couch. "Your man needs to get better soon. I don't think my back can handle this couch again."

Natalee giggled. "Come on. I will buy you some breakfast. We need to work on our plan for meeting my future in-laws." Those words caught Mary's attention as she quickly grabbed her purse, following her to the cafeteria.

CHAPTER FIFTEEN

Natalee borrowed a hairbrush and makeup from Mary. Less than an hour later they had endured the hospital cafeteria food and did some face repair in the ladies' restroom down the hall from the intensive care unit. Natalee debated whether to drive home and shower, fear of leaving Joe had won out as more important than looking nice to meet his family. Besides if it was her son, and the situation arose she would want a partner that cared more for her son then her own personal needs.

Natalee only considered leaving due to fear of meeting them. A part of her wanted to run. Instead Mary and her waited until the time arrived when she was allowed back into his little room again. Natalee sat at his bedside, telling him stories of their time together and every annoying thing he did that led her to take a chance on him. The urge to lay down next to him was overwhelming. Only the fear of hurting him kept her from indulging in his touch.

"Yes ma'am. Here is a list of our visiting hours. You have quite a large family and we will do everything we can to make you comfortable. We do only allow three family members in the patients' room at one time. And only for a limited amount of time."

The nurse tried to hide her frustration at the very large family crowded into the waiting room. Mary walked into the room carrying two drinks from the coffee shop downstairs, as the nurse stated. "Mrs. Costas is in with him now. Two of you

110

may go in when she comes out." The nurse quickly turned on her heels as she passed Mary, frustration marked, clearly on her face as she stepped back into the intensive care unit.

Mary jumped when a loud voice erupted. "What Mrs. Costas. I am Mrs. Costas. My son does not have a Mrs. Costas. I as his mother would know this if he did."

A male attempted to soothe her. "Now Alissa. It must be a mistake. Joseph would never marry without talking with us first. There has got to be, a logical explanation. So, let us sit and wait. It should not be long that is what the nurse said." Mary released the breath she was holding, quickly walking back around the corner from which she came, sitting the drinks down. Pulling her cell phone from her pocket, sending a quick text to Natalee. Mary chose a set of seats in the hallway and watched the door. Ready to intercept as needed when Natalee walked into the lions' den.

Okay, I am coming out. I might need back up. Mary smiled. **I am here buddy.**

»»

Natalee stepped from the intensive care unit after giving a well, deserved thank you to the crew of nurses that cared for her Joe. Verifying that they had her number, she gave them a brief story about his family. Only telling a small imaginative story that her and Joe had married but had not told his family yet. All four of the nurses professed they would hold the secret until Joe was able to help tell his parents. They seemed to laugh at her explanation to let his family think it was instead a mistake on the hospitals part. Professing her thanks once again, before she walked out into the group of people.

The nurse who had faced them alone, gave Natalee's arm a final pat. "Natalee, I feel for you, my in-laws look like kittens compared to this group. You will have no problems with us."

Natalee smiled. "Thanks Sarah. I appreciate you taking care of my Joe." Sarah smiled then turned back to the group at the desk. Taking a deep breath, Natalee decided to meet the opposition head on. After deciding with Mary that Joe's family was on a need to know basis with their relationship. Walking up to the group, Natalee slowly reached out touching Mrs. Costa's arm.

"Mrs. Costas, Hello, I am Natalee Brennan." Sticking out her hand. Surprisingly Mrs. Costas took her hand giving her a firm handshake looking her straight into her eyes. Natalee admired this beautiful tall woman. She stood eye to eye with Natalee, her striking black hair and olive skin. *Sophia Lauren* was the first name that came to mind.

Her question interrupted Natalee's thoughts. "And who are you?" Natalee had the sense to be slightly embarrassed.

Her cheeks reddened as she spoke. "Well, it seems strange at our age, but I am Joe's girlfriend."

Still not releasing Natalee's hand, his mother leaned her to the right then to the left as she inspected Natalee. Feeling extremely self-conscious, Natalee felt the comforting familiar hand placed onto her back by her best friend.

Mrs. Costas, responded with slight sarcasm. "So, my son has a wife and a girlfriend?" Natalee pulled her hand back, laughing. "Heavens no. Several of the hospital staff assumed I was his wife when he was brought in. My close friends Leo and Mary." Turning to introduce Mary to the family. "This is Mary, my best friend. Her husband Leo is Joe's partner. That is how we met last spring. Leo introduced us. Well Leo had hinted to the staff that I was his wife when he was brought into the emergency room. You see, they don't recognize girlfriends as next of kin. So, in this case when it involves an officer they are quite protective. Only wives, and the other officers. Leo felt he was doing best. He was the one to notify your family."

Natalee paused, and accepted her drink from Mary. Sipping the hot cinnamon spiced creamy tea, avoiding the stare of the family for a few minutes. Using the diversion of her drink to calm her nerves.

Mrs. Costas replied. "You have been here this whole time." Natalee felt the scrutinizing glare from her head to her running shoes covered feet.

"Yes Ma'am. Mary called me while Leo was at the scene with Joe. I came straight here. We haven't left." Natalee fought the tears in her eyes.

Mrs. Costas replied. "You are tired." It was not a question but instead an observation.

"Yes." Mary interjected. "Yes Ma'am, that couch there, is not too kind to the body."

Mrs. Costas directed her attention to Mary. "You stayed with her?"

Mary wrapped her arm around Natalee. "We are family. Leo was here for some time then he had to return to work."

Mrs. Costas surprised Natalee pulling her into a Mother's hug. The type of hug that Natalee had not felt in such a long time. "Thank-you Joe's Natalee. Thank-you for loving my son, staying here and watching over him." She nodded as she stepped back. Natalee was quickly introduced to Joe's Dad Alec, his sisters Aline and Callie. Along with their husbands. A set of Grandparents and an Aunt and Uncle. The names flew by her at such a pace she gave up trying to recall them. Relief set in as she watched them go in two at a time to see Joe.

She willingly gave up her time with him for his mother to stay. She knew something of the fear Alissa must be feeling. Now all Natalee could do was wonder how her and Joe were ever going to explain the rest of their crazy life to this wonderful family.

»»

Natalee left the hospital at close to six the following morning. The intensive care doctor came to the waiting room where her and Mary were napping. Stretching as she tried to stand. Mary struggled with great effort the two nights of sleeping on hard couches or chairs had taken its toll.

"Mrs. Costas." Natalee had long given up trying to explain that she loved this man and yet, she was not his wife.

"Yes."

"Your husband is responding well to the treatment. His lung is recovering from the accident. We are hoping to remove the chest tube by tomorrow and move him out of the intensive care."

"Thank you."

"So, he should be waking up anytime today. Take a break. Go home, eat a real meal, whatever you need."

Natalee pulled out from the hospital parking lot, glancing at the clock she made one quick phone call.

It was answered by the second ring. "Hello."

"Alissa, this is Natalee. Sorry to call so early."

"No problem Natalee. We were up."

"Good, I wanted you to know I just spoke with Joe's physician. We have good news. He said Joe was responding well to treatment. He should be moved out of Intensive Care by tomorrow. And they are planning to be able to remove the tube in his chest by then." Natalee could hear the family in the background happily sharing the news.

"Oh, Natalee that is wonderful news thank-you dear for sharing this news."

"I am so happy to bring good news. I wanted to let you know I am running home for a shower and a change of clothes. I will be gone about two hours if you get to the hospital before I am back."

"Natalee, it is no trouble we are preparing to head there soon ourselves after we stop for breakfast. I wish I could have stayed there with you over night. But I am afraid my aging back would have never made it all night on those couches." Natalee heard Joe's dad in the background laughing and making a joke about his wife.

Natalee smiled. "I do not blame you a bit. I can understand, my back is very stiff. I will see you in a few hours."

"Bye, Natalee."

"Bye Alissa." Natalee drove the past few miles towards her house with a renewed sense of life. Suddenly she could see a different world for herself and for Joe. Happiness lingered quite close and yet doom was not that far away. Just when she could feel the happiness near, she remembered. "Jenny and the baby."

Walking into the kitchen, she shook her head as she looked at her beautiful kitchen overran by dirty dishes, take out containers and trash. Quickly losing it. "Jenny, what in the hell happened in here?" Jenny came walking from the living room. Her flannel pajamas barely covered her expanding belly.

"What Mom, you are the one who left two days ago and never came back. I had to have food delivered. Oh, and I used your credit card."

"Jenny, you are pregnant not handicapped. You could have cleaned up after yourself. I told you Joe is in the intensive care. I have been at the hospital with Leo and Mary." Jenny laughed and placed the remainder of the ice cream bucket in the freezer and throwing the spoon in the sink.

"What are you worried he will die and leave you to pay all of the bills for his bastard child." Before Natalee realized what she was doing, she slapped her daughter across the face. Jenny's hand flew to her cheek. Natalee was steaming. She had never struck her child in her entire life. Her hand burned from the slap, yet there was no guilt. Instead feeling as if she would do it again if she dared say anything as hateful again.

"Mom, how dare you. You have no right to treat me this way."

"I don't? Really? That is all you have, to say to me? You purposely got pregnant by a man that had no interest in you. In fact, little girl. I had turned him down. I love Joe. And he loves me. And you, well, you are a spoiled brat. I can't figure out how, in the hell you could turn out this selfish. You have disrupted my life, Joe's life and you have the gull to act like your life is just horrible. You little girl, brought all of this on yourself." Natalee shook her finger at her. "I want you out of here this morning. Go back to your apartment. I don't want to see you right now."

Natalee stormed towards her bathroom. Slamming and locking the door. Stripping down, she stepped into the shower, sliding down onto the shower floor she cried until there were no more tears. She had done something she never thought she was capable of. She sent her daughter away and in turn she just took back control of her life.

Natalee dried herself, dressing in a pair of charcoal gray trousers and a cream sweater. Completing her look with a pair of small diamond stud earrings Joe had sent her for Christmas.

115

With regret Natalee stared out of her bedroom window into the dismal icy day, remembering the holiday morning that in the years past had brought her joy.

This year had been different, under a dark cloud Jenny and her, had opened a few small gifts then left for Mary and Leo's family celebration. It had been Leo pulling her aside later that day, handing her the small jewelers box wrapped in shiny red paper and tied with a matching silk ribbon. Tears had formed in her eyes when she opened the small box, revealing small elegant diamonds encased in a platinum setting. Natalee realized then and now, Joe understood her better than Patrick probably ever did.

Pulling herself from the painful memories, picking up her coat and scarf Natalee braved the cold once again to be with the man she loved.

Natalee glanced at the dashboard clock again for the third time in the past fifteen minutes. The endless staring at the solid bits of red lights in front of her, to the side of her and reflected off the many other cars behind her. The normal twenty-minute drive to the hospital had turned into an hour and a half. Regret coursing through her wondering if her daughter had made it safely back to her apartment. Deciding not to have to deal with her daughter herself. Taking the easy way out she sent a quick text to her daughters' roommate. Relieved when she received a comforting return text letting her know Jenny had indeed returned safely and was in a terror of a mood. All Natalee could do was send an apology text.

Tossing her phone down on the passenger seat, she turned up the radio attempting to relax against the growing frustration of the parking lot of traffic she sat in on the expressway. Checking her gas gauge, relieved to see she had a stray bottle of water on the floorboard. Tapping her fingers on the steering wheel, attempting to fight her mind from racing with all the complications in her life while she sat for another hour motionless on the road with hundreds of other drivers. Hearing her phone vibrate on the seat pulled her from her brooding. Natalee picked up her cell phone on the end of the vibrating.

Having forgotten to return her phone from silent, now realizing that she had four new messages.

Recognizing the first one was from Alissa, Joe's Mother. "Natalee, we are here at the hospital. Joe opened his eyes. The doctor just removed his chest tube. His color is good. They will move him to a regular room here shortly. I will call and let you know his new room number."

The next two voicemails were from Mary. "Nat, just wanted to let you know I am here with the Costas family. Joe looks great. And Jenny sent me a text message to let me know she made it back to her apartment. I guess you two had a doozy of a fight. Well call me. I am concerned for you, I thought you were only going to be gone two hours."

Checking the next voicemail. Again Mary. "Nat, it is already noon, please be okay. Call me." In her sadness of the fight with Jenny, Natalee had accidentally hurt Mary.

The last message was from Joe. "Hey stranger. Come back I need to see you. I love you." Tears filled Natalee's eyes as she replayed the message once again. To hear his voice, although weak and raspy it still felt like a miracle after three days of worry. Natalee tried his number first, sadly to be answered by his voicemail.

Next, she tried Alissa, answering on the fifth ring. "Alissa, hi it is Natalee. I am sorry, but I am stuck on the expressway. It appears there is a bad wreck, I am stuck in a massive amount of traffic." Alissa assured Natalee not to worry about Joe, to concentrate on getting to the hospital safely. After hanging up, Natalee felt an immediate sense of happiness, a positivity of possibility for the future.

Close to four hours later exhausted, Natalee pulled into the hospital parking lot. Walking into the lobby, she took a few minutes to purchase a coffee and calm her nerves. She squashed the bubbling emotions that boiled within her. The stress of the past few days had taken its toll, worrying at any minute she could lose control. She stepped purposely towards the elevator, glancing at the last text message she had received from Joe's mother with his new room number. The elevator doors opened to the fourth floor, instantly Natalee realized that something was wrong. Loud voices reached her ears from the direction of just past the nurses' station. Several staff members stood at the desk. One was on the phone, Natalee feared they were notifying security.

Stepping around patients and their family members standing in the hallway, Natalee looked in horror as she neared Joe's room. Realizing quickly the source of all the excitement was none other than Alissa, Joe's mother, recognizing her voice clearly all the way to the nurses' station. Surprised to see Joe's sisters and their husbands in the hallway and not attempting to quiet the commotion. Prepared to try to calm the argument, shuddering when she heard Alissa's words.

"Joe, you did what?" Natalee's heart immediately hit her stomach, as wave after wave of nausea hit her, realizing Joe must have told his parents about Jenny and the baby.

Muttering to herself. "He had to go and say something, just when things were going so well." Taking a deep breath, Natalee walked into the room. Unprepared for the sight, Alissa stood with her arms crossed at the end of Joe's bed, while Mr. Costas sat quietly in the chair under the window seemingly reading the newspaper. Apparent to Natalee who ruled the Costas family. Natalee could not help but realize why neither her daughters or their husbands had managed to stop this tirade.

Natalee felt no fear from this woman as she marched into the room. Setting her purse and jacket down on the chair next to the bed. She stepped close to the bed, near Joe's arm as she reached down and taking his hand in hers. She felt the squeeze, that was all the encouragement she needed.

"Alissa, the nurse is calling security. I am sure that in your frustration you do not mean to not only upset Joe after such a horrible accident nor do you mean to scare the other patients who are recovering from equally dangerous illnesses." Not waiting for a response, Natalee quivered inside, determination broke through as she continued. She noticed the change in Alissa's body language. Alissa opened her mouth then quickly closed it. Natalee continued. "I have a feeling that Joe told you about our situation. Yes, it has been a trying time, for us both."

118

Pausing as she looked at him. Even in his weakened pale state, he was still the incredibly handsome good man that she had fallen in love with. Natalee willed herself to remember that one of the reasons Joe was the man that he was, his mother. Taking that into consideration she chose her words carefully. "Alissa. You raised an amazing son. I love him. I can't help it. I tried to walk away from him. I tried to deter him, that first time I met him. I said and did everything I could to keep from letting him into my heart. But he did it. He kept wiggling his way in, until he had my whole heart."

Natalee watched as the woman of steel changed softly before her eyes. Using one of her long, manicured nails to gently wipe a lone tear from her cheek.

Alissa nodded as she responded. "He has always been determined when it came to something he wanted." Joe watched the exchange between his mother and the woman he loves, as his dad looked over his newspaper in surprise.

Natalee continued. "Alissa, the situation with my daughter Jenny, has tormented me the past eight months. I did not raise her to behave this way, but at the same time I do worry that if I would have handled many things differently then she would not be the person she is. For this I take full responsibility." Natalee paused again, as she pulled her hand from Joe's, taking a step closer to his mother. "When I found out, I had every intention of continuing my determination to not, I mean not fall in love with your son. I tried to blame him, it was so much easier to blame him then to accept the blame for my daughter. In all truth if I would have just said yes to the first date, well then Jenny would have known that I liked him and I think it would have changed her actions." Natalee paused again. She was admitting to Alissa, with Joe listening to her feelings, things that she had not told him.

"My reason for turning him down the first five times, was simply because I am eight years older than him. I used my dead husband and age of my daughter as a shield to protect my scared heart of ever being abandoned again by someone I loved. I told Joe and myself that I was thinking of him first, I had no intention of having another child, and I did not want to keep him from all of the things that he wanted." Natalee looked over her shoulder to Joe. His puzzled expression gave her the courage to continue. "So, as I professed to him and to everyone I know that it was the age that kept me from him, in all reality it was my fear. Fear of loving him. Having him near, then losing him. It took this accident to realize you can't push love away out of fear. Instead you love. If you lose someone, you cherish what you have, not what you don't."

Alissa stepped forward, pulling Natalee into her arms. "Natalee, I am so sorry I misjudged you and your daughter." Alissa looking over Natalee's shoulder talking to her son. "Son, I love you. I should have trusted you to be the good man I raised. I should have really listened to what you were saying before I became upset."

"It's okay Mom. Just please give us time to figure out all of this crazy stuff before you start making plans." Alissa nodded as she released Natalee.

Before Natalee could take a step back, Alissa asked. "So, when do I get to meet my grandchild?"

CHAPTER SIXTEEN

Natalee looked out the window above her desk, wishing for signs of spring instead of the gray dismal day before her. The first day of February failed to hide the fact that winter was still going strong. The frost on the window along with more ice on the branches, only concerned her more this day. Instead of writing, she sat here and worried. Natalee could not help but think back to the day less than a month ago when Joe had barely survived an accident in weather much like this.

Today marked his first day to return to work. A small part of her felt relieved that he was on desk duty at the station for the next three months. Selfishly, she had been pleased while listening to him rant and rave about his sentence as he had called it. He continued to wear a brace on his leg and arm other than that he had recovered nicely. Natalee was thankful for any delay to slow him down even if it meant only for a few weeks. Pushing her chair back, she gave up for now, standing up and stretching. Deciding to complete some house hold chores while she patiently waited for five o'clock. Natalee had just loaded the dishwasher and started a load of towels when her cell phone rang.

"Hello. Hi honey. What? Really, already? Okay I will be right there. How far away are you? You aren't driving yourself? Oh, okay. I will be right there. Yes, I will call him." Natalee hung up the phone, throwing on a sweater over her long sleeved knit shirt. Grabbing her boots, jacket and scarf as she walked to the kitchen while she quickly called Joe, zipping her boots as she ran to garage. Starting her engine as the phone continued to ring.

Thankful, he picked up. "Hello."

"Joe. Jenny's in labor. I'm leaving now."

"I will meet you there." Natalee backed out of the driveway. Realizing now, his voice was distant, and cold. She had wondered how the birth of baby Jake would affect their relationship and the closeness they had shared since his accident. Now with one phone call, all the problems of the past nine months surfaced.

Ignoring the fear inside her, she called Mary, leaving a message. "Mary. Baby is coming. Leaving for hospital now. See you there, I mean. Mare, I need you there." Natalee knew her best friend would be there for her.

Natalee watched the scene unfold in front of her as if she was a spectator at the movies. Seeing Jenny in the bed grimacing, sweat dripping from her brow while Joe stood next to the bed, wiping her brow with the cool cloth, encouraging her with each contraction. Conflicted between the overwhelming sadness and the joy that becoming a grandmother should bring to her.

As always, Mary sensed her pain, pulling her into a hug. "Nat, do you want to take a walk?" Natalee did not speak, replied only with a nod of her head.

"Joe, we are going to take a walk and grab some coffee. Would you like one?"

Joe responded with a quick. "Yes, thank-you."

Mary led Natalee from the birthing room and waited until they had gotten onto the elevator before she asked. "This must be hard on you. Are you okay?"

Shaking her head no. Natalee released the tears when she said. "I don't know why I thought I would be able to go through with this. Seeing Joe with her, caring and touching her. It just brings all of this back."

They sipped their coffees for several minutes before they slowly walked back. Natalee had wanted to be there for the birth, now dreading the very thought of having to go back upstairs only to be faced with horrible memory of her daughters' indiscretion.

Mary hesitated outside the birthing room door, giving Natalee one more hug before they braved the situation.

Speaking low into Natalee's ear. "Nat, I know all you want to do right now is bolt, from this floor, out into the cold wind and keep driving until you feel human again and the pain stops. I understand completely." Mary pulled back and looked her best friend in the eyes. "But, you in there, it is not about Jenny or even Joe. It is about baby Jake, coming into this world. No matter how he got here you will be able to look at him and not see pain. You will see him. A beautiful baby, he is a part of you. Be strong for him. I love you."

Natalee nodded and softly snarked. "You think you are so smart don't you. I love you too. I'm going." As they stepped into the room, the nurse informed them the baby was crowning. Natalee's motherly instincts over rode her sadness as she stepped closer watching in awe as her grandson was born. Natalee looked him over as Joe cut the cord and baby Jake was weighed and examined. The nurse wrapped the baby and attempted handing him to Jenny, pain registered across Natalee's face as her daughter instead turned her head away. The nurse laid the baby into Joe's arms, the joy was all too apparent in his smile.

Natalee walked closer to her daughter. "Jenny? Jenny, don't you want to hold the baby?" Natalee grew increasingly more concerned when Jenny shook her head then quickly closed her eyes. The nurse encouraged Jenny to breastfeed the baby, attempting to explain the importance of the first few days of feeding. Jenny continued to ignore the events in the room.

It was Joe, that motioned to Natalee. "Lee, you ready to hold him?" Joe gently handed her the baby. As Mary documented the event with her camera, tears filled Natalee's eyes as she looked over her grandson.

"Hi, honey. Jake, you are a beautiful baby." Instantly she was mesmerized by his large dark eyes looking up at her when she spoke. She was in love. For Natalee, this was the defining moment, gone was the anger, disappointment and hurt, taking its place was joy, love and immediate bonding. The nursing staff settled Jenny into a large room with an area for the baby and family.

Natalee walked down the hall toward the new room passing by several rooms with doors opened. Catching a glimpse of fathers holding their babies with tired but happy mothers, only saddened Natalee more. When Natalee entered the room quickly realizing the nurse had convinced Jenny to pump her milk so that they could feed the baby while Joe had left the room in search of food. Natalee on the other hand had done her best to avoid both Joe and Jenny. The only one she was concerned for at this moment was Jake, although she was continually disturbed by her daughter's behavior in the few hours since his birth.

Two days later, Natalee drove home, glancing at her daughter in the passenger seat before pulling into the driveway. Looking up into the rear-view mirror she caught a glimpse of the worried expression on Mary's face as she unbuckled baby Jake from his car seat. Mary bundled the baby while Natalee unlocked the kitchen door. Jenny moved slowly, walking from the car, without a word she went straight to her room. Natalee sighed, fighting the cold winter wind while she carried the remainder of the bags into the house.

Mary was fast at work warming the baby his bottle. Natalee collapsed into the kitchen chair as she watched Mary dance around the kitchen with the hungry newborn while his bottle was prepared.

"Mary, I can't do this." Natalee laid her head down on the table, with tears threatening. Muffled sounds came from between her arms as Mary pulled on her hand. Lifting her head, Mary handed baby Jake to her along with the bottle.

"Nat, feed him. He needs you."

"I didn't sign up for this. I did not want more children. I had a good life."

Mary laughed out loud as she poured two glasses of wine. "What you had my dear was a safe, quiet, lonely life. You wrote, worked in your garden, swam, ran and got back up the next morning and did it again. Your life was clean and neat, tidy. But you were lonely. You just never admitted it to yourself or anyone. You had the perfect excuse, not to have messy relationships, because you wrote about them instead of having them." Mary let her words sink in as she set the glass of wine in front of Natalee, pulling herself a chair out and sitting down. Mary waited for a response.

"You are right, you know."

"Yes, love, I know."

Natalee snorted. "Gees, how does Leo live with you. So, conceited."

"Ha, he loves me and so do you. And both of you know I only speak the truth because I love you." Natalee ran her finger over Jake's tiny fist, mesmerized at how perfect he was.

Recognizing the fact that Mary was right. "Okay I hear you, I understand where you are coming from. But can't I have some balance. Maybe be a grandma on weekends and still have my nice tidy life the other five days."

"Ha, let me know when that works out for you."

"Okay, okay. So now what?"

Mary pondered the question. "Well, first thing Jenny needs counseling. She has not bonded with the baby, let alone acknowledged him. Second, you need a plan, probably some parttime nanny or you will go insane. And third, well you and Joe probably need a post baby night out. You both were in a good place before he was born, but now I worry about the wall that went up in the past three days."

Natalee looked down at the baby, wondering to herself if she was going to be his grandmother that raises him.

Natalee waited patiently as Jenny dressed that morning. It was the day of Jake's one month pediatrician appointment. Natalee looked out the window with longing, the dark gray clouds threatening for yet another early spring thunderstorm. After having not ran in three days, she was going stir crazy. Her head pounded, an aching heart longed for the life that she had just a month ago.

Jenny was speechless while they waited in the well child side of the pediatrician's office. Throughout the appointment, it was Natalee who dressed and undressed the baby. The Doctor attempted talking to her daughter. At one point having Natalee, leave the baby on the table and asked her to step out of the room.

When Natalee returned to the small room, her daughter rushed past her. Natalee rushed to baby Jake. Listening to the physician as she added the coverall suit to her grandson.

"Thank you for trying. She has been seeing the counselor recommended by the hospital. So far, nothing appears to be helping. She didn't tell you anything, did she?"

"Sadly, no. She sat stone-faced waiting while I talked. She did not answer any of my questions, she never looked at him."

Natalee glanced down to the beautiful baby in her arms. Not sure where she found the sudden strength to add. "He will be well taken care of." Saying her goodbyes, with her fist full of pamphlets and a copy of the immunization schedule she walked to the car. Not surprised to see her daughter sitting with the engine running. She murmured to the baby. "Well, two things to be thankful for Jake. She has the heater running and she did not leave us." Looking, into his chocolate brown eyes so much like his Daddy's before she covered his sweet little head with the blanket she crossed the parking lot.

Two hours, a bottle and a diaper change later, the house was quiet. Jake was asleep in his crib. Baby monitor on, next to her computer Natalee stared at the monitor waiting for the words to come. Between the diapers, bottles and two am feedings, for the past four weeks she had spent more time in the rocking chair then writing. All the while Jenny spent her nights sleeping with the pillow over her head ignoring the screams of her son as he battled colic. Her days she left the house early, making use of the gym membership. Natalee had been so angry by the end of the second week, she had called the post-partum counselor to verify that her daughter was indeed going to their weekly sessions.

Natalee had attempted to talk to her daughter. She would start a conversation, before she could get past the basic of what would you like for dinner, Jenny left the room and shut her door without looking at the baby. Fighting hard to not give in to her own desire of eating a pan of brownies at one sitting.

"Oh, and top that off with hot fudge and ice cream and then it might make me feel happy again." Speaking to herself. "Joe will never look twice at me as long as I look like this. I will never get sex again." The saddening thought pounded in her along with the ache in her head, was not even the worse of the problems at this moment. Rising from her chair, stretching she opted for a second cut of coffee, tea failed to reach her foggy brain to make up for the lack of sleep and the threat of more stress in her life.

Tired, exhaustion taking its toll, her concern for her daughter's actions and now her lack of action. Barging into her daughter's room, slamming against the door against the wall not caring about the dent she had created. Her burning questions went to the wayside, watching in horror, as Jenny pulled out her filled suitcases, loaded with most of her clothing.

"Jenny, what the hell is going on?"

"I am leaving."

"Where do you think you are going?"

"California."

"What the hell? Why?"

"It is a job offer. A very lucrative one." Natalee, staring at her daughter in dismay as she continued to pack her third suitcase.

"What about Jake. You can't put him in daycare. He is too little." Her voice broke at the thought of her daughter taking the baby across the country. Thinking about Joe's heartbreak.

"Hmph."

"Jenny, answer me. After everything that you have put me through, I at least deserve the respect of looking me in the face and having an adult conversation." Jenny did not say anything, instead picking up two envelopes from a stack of papers on her desk handing it to her mother. Confused, Natalee opened the envelope. Her heart pounded in her chest, churning waves of nausea assaulted her stomach.

"Jenny, what did you do?" Her daughter lifted the first two suitcases walking past her. Natalee followed her with the envelopes in her hand, her mission to have a much needed conversation with her daughter was interrupted by the crying baby. Torn between the two, choosing the helpless infant over the spoiled adult she picked up Jake, patting his back receiving a burp in response as his body relaxed in her arms. Natalee wrapped the blanket around him settling into the rocking chair. Fear of the unknown, as dread filled her while her daughter made trip after trip to her car. Thoughts raced through her head.

Natalee whispered to herself. "I bought her that car. I could take it away." Laughing to the sleeping baby. Knowing all too well, her head strong daughter was off no matter how she had to get there. Natalee rose, waiting in the kitchen for her daughter's next trip to her room. Jenny walked past her saying nothing. She felt relieved with each time her daughter passed without any baby items in her hands.

"Jenny, will you please stop and talk to me. You owe me that much." Natalee waited with no response to her pleas. Placing Jake in his baby carrier in the den near the warmth of the burning fireplace. Covering his legs with his quilt, she whispered. "I made this blanket when I was pregnant with your, your." Natalee swallowed her words uncertain of how to address her daughter. When Jake closed his eyes without fussing Natalee settled at the kitchen table. Overwhelming fear bore into her, while she opened the first envelope, reading with her own eyes the employment offer, involving continuous travel around the world. Natalee sat speechless at the table, watching Jenny pack up the remainder of her belongings.

When her daughter passed her on the way to the door, Natalee asked. "Jenny, have you talked to Joe about this?"

"Why should I?" Looking at the daughter she barely recognized. The one that she had raised and yet somehow did not know at all.

Uncertainty for the future pooled in the pit of her stomach. Natalee responded with the first thing that she could think of. "Because he is the father."

Jenny slammed down the top of the last suitcase, responding. "Yes, he is and you are his mother. So, you two will have to figure out the custody together." Natalee watched as her daughter took yet another suitcase to her small sports car. Jenny loaded several boxes and her bags into the back.

Waiting until her daughter returned inside for another load of belongings, Natalee followed her to her room asking. "Jenny, what are you talking about?" Natalee could not hide her confusion. Her daughter stormed towards her and pulled the unopened envelope from her mother's hand with force, shoving it in front of her face.

"This one Mother, read this one." Saddened by the sound of her daughter's disdain. Natalee opened the envelope. Reading the words. Jacob Alexander Costas. Father. Joseph Alexander Costas. Mother, Natalee Jayne Brennan

"Jenny, What, did you do?" Peppering her daughter with questions. "Jenny, did you ever have any intention of being his mother?" Jenny looked at the ceiling and then the floor.

Tapping her manicured nails on the box she carried, thoughtfully responding to her mother's question. "At first, during the pregnancy. I liked the feeling of being pregnant with him. Then, the larger I became, the worse I felt. I would see other pregnant women and I could tell they had already bonded with their babies. Mom, I didn't feel that way. Even after the birth I didn't look at him the way you did. Mom, he bonded with you not me, and you with him, I didn't." Remorse filled Natalee. Jenny continued. "Mom, he doesn't even look like me. Even Aunt Mary thinks it. He looks just like you and Joe, not me. It is just like I had nothing to do with any of it." Natalee's heart splintered apart. Worried that Jenny will never know love.

Her voice softened as she responded. "Jenny, it might take time, because of the way you got pregnant, maybe you feel guilty about that." Jenny picked up another box, turning she walked towards the door. Natalee waited patiently for a response.

Almost as a second thought, her daughter stopped, looking over her shoulder as she said.

"No, I don't regret it. Now, I do know that I really don't want children. So, just consider me like a surrogate, you have the second child you've always wanted."

Stunned, Natalee hesitated, when she finally formed her thoughts into words, she ran down the hallway following her daughter. She announced out loud. "But you didn't ask me what I wanted." Quickly realized she was speaking to the empty house with a closed door.

Glancing at the clock once again, Natalee finally found the strength to call Joe. Dreading the past two hours since she had looked at the birth certificate. At that time, she had not expected her daughter to walk away. Her anger had mounted in the hours since her Jenny left. Natalee had carried the mountain sized weight of burden on her chest as she had cared for baby Jake throughout the afternoon. Sadness over coming, realizing the freedoms she had once taken for granted were now gone until Jake became a teenager. The anger continued the more she recognized the lack of control she had over her life.

"The fact that she had the audacity to make life decisions for me, was beyond unreasonable." Natalee argued with herself, her mind raced with possibilities of what to do. Everything from signing over custody to Joe, to adoption. Hearing Jake's soft cries through the baby monitor, interrupted her frantic musings. Warming the baby's bottle, she could not help but look out at the storm over the river.

Picking up her grandson, Natalee changed his diaper, wrapping him in a soft blanket. "Hi honey. Did you sleep good?" Natalee smiled as he opened his mouth even though the tears she struggled to hide burned at her eyes. "You are a hungry boy, aren't you?" Carrying her bundle to the living room, settling in the large rocking chair next to the window. Listening to the baby suck his bottle of milk, Natalee imagined

Jake at three years old running across the grassy hill, down to the river for a boat ride. Suddenly a sliver of hope broke through the gloom she felt. The tiny bit of remaining sunlight left of the day was almost gone when Natalee picked up her cell phone and called Joe.

"Costas"

"Joe. Hi it's Natalee."

"Hey, sorry I didn't see the caller id before I answered. Just getting off duty. How is everything?"

"Uh, well Joe. Are you busy?"

"No, I am almost home why Lee is Jake okay?"

"Oh, yes the baby is fine. I am getting ready to give him a bath now. I really need to talk to you. Would it be too much trouble for you to come by?"

Natalee did not realize that she had been holding her breath, until relief flooded her as she released her breath when she heard him say. "I'll be right there." Not knowing whether to be apprehensive or relieved. A part of her could not wait but the other part dreaded seeing him again. Not knowing how he would react to her news.

Natalee had just wrapped the baby up in a towel when she heard the back door, open. "Lee"

"In the baby's room." Pulling out his sleeper, from the antique bureau. Natalee unwrapped Jake from the large soft blanket giggling as Jake swung his arms and kicked his legs.

Feeling Joe's presence walk up to her before he spoke. "Hi buddy, wow you are happy after your bath." Standing side by side next to the small changing table as Natalee applied baby lotion and a fresh diaper to the squirming baby. Feeling Joe move closer, with his arm brushed against hers. Whenever he was near, each part of her body burst alive with desire. "Hey buddy, how was your bath?" Watching his eyes search for the source of the voice.

Jake waved his arms in excitement. "He recognizes your voice." Natalee finished the last of the snaps between his small legs. Gently picking him up, she handed him to his father. Natalee stalled for time while she tidied up the changing table, picking up his towel, walking into the bathroom, Natalee emptied the baby bath tub and straightened the counter.

Knowing that she could only avoid this dreaded conversation for only so long. She threw the towel in the hamper.

"Would you like a beer?" Realizing how much she had been trying to avoid this conversation.

Smiling down at his son, he asked with a laugh. "Do I need a beer?"

She whispered. "Yes." Staring into each other's eyes for the first time since he arrived.

"Okay." Following her into the kitchen she motioned to the kitchen table. Joe placed the baby into the carrier, belting him in and covering him with his blanket. Natalee handed him the opened beer. Waiting until they had both drank at least two sips, picking up the envelope from the counter, handing it to him.

Looking at her inquisitively. "It is Jake's birth certificate." Still unsure what was happening, he opened the envelope. He smiled as he read his son's name. Then he read further.

Looking up at Natalee. "What the hell?" Nodding. Completely at a loss for words. She waited for him to work it out in his own way.

"She gave him away?"

"Yes."

"You knew about this?"

"Not until I opened the envelope."

"She did not tell you before?"

Shaking her head no. "I found out about it at the same time, she let me know about the job she took out of town. She is gone, Joe."

Natalee watched as a myriad of emotions flickered across his face. It was strange that she knew him so well. Less than a year ago he was the man that she had just met. She had a crush on him. Never thinking that anything could possibly happen between them. They had fallen in love, were together, forced apart, then stayed apart purposely until the situation of her daughter was settled. Now there was a baby and both of their

131

names were on the birth certificate. And they were going to have to somehow co-parent.

Joe finally spoke, interrupting her thoughts. "She never had any intention of raising him, did she?"

Shaking her head. "No. I don't think so." Her throat tightened when Joe stroked the baby's cheek while he slept. Watching the tenderness, he had for his child. Deciding, she had to stop blaming Joe for the situation that had created Jake.

It was Joe that voiced the solution first. Taking her hand in his, he leaned in kissing her lips softly. "Lee, we can raise him together, as a family." Natalee was not sure why, but she was filled with fear of a new life. She began to shiver. He whispered. "Are you cold?" Getting up from the table.

She went to the refrigerator. "Just a chill. Are you hungry? You haven't eaten, have you?" S

"No, I am starving." Changing the conversation to the events of the day.

Joe cleaned the kitchen as Natalee picked up Jake tucking him in, standing next to his crib watching him sleep for a moment. She enjoyed this time of day. She had missed this chance for a second child when Patrick had died, Now, it just seemed out of place, yet at the same time felt so right. Turning on the baby monitor she walked towards the kitchen. Leaning against the counter watching Joe at the sink, loading the dishwasher. "Now that looks right, a handsome man doing kitchen duties."

"Ha, Ha, only as long as you keep feeding me great meals like that one, although I will gain a ton of weight." Looking over his shoulder, her insides started to melt. An hour later, after a few decisions made about him helping with the baby after work and on his days off she walked him to the kitchen door. Natalee held on to the door as she began to tremble when Joe bent down and kissed her lips. She had not realized how badly she had missed his touch in the past month since Jake was born.

"I will call you tomorrow. Call me if you need anything." Nodding, she quickly closed the door to keep the cold damp air out. Walking through her large house, it suddenly did not feel so lonely anymore. Looking at the clock she focused on getting several hours of writing in before Jake awoke before his next bottle.

"This might just work after all."

CHAPTER SEVENTEEN

Two weeks later all the positive feelings that she had that she could do this again, raise a baby and keep up with her writing commitments was a pipe dream.

"A crazy, pipe dream." Looking in the mirror, she was exhausted, deep purple circles below her eyes. The new treadmill she ordered so she could keep up her runs sat unused for the past four days. A solid week of no sleep had taken its toll. The original plan of Joe coming by every day after work and on his days off to help with the baby so that she could write and have some time alone. It lasted well for the first week. Then he took on two new cases. His work load doubled in a short amount of time.

With Jake now six weeks old, colic was full blown. He had screamed every day and night for the past five days. Two trips to the pediatrician, a change in formula. She had tried everything to get him to sleep, even on her chest in the old rocker. She was so tired.

The knock on the door did not help her mood. It was close to eight and all she wanted to do was sleep. She had held the baby and walked the floor for the past two hours, anything to relieve his pain. She had driven him around in the SUV for an hour, the motion allowed him to sleep for about twenty minutes.

As soon as she pulled in the driveway he started up again. Natalee had tried every trick that she could remember and the ones Mary had used with her boys. Mary had been coming by every day for an hour to give Natalee at least time to shower. Her newest trick was putting the baby in the belly holder and getting on the treadmill. He seemed to like that. The first of April was still cool and damp, and she did not need to add a cold on to the colic so Natalee had to refrain from taking him outside.

Walking to the door she was surprised to see Joe. With his suit jacket over his arm, dress shirt unbuttoned a couple of buttons, assuming his tie must be in the truck. He looked almost as bad as she did.

"Hey"

"Hey yourself."

And with that Jake started again. "I know buddy. It's time for your drops again." Turning to the kitchen she did not have to invite Joe inside.

By now he knew he was welcomed anytime. Pulling a bag of Chinese food from behind his back, sitting it on the counter. "How did you know?"

"Mary, called Leo and told him that if he did not give me some time off that she would be moving in with you for the next month to help with Jake. And that Leo would be eating cold tuna casserole for the entire time."

Natalee laughed. "And she would do it. She has been coming by every day after work to give me a break." Joe laid his jacket over the back of the chair.

Rolling up his sleeves, he started washing his hands. "Lee, why didn't you tell me how bad it has been?"

"I am sorry. I just didn't want to make things harder with the extra cases you have."

Joe took the baby from her arms with ease. "Okay little buddy. We have, to have a man to man talk. You have, to give your mom a break. She needs some sleep and most important a shower." Natalee stood with her mouth wide opened. She had not thought about being called his mom, it left a surprisingly warm feeling that replaced the anger when she read her name on the birth certificate.

"Why don't you get cleaned up and try to rest some while he is sleeping." Joe hesitated, unsure of how she would react. "If it is okay I will stay on the couch and listen for him. Maybe

I can give you some sort of a break." Too tired to do anything but nod. Natalee walked to her bathroom. Shutting the door softly she walked into the hot water spray. Letting it beat against her body, she tried to ignore the fact that he was on her couch right now looking completely exhausted, stressed and sexy. How any person could pull that off was beyond her.

Drying off she cracked the door open. No baby sounds. So far so good. Applying coconut lotion to her body, made her wish she was on the way to some exotic island, instead all she needed was sleep. Stepping out of the bathroom, towel drying her hair. Putting on a tank top, pajama pants and a cardigan sweater. Walking into the living room, surprised to see Joe in the giant swivel recliner. His dress shirt off, his white undershirt that probably would not stay clean for long around his son. His bare toes pushed in the rug as he rocked the baby.

Looking up at her with a smile. "Just show me where his bottles and that medicine is, then you go to sleep." Nodding she pointed to the frig, then writing out a few instructions. Taking one last look at those two, it was on the tip of her tongue to call them her boys, she held it back. Lying down in bed, her last image was of them two as she fell asleep.

Waking to the tapping on her shoulder, forgetting for a moment who it could be. Natalee opened her eyes to Joe sitting on the side of the bed holding Jake.

"Did he sleep at all?" Rubbing his face.

"Not much. He was good as long as I held him while I was up in the chair."

Natalee realized she had rested well, when she asked. "What about you?"

"A little bit. Sorry to wake you. I just got called in."

"Oh, I didn't hear your phone ring."

"I had it on vibrate, hoping not to wake you or Jake."

"What time is it?"

"Almost four." Getting up. Natalee shrugged on her sweater.

Joe placed the warm and sleeping baby into her arms. She followed him toward the kitchen door. "Thank you for tonight. I really needed that extra sleep. I just feel bad that now you are short on sleep."

Joe picked up his jacket. "I will be okay. Call you later." Nodding. Natalee watched as he leaned down and kissed his son's head. Wondering if he would kiss her. Instead he just squeezed her shoulder. "See you later." Closing the door behind him. Natalee curled up in the big chair with her little man and dreamed about his daddy.

Natalee walked the incline on the new treadmill while Jake slept strapped to her chest. Not her desired workout, it was a good alternative. Trying to control her frustration, the feeling of her life had been decided for her. She gave Jake a bottle, laying him down on the floor with a mobile above him. Hoping for a long enough entertainment for her to answer emails from both her agent and her editor. At just past two months old, switching him to the battery powered bouncer, keeping him in motion while she emailed away. Trying to write with an infant was virtually impossible.

Every time inspiration would hit, Jake would pick that exact moment to cry, needing a bottle or a change. She tried holding him on her lap, that didn't work. Returning phone calls and bouncing him around the kitchen while the weather poured. Natalee had hoped for a sunny day, at least that would allow her to take him for a walk in the fancy new stroller, a surprise from Aunt Mary. Giving her time to return calls while she walked.

Jake had recently discovered his fists. Laughing while he tried to eat them. "Really honey. You are hungry again?" Shaking her head. Mary had warned her that boys were completely different than girls. "Wow, if I would have had a boy first I definitely would have never wanted a second child." Natalee had recently started putting rice cereal in Jake's bottle with his formula. Hoping that his belly being fuller would help him sleep at night. Her thoughts interrupted, when her cell phone rang. "Hello."

"Lee, hey it's me. I can't come by this evening. I have a work issue tonight. And then I have to be in early in the morning."

136

"Fine."

"Really, I am sorry. I will be there tomorrow after work."

The frustration only mounted with her anger. "It is fine. Don't worry about. All is good here." Natalee cut him off when she ended the call. Natalee was not surprised by the third day in a row he had backed out of their agreement. Her rational brain knew it was hard for him to work all day only to stop by his apartment to change clothes then race to her house. Staying up half the night with the baby, sleeping the other half of the night on the couch. Then to get up and do it all again. His frustration was showing also. The last time a few nights ago they almost got in a fight before he left for work.

Fighting tears as she dialed Mary's number. Her friend answered on the third ring. "Are you okay?" Mary knew her well. No need for hello. Natalee responded replaying the conversation with Joe.

"Natalee, think about something, you two had just finally reached the place in your relationship Labor Day weekend, then Jenny messed that up. Then after the accident, it seemed you two were fine together again. Then when Jake was born, you both pulled away from each other."

Natalee interrupted her before she finished. "See, that is why we should not be together. We can't keep things right."

Mary laughed. "No silly, you two had too many obstacles. After the baby was born he pulled away because he was still feeling guilty about the incident. And you pulled away because you were trying not to be reminded of the incident. Now Jenny is gone, and Jake is just Jake, a baby who needs both of you together. What you both need is a night of passion to find each other again." Natalee snorted. Mary laughed. "I promise, you two, need to have the time to reconnect and the bedroom would be the first place to start. The rest will fall into place."

Natalee hung up, wondering to herself if Mary was right. A small sliver of fear seeped inside of her.

"Jake, what if your daddy doesn't want me anymore?" Receiving a slobbery fisted smile. "Buddy, I sure hope that you think he does."

»»

Joe sipped his coffee, walking into work the next morning. Between the last three nights of a stake out trying to catch the suspect for his latest case. He was irritable, grouchy and sexually frustrated. And to top it off he was missing Natalee. Sitting down at his desk, handing over files to Leo. Hopefully with all the hours he had been logging, he finally had enough to put this guy and his followers away. Leo looked up, giving Joe a one minute hold on signal as he finished his phone call.

"Okay Mary, I don't know what you want me to do about it. Well, I understand. We never left the boys with strangers when they were babies. But Nat can make her own decisions. I am sure she has deadlines that she is having trouble making. She needs help. Maybe she can get live in help. Okay, well try to help her how you can. I've got to get back to work."

Joe could not ignore when he heard Leo's side of the conversation. Asking his partner as soon as he ended the call. "So, you want to tell me what that is all about?"

Leo didn't even try to hide the conversation. "It seems Mary is worried about Nat. She is exhausted. And is considering taking Jake to a babysitter half the day so that she can write. Mary is trying to get her to hire someone in, maybe a live in."

Joe slammed the folder down on the desk, jumping up knocking his chair over. "This is not happening. My son is not being raised by strangers."

Leo looked up in surprise. "Well, son what are you going to do about it? I mean when you are a married couple you share all the parenting duties. Well me and Mary did."

Exhausted, Joe asked. "How did you do that, I mean how did you do it with this job?" Laughing. Leo shook his head. "Sit down. Let me tell you a little story."

An hour later, Joe walked out of work. He had rushed through his reports. Taking what Leo had managed to explain how he and Mary had managed to raise three boys, together.

Joe replayed the words from Leo. Wondering what it must have been like for Mary, as a stay at home mom. Staying home with them all the time, Leo had learned quickly how to help around the house and when to take over the duties giving Mary the much needed, breaks. They had somehow made it work. And now they were enjoying their freedom.

Joe got the message, he realized what all was at stake. It was more than giving Jake two parents. It was about giving him instead, a family. A family that loved each other, even though his parents had not figured out how to tell each other yet.

Walking out of his apartment three hours later with the last box of personal belongings. The back of his truck was loaded with his clothing and workout equipment. Handing the keys to James, the rookie who just sub-let his apartment. Joe hoped that this, like so many things in his life was not going to back fire.

CHAPTER EIGHTEEN

Natalee heard a noise, unable to place the origin. She kept writing, enjoying a rare moment of peace. She was determined to get at least something started on the new book. The words were finally flowing, Jake had stopped the colic just as fast as it had begun. Now the teething was full force, but he didn't seem to mind it quite as bad. Fortunately, with the weather finally warming up April was giving her more outdoor time with Jake. Sitting on the patio with him in his stroller he laughed and cooed at his toys while he was outside. The late afternoon sun had begun its descent. Knowing that she should take him in for a dinner and a bath, Natalee held on for just a few more minutes as the words poured onto the screen.

Writing was such an emotional experience, feeling at a loss when she was unable to create. Now feeling better, she wrinkled her nose when she heard the strange noise again, closing her laptop as concern crossed her face. Pushing the stroller towards the house she looked in the patio windows, everything in the house appeared the same. Hearing the noise again. This time the sound came from the direction of the driveway. Parking the stroller next to the house, Natalee rounded the corner past the kitchen door to look down the driveway. Instant relief at seeing Joe's truck in the driveway. Her mood quickly changed from relief to irritation when she witnessed the source of the sound. Returning to get the stroller as she looked at Jake sleeping peacefully.

»»

Pushing the stroller towards the driveway. "Would you like to tell me just what the hell you think you are doing?" Joe smiled when he heard her voice to his back. Turning around to see Natalee standing in front of the stroller with her hands on her hips. Jumping down from the bed of the truck, picking up the weight bench he carried it towards the garage.

Natalee followed him pushing the stroller. "I asked you a question." Setting up his weight bench in one half of the garage. "Joe, why won't you answer me?" Joe could feel the daggers of anger flying from her eyes to his back. He avoided laughing out loud instead turning around to walk back to the truck.

Stepping up close, looking down at his son and whispered. "You don't have to yell. I would think you would not want to wake up the baby." Gritting her teeth, she squeezed her eyes tightly and shook her fists at the sky. Suppressing the yell, the only reason she held back was to not wake the baby, she did not need him to point it out.

She whispered. "Why are you moving your workout equipment into my garage?" Joe continued to walk past her again with another load.

This time he replied. "Finally, you asked the right question." Leaning in close he whispered. "I am moving in." Touching his index finger to her nose, he turned to pick up another box, continuing his mission. Natalee was furious, ready to give him a piece of her mind when she was interrupted by Jake crying.

"Okay, I will wait to string up your daddy. Let's go give you some dinner first. What do you say?" Talking to the baby as she wheeled him next to the door, picking him up and cuddling him, entranced with his smile as she walked inside. She missed seeing Joe watching them as she picked up the baby kissing his soft cheek and talking to him. Nor the tenderness in his eyes as he realized how happy he was, to have made this decision. Joe continued unloading as he secretly worried how he could keep her from making him leave.

»»

Jake sat in the carrier on the kitchen table, the view of the sunset through the window drew her attention away from Jake while he ate baby cereal. He pushed out much more than he took in, they were making head way. With a fat little fist in his mouth more oozed out around his fingers.

"You are a messy one." Not sure of what to say to Joe as he walked past her with two boxes.

He spoke first. "Is Jenny's old room okay?" Hesitating, unsure of how to respond. "Or I could make it your room?" There was a glint of a dare in his eyes when he said it.

"No Jenny's room is fine. After I get him to bed, can we talk over dinner?"

"Yes. I would like that." Joe carried the boxes to Jenny's old room, across the hall from his son's nursery. "Well, step one, she has not thrown me out yet." He said as he opened the first box. An hour later his truck was unloaded, clothes in the closet. Gone were the girl's quilt and frilly pillows. His service revolver was securely locked in the safe in the closet. Taking his toiletries to the hallway bathroom, he could hear Natalee singing to the baby in his room. He kept telling himself this was all for Jake. But with renewed hope for him and Natalee, he realized moving in was as much for him, as for his son. Walking into the kitchen a bit later after locking up the garage and his truck, he was assaulted with the smells of home cooked food as soon as he stepped inside. The table was set, the baby monitor on the counter within ear shot, Natalee brought their plates to the table.

"You don't have to cook for me. But I would be lying if I said I didn't enjoy it." A small smile escaped her lips before she could shut it down.

"So, do you want to explain why." Joe skirted the question and responded with.

"Why I like your cooking?"

"Ha. Joseph Alexander Costas, you know exactly what I meant."

"Yikes you used the middle name, you must have learned that from my mother." Sighing as he pulled her chair out for her. "Yes, I should have talked to you about it before I just showed up. I didn't want to risk the chance of you saying no. The only way that we can share the responsibility of raising Jake is if I live here. I can't help out here, sleep on the couch and go back to my apartment then make it to work on time." She started to interrupt, but Joe reached across the table placing his hand over hers causing her to lose her train of thought. "Give me a minute to explain before you find fault with my plan." She nodded. "I thought about it a lot. I even asked Leo how he and Mary managed to raise the boys like they did. He explained it all. I tried to figure out how we could do this. Even when Jake is older, if I have him overnight and I get called in to work then I have to wake him up and bring him to you."

Natalee understood, he made a great point. Suddenly released from the anger, frustration and the feeling that he was taking over her life.

"Lee, this isn't about just raising our son. It's about giving him a family."

»»

"Lee, wake up Lee." Natalee rolled over in bed. Surprised to see Joe sitting on the side of her bed holding Jake. "Jake tell your Momma if she wants to start running again, and not on a tread mill then she has to get up, run and be back by seven thirty when Daddy leaves to go to work." Natalee smiled a sleepy smile as she nodded. Turning over in bed, pulling the covers up she thought about it for a moment when she felt the swat to her blanket covered bottom. "Last chance Lee."

"I am going, going." Five minutes later she was dressed, tying her running shoes and heading to the kitchen door while

Jake sat in his carrier listening to his father explain the art of his fancy coffee maker that now took over a portion of her beautiful clean granite counter top. Keeping an eye on the time while she did a quick run, making a mental note to set an alarm for the next morning. She planned on calling Mary, to find out exactly what Leo had suggested to Joe.

For the first time since Jake was born Natalee felt positive that they would be able to make this work together. Opening the kitchen door, not immediately seeing Joe and the baby, she could hear his voice from his room.

"I'm back." She followed the sound of his voice, walking into Joe's room without thinking. Seeing him standing next to the bed with his jeans hung low on his hips and a bare chest, talking to the baby lying on his bed while he threaded his belt through his jeans. Natalee leaned against the door frame, a smile on her face while she enjoyed the scene before her. Hearing Joe ask Jake.

"What do you think buddy. Which one should I wear today?" Watching as Joe picked up two different polo style shirts. Natalee could only think either one would look amazing on him, or better yet no shirt at all. Jake kicked his feet and shook his arms in the air. "Okay the blue one has it."

Seeing Natalee as he pulled the shirt on over his head. "How was your run?"

"It was wonderful. Thank-you for watching Jake."

"No problem. This is one of the many reasons why, this will make things better." Picking up the baby, he walked towards Natalee as he said. "I will get extra time with him and you will get some free time that will help keep you from going crazy." Handing the baby to her, he gently kissed his head.

"I wasn't going crazy."

"Uh, huh." Pulling on his boots. Grabbing his bag, pulling his service pistol and badge from the safe. Attaching his holster. "Yep, you keep telling yourself that." She followed him to the kitchen. "Oh, Lee he has had his cereal. He should be ready for a diaper change, a bottle and he will probably take a nap for you. Most likely you will get some writing in." Natalee looked at him suspiciously as he moved closer to the kitchen door.

"Who are you, super Daddy?"

Laughing as he picked up his travel coffee mug, opening the door. "Oh, and Lee I should be home early. I will work out for a bit before dinner and then I can take over the baby duties that should give you several hours this evening." Natalee opened her mouth in surprise as Joe leaned down kissing her on the forehead, the baby received one also. As he whispered. "See you tonight." With her mouth open, nodding was all that she could manage.

»»

"I just don't get it. You will not believe what he has done. Moving all his stuff in like he owns the place. And to top it off, he is telling me, me when I should write!" Mary listened patiently, attempting several times to respond. Natalee continued her tirade as Mary tried to remember the last time she had seen her best friend this angry.

Promising Leo before she left home, she would appear surprised at whatever Natalee had to tell her. Now close to an hour later, Natalee had not stopped talking, as Mary sat on the floor playing with baby Jake. Natalee paced the living room ranting about every little thing that Joe had done in the past few weeks since Jenny had left.

Natalee continued with her tirade. "And to top it off I talked to Alissa, they are coming in two weeks to see the baby again."

Mary attempted to hide a smile. "Well, what are you worried about the first visit went well. And they are crazy about Jake."

"I know, but then I told her how the Pediatrician said I was starting cereal too early."

"What did she say?"

"She said her darling son Joseph started cereal at precisely the same time because if not he would nurse every hour. And he always ate twice as much as any other child his

144

age. And he was always the tallest and the best athlete, she said she cooked him six, six meals a day!" Natalee shook her arms towards the ceiling, as she announced. "So, one little baby from super Daddy and I will be chained to a stove until he moves out."

Mary laughed, she gave up trying to hide it. "Nat don't you remember when the boys when they were little. Jenny ate her little half sandwich and carrots, while my boys each ate three hamburgers."

Natalee kept pacing. "You are going to wear a path in this perfectly good rug you have." Natalee stopped mid-step, realizing that she was acting crazy. Sitting down on the floor next to Mary watching Jake attempt to hit the toy above his head.

Feeling defeat she responded. "Why does this man make me so crazy?" Burying her face in her hands.

"Because you are in love with him, and I am talking real forever love not hot sex weekend on the boat." Natalee raised her head slowly, blowing her hair off her face. Absolute speechless, a very rare occasion for Natalee. Mary watched as a dawning recognition changed the very expression on her friend's face.

"You really think that I am?" Mary nodded. "How long do you think I have been?" Mary moved closer to Natalee, grasping her hands in hers.

"Nat, I hate to be the one to tell you this. I think you have been in love with Joe since the first night Leo introduced you two." She continued. "Nat. I think it was instant between you both. I believe that you fought it so hard because you tried doing what was right for Joe. Although I do not agree with what Jenny did, and I know you feel betrayed by what she did but something you do not realize is no one else knew you were in love with Joe. You did everything in your power to hide it from the world and worse, from Joe and yourself."

Mary bit her tongue to keep from going too far. Giving Nat a chance to think about it.

"Nat, Leo and I love you, but you have made yourself a martyr for most of your adult life. You have been so convinced that you could take care of everything and everyone by yourself, you have never let anyone except us in." Natalee let a few lone tears down her cheeks. Nodding as Mary continued. "All these series of events that have been eating you up since Jenny came and confessed. You never told her, did you?" Natalee looked up confused. Mary explained. "You never told Jenny how bad this hurt you, because you are in love with Joe."

Natalee thought for a moment then responded. "No. I didn't realize I was. I think I thought of him as this sexy younger man that was unreachable for me. That, that he needed this young athletic beautiful woman that he could start a family with. Even that weekend at the beach, I thought it was a fling. I never thought it would last."

"Nat, think about it, it was you that made that assumption. At the party, you took Joe's choice from him, he was interested in you. He did not pay any attention to any of the other single women at our party, nor has he had an interest in anyone since. He drives Leo nuts asking about you. He only had eyes for you at the party, even after Jenny threw herself at him. And you let her, you just walked away. Why do you believe you are unworthy of a man like him?"

Tears streamed down Natalee's cheeks, as she looked at Jake. Realization that although all the hurt that occurred with Jenny and her actions. Natalee had to admit that she did blame Joe. Opening herself up now, seemed to be the right thing. Talking softly, she recognized the truth for the first time. "I blamed Joe for not trying harder to stop it."

"Oh, honey. I love you so much you know that." Natalee nodded and continued to cry. Jake began to fuss. Getting up, Mary went in search of a bottle for him. Picking up Jake and holding him in the rocker while Natalee laid on the couch with a blanket. Mary spoke first. "Honey, you have to get all of this out. Tell me everything. All of it. Don't hold back anymore." Natalee nodded, sitting up and crossing her legs. Jake fell asleep, Mary raised one finger and went to lay him in his crib. Bringing back the baby monitor. Mary walked into the kitchen and opened a bottle of chilled wine. Pouring two glasses, coming back into the living room. Settling onto the love seat next to Natalee, they both took a sip of wine.

"I thought you were past all of this when Joe had his accident."

"I thought I was too. I think it was Jake's birth. All the fear just came back."

"Okay, I want to hear all of it. Everything you feel. No more holding it in." Natalee opened herself up to feelings she did not even realize that she had. Blaming herself for not acknowledging the fact that she did have feelings for Joe from the very first night. She could not help but wishing he would have fought harder for them. As Mary pointed out, he had tried but she shot him down at each try.

"Oh, Mary why did he get so drunk that he had no control."

Mary snarked. "Honey he was drinking because he saw you out with Garrett. Joe didn't know the circumstances. He just saw it as he wasn't good enough. He thought that all of those reasons you gave him when you shot him down were just that, excuses."

Natalee paused, thinking as she took another sip of wine. Much larger this time. "And I guess you know this why?"

"Because of the stake out that him and Leo have been on that is why he did not come help with Jake the past two weeks."

Natalee felt horrible, the more she thought about how much she had blamed him and not her daughter. "So, he told Leo?"

"Yes, he told Leo everything. Including how he truly felt about you. And how stupid he was to not try harder to get Jenny to leave."

"Oh, Mary I have spent so much time being so angry at Joe and not holding Jenny accountable for her actions. I don't want to end up resenting the baby."

"Honey, you will not. You love him. He is the second child you always wanted. No matter how crazy the circumstances were that created that beautiful baby boy in there, you are his Momma and Joe is his Daddy. Now the question needs to be. Is Mommy going to finally show Daddy how much she wants him?"

CHAPTER NINETEEN

Joe pulled into the driveway, relieved to be home. "Home." Saying the word with a new found meaning, while he admired the older ranch house with the large yard and long driveway. Joe easily imagined Jake learning how to ride his bike, or the front yard would be a perfect size for football or baseball. Joe looked forward to using the boat dock. He had wanted to ask Natalee if she would mind if he kept his boat here instead of the marina. Now that Jake was getting a little bigger they could do evening boat rides on the river. He didn't think that she would want to take him out into deeper water until Jake was large enough for a baby life jacket. Lost in plans, he parked his truck to the right side of the driveway next to her SUV. Lately she had taken to leaving her car out. Hoping he had not put her out too much by moving his work out equipment into the garage.

Joe opened the kitchen door, he was met with Natalee wearing a red spaghetti strapped sun dress. Leaning against the door, watching her singing to herself while she stood at the stove. Joe chuckled when he noticed her bare feet with bright red toe nails moving to the music while she cooked.

With a gleam in his eyes he said. "Hi." Natalee jumped at the sound of his voice, heat immediately rose to her cheeks.

"Oh hi, I didn't hear you come in."

"I guessed that." His eyes twinkled as he teased. Blushing, Natalee opened the refrigerator and pulled him out a beer.

Taking the beer, his voice softened as he apologized. "Sorry I was running a little late today. Lee, you don't have to cook for me."

Smiling up to him as she teased. "I know, sometimes I will expect you to cook for me."

He noticed a slight teasing tone to her voice. "I can do that."

148

"You do like pork chops, don't you?"

"I do." Watching as she motioned to the table.

"Take a load off. Dinner is ready." Sitting down, Joe stretched his legs out in front of him, enjoying the site of her bringing the food to the table. His mouth began to water when he saw the fried pork chops and rice with gravy. A large leafy green salad sat in the middle of the table.

"Lee this looks amazing. But you don't usually eat like this."

She laughed with her reply. "I love fried pork chops. Not much sense in cooking like this for one. See it works out I cook it and you will eat most of it. Keeping me from over eating."

"Well, there is that." He murmured.

Joe enjoyed every bite of the meal, when Natalee got up bringing the dessert to the table. "Dessert too? You are really trying to spoil me." Joe ate two helpings of the warm brownie, ice cream and warmed caramel sauce. Licking the spoon as he finished the second helping. "I think that is my favorite dessert."

Natalee finished clearing the dishes, while Joe loaded the dishwasher. "I am going to get in a swim, I can take the baby monitor with me if you would like to work-out in the garage."

"That would be good, especially since you fed me so good tonight." Patting his stomach. "I will go change." Walking across the living room towards the hallway. When he turning quickly, Natalee walked right into his arms on her way to her room to change. "I forgot to ask how long will Jake sleep?"

Glancing at the clock over the mantle, she responded. "Oh, it is barely eight. He should be good until at least eleven."

Taking in her scent, Joe lowered his voice responding. "That is great." Slowly he took a step to the side allowing Natalee to walk past him down the hallway. Joe stepped into his room pulling the door closed. After changing his clothes, staring at himself in the mirror thinking about how his life had changed in such a short time. Joe continued to debate with himself on how to advance his relationship with Natalee again, while he tied his running shoes, opting for a run first before the weights. He had never experienced nervousness around women before.

Peeking in on his son sleeping peacefully, he walked through the house to the kitchen door. Attempting not to look outside, to see if Natalee was out by the pool, taking all his willpower to not follow her into the pool, pulling her close and making love to her as the twilight faded to night. His lower half jumped into action, he was certain considering their current relationship, he should not follow his desire to jump into the pool after her. Instead he chose to start jogging toward the driveway for a very long run in the muggy spring air.

>>>>

Natalee enjoyed the cool water caressing her body, cooling her as she sliced through the water with each stroke. She could not help but imagine Joe's fingers trailing down her shoulder towards her back, rippling against her skin heating a trail as they moved lower. Her body ached for him, missing his touch by their brief encounter that one weekend, so long ago. Yet, if she counted the months it only seemed to be yesterday, she yearned for their closeness, skin to skin. Shivering she finished her last lap, grabbing the baby monitor and her towel throwing it around her shoulders running towards the house. With no sounds from the monitor, Natalee quietly headed toward the shower. The hot water helped to take away the chill from the cold swimming pool water.

Stepping from the shower, she wrapped up in her favorite robe. Quickly running a comb through her hair, she walked quietly down the hall to Jake's room. Stepping up close to his crib, she watched his soft baby breathes. His little arms were up above his head, she was curious if he would sleep this way when he was older.

Natalee took photographs of him daily since they had brought him home from the hospital. Today he looked more like an infant and less like a newborn.

Whispering. "Time goes by so fast."

Surprised when she felt Joe's warm breath on the back of her neck. "Still sleeping. You did good tonight." His whispers lifted the small hairs on the back of her neck, sending shivers down her entire right side. Taking in his clean fresh sent, her brain registered his recent shower, while her body cravings intensified. Joe asked. "You cold?"

Looking up at him she replied softly. "Yes, the pool was a little colder than I expected." Natalee watched in awe, as his lips parted just before he meant to say something. It took several minutes for her to realize what he was doing when he took her hand, leading her toward the couch. Joe picked up the soft throw from the corner of the couch, laying it over her legs. She admired him, moving over towards the fireplace to light the logs. Placing the screen back in front of the fire, hesitating for the briefest of moments almost as if, he was searching for courage. Joe sat down next to her. No words were spoken as the muggy evening gave way to a night storm.

Watching through the large living room windows, into the night, while streaks of lightning raced across the sky. The trees swayed in the wind. Joe lifted his arm, placing it behind her. Without thinking, she leaned into his chest, his arm came protectively around her. He whispered softly to her.

"Wow, this is better entertainment than watching television."

Natalee smiled, looking up at him. "Really? What if football was on right now?" He hesitated. She nodded. "See I am right."

Joe pulled her close when she giggled. Talking low into her ear. "I would turn off football every time if it meant sitting on a couch this close to you with a thunderstorm outside." Her shivering had been driven away by the fire building inside of her. He lowered the blanket as he asked. "You warmer now?" Nodding, she looked up into his dark chocolate eyes and melted. Joe pulled his arm from her shoulders, touching her neck with the gentleness of touch. Leaning into his touch. "Feel good?"

"Mm yes,"

"Hold on I will be right back." Natalee raised her head from the back of the couch when he sat down moving her in front of him. Natalee gasped when he lowered the robe past her shoulders. Her senses assaulted by the smell and sound of the liquid oil in his hands, before she felt its silky warmth on his long fingers caressing her skin.

"Mm." Natalee moaned as the tension released from her neck. The unmistakable scent of baby oil permeated her soul. Gently leaning her head forward, he massaged towards her hair. Joe playfully tugged a small strand of hair pulling her head up towards the ceiling before, he moved his hands to her shoulders.

A smile came to his lips when audible sounds of pleasure passed through her lips. Pouring baby oil onto his hands, he gently worked his magic across her shoulders, kneading deeply with the perfect amount of pressure.

"Oh, oh." Joe smiled, memories of that sound in the tiny boat cabin, bringing stimulating excitement to his lower half. He focused on reaching each muscle, relaxing her while he continued his mission. Lowering the robe down her arms, exposing her back towards the top of her buttocks.

"Ooh." Natalee arched her back, his fingers applying warm moist pressure relieving the ache in her lower back. Her nipples were taut with want, craving his touch. His fingers needing as they traced her hips. His hands spanning the slight soft mound of her stomach, pulling her close against his bare chest. Her head resting onto his shoulder. "Oh, oh." Releasing a soft moan, his hands pushing up to bare breasts. One in each hand.

"Mm," Sighing deeply. Natalee pushed her soft mounds filling each of his palms. The oil soft fingers tenderly sought out her nipples, running tiny circles turning them into tight nubs. His lips opened on her neck, with a slight sucking, he sent thousands of shivers down her spine.

"Oh Joe." His name moved past her lips on the edge of a deep throated moan. Joe moved his tongue along her jaw while she turned in his arms capturing his lips to his. In one swift movement, turning her, he removed the robe from between them. Joe lifted Natalee then slowly, sliding her oil slicked breasts down his bare chest, lowering her onto his lap.

Nervously, she licked her lips watching as he leaned in closer, crushing her to him. Taking her lips into his, staking his claim. Natalee delved her fingers into his hair pulling him nearer as the kiss deepened. Overwhelming feelings of unbearable desire for his hands on her body, slowly she guided his hands back to her breasts, pushing against his hands, yearning for his touch, lightly he squeezed her taught nipples. His lips left her mouth, trailing kisses from her jawline to her neck, lifting her he kissed down her chest to her breast, sucking gently to the taut bud.

"Mm. Mm." Joe heard her moan, the sound resonating in her chest. Her hips bucked, he suckled harder grazing the taut bud with his teeth. Feeling the flood of hot moisture flow seep into the thin material of his shorts. Joe fought the overwhelming desire to rip off the wet shorts, unleashing his hardened member and lay her down on the floor, sinking himself deep inside of her. Instead he willed himself to slow his pace. He took the tight little bud deeper, not easing on her. His free hand, his oil moistened fingers moved between them, searching for the heart of her desire.

His fingers moving on their own volition, past her moist swollen lips pushing inside, he reveled in his reward of a second gush of the warm wet flood of moisture.

"Oh, oh, Joe." Natalee, clutching at his head pulling him closer, while her hips pushed against his hand urging him further into her depths.

"Oh Joe, please." He smiled against her breast. He remembered all too well what his girl liked. Feeling powerful by the revelation, that her desire had been building since, their last encounter.

"Oh, Joe, more, please, deeper, more." Her words coming out in ragged breaths. Joe obliged by sliding in his fingers deeper, lifting her higher against his body. His mouth continued to tease her tight bud.

"Oh, oh, yes." Her body released into a string of spasms, squeezing his fingers deep inside her. Releasing her breast from his lips he kissed up her chest claiming her lips once again. Marveled in the site of her expression changing from exhausted torment to a happy relaxed release. Moving his fingers from her moist center, towards her rounded bottom pulling her closer. Her oil slicked breasts crushing against his bare chest. He was ram rod stiff pressing against her moist center, the only thing between them, the silky material of his shorts.

Natalee shifted her weight against him pressing his length against her center. Joe moved his hands, cupping her face.

Changing the atmosphere from a fevered sensual heat to a calm, soft moment when he said. "Lee, I want to be inside you more than you can ever know." Holding each side of her face in his hands. He gently kissed her lips. "But, I have to know that you want this without any regrets." Kissing her lips again, opening her mouth and pulling her tongue to his. He released the kiss. "I want you to know what this means to me. That first time on the boat was just the beginning. We rushed into it. I saw the pain that you went through. I love you. I want you to be my wife. I want us to be a real family." Natalee returned the kiss, sliding her moist center across the friction of the silky material guarding his shaft.

He kissed her again, pausing she pulled back, in the dim light of the fire she stared into his eyes. The words Joe said, penetrated her sex starved brain. "Lee, I will not make love to you again, until I know for sure that we are going to be husband and wife."

»»

Natalee pulled back from his arms, separating the contact. Watching as his lips parted, concern moved across his face. She mourned the loss of his touch immediately, yet she was unable to stop her actions. Threading her bare arms into the sleeves of her robe, pulling it up over her shoulders, holding its edges tightly in her fist covering her bare breasts. The evidence of his desire continued to press against her while she straddled his lap. Feeling angry that her body continued to betray her, unable to stop the warm moisture emitting from her. She struggled with the right words to say all the while thinking to herself.

"I make my living with words and now I can't put two together." Lifting herself from his lap, biting her lip, afraid to look at him. Instead, she stood and walked toward the window, staring out at the storm. The lightning had moved on, wind and rain pelted the pool and yard. Watching in surprise as large chunks of hail began to drop into the pool with large splashes.

Natalee felt the warmth from his body against her back before he spoke. "Lee, talk to me, please." He whispered into her ear, igniting shivers down the side of her body. She craved his touch, knowing, with every conscious thought of her being she wanted him with every breath she took. Natalee had attempted to fight these feelings since the first time they had met. Every day, each week, for months she fought the urge to tell him how she felt. She wanted to show him with her body, what she wanted him to do, she was not that brave person.

After holding in her feelings for so long now, threatening to come out. Every inch of her was his, without him even knowing she had already given her entire soul to him. Always thinking she was a brave person but now instead, gripped by fear.

"What if I gave away my heart and he breaks it?" All Joe heard was silence as she repeated the question to herself, for her ears only.

"I guess that is my answer." Natalee heard Joe's words. He walked down the hallway to his room quietly shutting his door.

"I didn't answer him. I did not say anything." She told herself to follow him, to tell him that she loved him, that she wanted to be his wife. "I'm just scared. I could not handle losing another man that I love." Speaking to her reflection in the window with the moonless night beyond the glass. Natalee wondered how her life had turned out this way. Her heart could only stand so much loss, and hurt. She felt as if she had a lifetime of pain, and at the same time hating her feelings of sorrow for herself.

Natalee crawled into bed holding her pillow, crying herself to sleep. Awakened once during the night by Jake crying for his middle of the night feeding. Natalee sat up, ready to get out of bed when she heard Joe's soft croon to the baby singing while he fed his son. Hearing the tender moment between father and son only increased her sadness and indecision. Once again, the tears flowed as she turned over willing herself to sleep for the remainder of the night.

CHAPTER TWENTY

Natalee checked the baby mirror, watching Jake sleeping peacefully in the backseat of her SUV. Taking in a deep breath. His chubby little legs now had baby rolls and dimples, looking adorable in his red and blue romper. His eyes the color of milk chocolate with hair as dark as his daddy's. His skin had the olive tint. When he smiled, Natalee saw Jenny. She had inherited her smile from her dad, Patrick. Jake's dimples were pure Natalee. Returning her eyes to the road as she pulled out of the parking lot. His doctor visit had gone well. He was at the top of the weight and height chart.

"Healthy." That is what the doctor had said.

Pulling into the traffic. It had been difficult when Jake's doctor had asked questions about their home life and his father's involvement. Trying to avoid thinking about it. She instead focused on the road only to be frustrated a few minutes later, realizing it was now just after five o'clock on a Friday afternoon. Thinking about Joe happened approximately every fifteen minutes, whenever she had more than five minutes of quiet, it seemed to happen the most.

Ever since that night last week, they had been avoiding each other. He left early for work each morning, arriving home late at night after she was asleep. She missed him more than she ever thought she could. Yearning for their evenings sitting on the patio and late night, swims. She longed for their dinners together, she now felt her life was much more, lonely than it had before.

Bumper to bumper traffic had her moving slow as she neared the large intersection. Debating to herself on whether to stop by the grocery store on her way home or wait till in the morning as she glanced back at the sleeping baby. Realizing, Jake sleeping now meant a late night for her.

"Ugh." Massaging her temples to ward off the headache that threatened behind her eyes. Natalee fought the urge of frustration as she waited for the long line of cars to go around a fender bender in the middle of the intersection. Looking for an option other than the road ahead, she happened to glance over to a parking lot to her right, a car and a truck caught her attention.

She watched as a young woman picked a small child from the back seat of her car. Natalee instantly felt her pain as she murmured to the baby who appeared to be not much older than Jake, handing him to a nice looking young man. The last kiss and a touch to his head, making a quick turn toward her car. Natalee watched as the young woman waited, wiping tears from her cheek while she monitored the young father buckling the baby in the infant carrier in the back seat of his truck. A painful sinking feeling developed in the base of her stomach as she watched the father place the baby bag on the floor board, then he closed the door. The young mother stood next to her car, as the young man waved saying a few parting words to her. Natalee watched in sadness as the young woman leaned against her car until the truck pulled out of the lot onto a side street. With tears in her eyes and her fingers to her lips she finally got into her small car and drove in the opposite direction. Natalee envisioned the tears flowing down the young woman's cheeks.

With a lump in her throat Natalee was helpless to imagine herself in a similar situation. Fear gripped her, for the first time the fear of losing Joe was now somehow scarier than them in a relationship together.

"Loving Joe and sharing custody of Jake if we were not a couple would be horrible." Tears streamed down her cheeks. Finally driving through the intersection, Natalee realized she needed to put her fears aside and tell Joe how she felt.

Choosing to get the torturous task of the grocery shopping over, she took Jake's carrier out of the car. Carrying it to a shopping cart and walking into the grocery store. Recalling fondly the trips to the store where she would walk in wearing her short heels and took her time shopping. Now these days, she rushed through the store with a preplanned list that was in order by the location of items in the store. All of this now was done in a very fast organized manner that ensured getting through the store, items loaded in the car and engine running before the baby began to fuss. List in hand Natalee wandered through the vegetables.

Lost in thought when she heard. "Your baby is beautiful. How old is he?" Surprised by the woman walking past her with two blond hair, blue eyed little girls in the cart. Natalee had been extremely self-conscious of trips out in public with Jake because of her age. Feeling as if she had a neon sign blazing across her chest stating the fact. "Biological Grandmother and yet also the legal Mother." Smiling to the woman. Natalee was surprised to see that she had just as many wrinkles as she herself did.

"Jake is four months old. And looks just like his Daddy."

The woman giggled. "Well, it looks like you have yourself a hottie."

Natalee smiled and nodded. "I do." Sticking out her hand. "Natalee."

The woman with the kind and exhausted smile reached for Natalee's outstretched hand. "Meredith. Crazy woman over thirty-five who decided she wanted a family."

Natalee responded. "How old are they? They are gorgeous."

"Thank you. Adaline is three and Lacey just turned one. So basically, I get no time to myself or any sleep." They laughed together as they both moved through the fruit section. Checking her list again, she added a few more things to her cart.

Natalee added. "I know what you mean. He is one little boy and yet by eight o'clock I am completely ready for bed."

Before Natalee had left the store, she felt a new sense of belonging with Meredith's phone number and a play date scheduled for the following week.

Being able to talk motherhood with someone that was closer to her own age sounded promising.

Natalee waited up for Joe. The distance between them had played havoc on her writing. Having not accomplishing anything for two entire weeks since the night as she referred to it. She missed him. Missed his voice, his laugh, his touch. Looking out the back window onto the moonlit patio.

"I love him." Natalee awoke a few hours later looking around she realized she was in the large soft chair by the window. Having covered herself up with the blanket before she fell asleep. Looking out, seeing the first soft pink rays of the sunrise. Stretching as stood up from the chair, Natalee walked down the hallway. Peeking into Jake's room, watching as he stretched. Realizing he should awaken at any moment. Looking at Joe's closed door, quietly opening it to see the still made bed. Sadness gripped her heart.

"What have I done?" Tears streamed down her face as she changed into her running clothes. Jake let out his morning yell. Smiling through the tears at the thought of her son ready for his diaper change and his morning bottle and his dad was not here. Jake's normal was Joe taking care of him in the morning so that she could get that precious alone time in to run. Not sure at this point which made her hurt worse. Joe not being there for her or for Jake. Picking up the baby and laying him on his changing table.

"Good morning little man. How did you sleep?" His smile surrounded his fat little fist. Lately his cooing had gotten more pronounced, sounds had started to form. Filled with sadness, she changed his sleeper into a cotton onesie and headed for the kitchen to feed him.

A text came later that morning pulling Natalee from her deep thoughts while she was writing. Jake had graciously taken a nap right on time, allowing her the two hours she needed. Happy for the text from Joe. His simple. **Sorry, work emergency last night. Will be on time tonight. Parents will be arriving today, staying at the Marriott. Planned on seeing them at six. Would you prefer to meet them at a restaurant?"**

Natalee's finger hovered over the keys, wondering to herself how her and Joe would be able to pull off this happy family routine when she had not been able to tell him how she felt. Responding. **I can cook. It would be nice to have a family dinner. Any requests?** A quick response was all she received, hiding her disappointment when she read.

Pasta and dessert. Hint, I inherited my love of chocolate from my Mother.

Smiling. Natalee text back.

Will do. Can't wait to see you tonight.

K.

Was what she received, hoping that he understood her unspoken message. With renewed hope she continued to write, finishing her chapter and then started preparing for dinner.

When Joe walked in shortly before five-thirty that evening, he was met with soft music playing in the background, the table set and several candles lit. Scent of dinner filled the air, Joe walked down the hallway as Natalee carrying Jake came out of his room.

"Jake, look who is here." Seeing his father, the baby shook his chubby little arms and legs, cooing.

"Hey buddy, did you have a good day today? Boy have you ate a hamburger yet?" Joe caught Natalee's gaze as he said. "I bet it will not be long." The warmth passed between them, passion bubbled up giving Natalee the urge to tell him now how she felt.

Breaking the spell, she spoke softly. "Your parents should be here soon, I have just a few things left to do in the kitchen. I can take him with me if you want to freshen up." Joe nodded.

Hearing the knock on the front door, Natalee wiped her nervous hands on the hand towel as she walked toward the door. Opening the door, much to her surprise, she was met with two wonderful hugs by his parents. Alissa, gave her son a quick hug and walked straight to the baby, lifting him from his carrier into her arms. Alissa moved to the rocking chair, sitting, Jake stared up at his grandmother as she began to sing.

Natalee stepped close to Joe, placing her hand on his arm relieved when he placed his hand over her smaller one. Listening to the song together, Natalee looked up in question.

Joe leaned closed, whispered in her ear. "It's a Greek lullaby. She sang it to all of us, it's been passed down for generations." Natalee placed her free hand over her heart, feeling the wonder of generations thankful that Jake will know and understand that love.

Natalee placed the trash in the outside can, taking a moment to breath in the fresh spring night air. Deciding tonight was the night to tell Joe how she felt, all she was waiting for was his parents to leave. A part of her wanted to yawn, stretch her arms and escort them out the door. Taking a deep breath, she realized she could wait a little longer.

"I doubt time will ever be on our side." Returning to the kitchen thinking her wish just might have come true, Mr. and Mrs. Costas were walking down the hall to kiss baby Jake goodnight. Natalee stood next to Joe as they escorted them to their car, looking up in surprise as he wrapped his arm around her after she hugged his mother.

"Goodnight my sweet Natalee, dinner was amazing. You are a very talented chef. My son will have to keep up his workouts to maintain his figure." Smiling, she winked.

Natalee responded. "Don't forget tomorrow Jake's first boat ride, and I am packing a picnic." Joe's dad added, "Don't forget to bring more of those brownies." Natalee laughed.

Joe growled, "Nope Dad those are mine."

Mr. Costas, laughed, giving Natalee a hug. "Hide them from my son he gets them all of the time, she keeps me on a diet at home." He said while pointing towards his wife. Natalee whispered, loud enough for them all to hear.

"I've got you covered." Saying goodnight as they backed out in their car. As soon as their visitors had driven away, Natalee stopped Joe from returning to the house.

"Can we get the baby monitor and sit out back for a bit?" Joe nodded and went to retrieve the monitor and two drinks. She didn't see him smile with hope that their problems had worked themselves out. Joe walked out the patio door, not surprised to see Natalee in her chair, her bare feet playing with the grass. Sitting the baby monitor on the nearby table, he handed her a beer tapping his to hers.

"Thank you for all that you did to make my parents feel welcome and especially for my mother, helping her to feel reassured that her baby boy is happy and well taken care of."

"No problem." She giggled.

"What is so funny." Shaking her head as she continued to giggle. "Nothing."

"Lee." Joe reached over and ran his fingers up her sides sending her giggles into full blown laughter.

"You call uncle yet."

Between snorts she managed. "Nope." Setting his beer down he reached over with both hands tickling. She managed. "Okay, okay."

"Okay what?" He continued his mission.

"Okay, all I was thinking that it was funny how you know you are a momma's boy and you don't try to do anything about it."

"Oh really, you think that is funny huh. Just wait, madam till Jake is in his twenties and some young thing is trying to steal his virtue and the family fortune. Your momma claws will come flying out."

She stammered. "Well, well that is different."

"Oh really, how is it so different. Huh?"

"He's my baby." She announced defensively.

"Yep and I am my momma's baby."

"Oh, you crazy men." He stopped tickling and pulled on her hands guiding her onto his lap.   Talking low.

»»

"It's a good thing my momma loves you. She wants to know when you are going to make an honest man out of me." As soon as he said the words he worried, she would bolt like the last time he had brought up forever. Instead he was amazed as she reached over pushing a button on her phone, sultry music of Nora Jones played. The words come away with me, echoed through the night air as Natalee pulled Joe up to stand. Wrapping his arms around the woman that he loved, she laid her head on his chest, they danced in the grass with their bare feet as they both kept one ear listening for the baby monitor. The song ended, Joe leaned down claiming her lips.

Natalee broke the kiss. "Joe, there is something I need to say. I am sorry for not trusting you enough to take the leap with you. I was more afraid then even I realized. It was Mary that opened my eyes. I am sorry for the pain I put you through while I tried to decide what I really wanted."

162

The soft music continued as a second song began. Joe did not recognize the tune, all he heard were the next words she spoke. "I would rather spend a year of happiness with you than a lifetime of misery without you." Without saying a word, he lifted her off his feet crushing her to him with a deep kiss.

When they finally came up for air he asked. "Will you marry me?"

Natalee nodded. "Yes Joe, yes. I love you."

Joe screamed out. "Yay, finally." Swinging her around laughing.

She asked. "Can we please make love now?"

"Oh, oh, I am so on to you. You just want my body that is why you want to marry me." Joe bellowed as Natalee tried to tell him throughout his laughter that was not the only reason why. Joe lifted Natalee, handing her the baby monitor. Their half drank beer bottles were forgotten as he carried her inside.

Joe pulled her dress over her head revealing a pink bra and matching lace panties.

"You've had these on all night?" Nodding. "So, glad I didn't know about that earlier. I would have to cut my parents off at dessert." Natalee giggled as she helped him remove his shirt, enjoying herself, running her fingers over the definition of his muscles. Taking their time, swaying to the soft music in her bedroom.

Natalee whispered. "Will you move in with me?" Joe raised an eyebrow, and pointed to the large king- sized bed. Natalee nodded. "Please. I don't ever want to sleep without you ever again." Running his fingers down her shoulders around to her back, unhooking the pink lace releasing the objects of his desire. An overwhelming urge came over him to take one of the tiny buds into his mouth. His hands found her soft mounds as he teased, until they became taut buds. Natalee arched her back as he lifted her to his waist, wrapping her legs around him he slowly sat down on the side of the bed.

Joe opened his mouth, wrapping his tongue around the tight bud, Natalee's hips bucked against his bare abdomen. Joe felt the warm moisture across his stomach as continued his mission from one breast to the other. Natalee moaned with pleasure as he moved their position lowering her onto the quilt covered mattress. Her legs remained tight around him as her hips continuing to buck with each swipe of his moist tongue. Joe left the taut nub moving his tongue slowly down her flat stomach, igniting a heat as he went. Natalee moaned, arching her back missing his touch.

Smiling against her lower belly he blew hot air as he moved down. Reaching up, placing his hand surrounding her soft mound. He took one small nub between his two fingers rolling it, causing her to buck hard off the bed. Joe knew exactly what he was doing to her. He had been waiting for this moment since September. Never again, would they be apart. Moving his tongue lower until he reached the apex of her thighs, she willingly opened the heart of desire for him as he lapped, her inner core, sending her into uncontrollable spasms.

Joe lifted his head and whispered. "You better not be done."

"Oh honey, I am just getting started." Joe laughed sliding his hard member deep inside of her. Hearing only one thing before he lost himself inside of her. "Joe, all of you Joe. I want all of you. I love you."

»»

Natalee awoke the next morning, blissfully sore. Hearing the soft snores next to her she wondered about the time. Looking at the clock through blurry eyes, she rose quietly slipping into a cotton robe to check on her son. Feeling thankful Jake was still fast asleep at six am this was a definite improvement. Natalee smiled at the memory of Joe with Jake asleep on his bare chest just before two this morning. She had quietly placed the baby back in his crib, where Jake quickly found his fist. Natalee had crept back into bed removing her robe, pulling the cover back revealing his naked form she lightly ran her finger over the top of him, watching in wonder as it sprang to life. Boldly she had laid down on top of him placing tiny kisses from his ear down his jawline. By the time she reached his lips he had opened his eyes and lifted her up, sliding her down taking him deep inside of her once again. Now reliving the memory of the second time overnight she tried to estimate how much time they had before their son awoke.

"Joe, honey. Do you want to take a shower?"

"Maybe in a minute. What time is it?"

Playfully she answered. "It's six."

"Oh, go back to sleep my parents won't be here till nine. Right?"

"Yes, but Jake is still asleep." Natalee dropped her cotton robe, running the tip of her well- trimmed nail down his chest arousing him enough to open one eye. Even in his sleepy state, she managed to catch his attention quickly.

"Damn woman, you are wanting more?" Natalee nodded, luring with her finger towards the shower. Joe sat up, exhaustion showed on his face as he jumped up quickly.

He asked as he stood. "We are taking shower, together.?"

"Yes, honey. We are going to do everything together."

"Yes ma'am, lead the way."

Natalee carried Jake while Joe unloaded the boat closing the cabin. Natalee felt a sense of deja vu from Labor Day weekend. Without thinking, she looked around half expecting her daughter to walk up and create yet another scene. By the time they had walked to the house Natalee finally begun to relax. After a day on the water which including an on board, picnic with her future in-laws only helped to solidify the relationship between herself and Joe.

Enjoying the day without reservation, until Joe announced to his parents they were getting engaged as soon as he could purchase a ring. Feeling relieved by the positive reaction from his family. Natalee could not wait to tell Mary the good news. Joe hugged and kissed his parents with a promise to bring Natalee and Jake to visit the family in Florida soon.

Joe took his son from his bride to be, taking him to the bath.

Slipping away to call Mary while Joe bathed his son, determined to not become angry at the amount of water that she predicted would end up on the bathroom floor. Natalee had to laugh when she thought about their new nightly routine. Jake loved it kicking and cooing at his loudest as Joe attempted to sing.

Natalee waited for Mary to answer her phone. "Hello."

"Hey, it's me."

"Dang woman it is about time I heard from you. How was the boat ride and picnic with the family?"

"Wonderful, they are truly amazing. I love them and they love us. And well they loved the good news Joe gave them."

Mary must have been temporarily distracted because she said. "Wait hold on a minute, what good news?"

Natalee hesitated briefly. "Joe proposed and I said yes."

Before she could finish telling Mary she heard. "Leo, he asked and she said yes." Yelling from the top of her lungs. Mary finally calmed down enough for Natalee to tell her the rest of the story.

CHAPTER TWENTY-ONE

"Mom, what did you do?"

"Jennifer Nicole, what do you mean what did I do?" Natalee's hands flew to her trim hips. She had just laid Jake down for a nap after swimming. Stepping back outside to pick up his water toys when she heard her daughter drive up and immediately begin to yell as she walked across the patio towards the pool. Natalee continued walking toward the house. Opening the kitchen door, she dared her daughter to awaken the baby.

"I am going inside now to make lunch. You are welcome to come in and have an adult conversation. But I will not allow for you to wake him." Jenny nodded in agreement. Watching as her mother started a salad.

Jenny hissed. "How could, how could you sleep with him? After him getting me pregnant." Holding the butcher block cutting board in her hand, her fingers itched to throw it at her child.

"What do you mean?" Natalee asked.

Jenny pointed her finger in a circle at her mother. "Don't get all uppity on me. You know what I am talking about. I mean your relationship with Joe. Aunt Mary told me the whole thing."

Nodding her head. "Okay. I understand why Mary told you. It was time for you to know." Natalee chopped the lettuce. Adding some chopped carrot and cucumber to the bowl. Attempting to avoid her pacing daughter, her fists tight as her knuckles continued to turn white.

"I don't understand how you could have a relationship with him?"

"Joe?"

"Yes Joe, how many younger men have you been sleeping with?"

Natalee giggled at the absurdity of the conversation.

"Jenny, watch your tone." Jenny poured herself a glass of tea. Watching as Natalee cut up grilled chicken adding it to the salad. Bringing the dressing and the bowl of salad to the table. Jenny set the table with plates and utensils. Natalee stalled for as long as she dared. Picking up a loaf of French bread and butter. Finally sitting down at the table. She waited while her daughter dished her plate.

After the first bite, the questions continued. "Mom. I just don't understand how you could do it."

Natalee was prepared, she responded quickly. "We chose to raise Jake together." Shifting the questioning towards her daughter. "You did plan for me to raise him, right? That is why you put my name on the birth certificate." Pausing, she watched as dawning recognition crossed her daughter's face. "Jenny seriously, how did you think all of this would work out? You knew I would raise Jake. That is why you did what you did. You easily signed your parental rights away and took the easy way out so you can do anything that you want to do. And I end up with the responsibility of raising him. But you did not think about that, did you?"

Jenny continued to eat her salad in silence. Natalee finished hers. Picking up her plate when she heard Jake's baby noises on the monitor.

She did not realize her daughter had followed her to Jake's room until she heard her daughter's accusatory tone. "Mom, where is my stuff. How could you?" Natalee focused on Jake and his diaper. At close to four months old she loved both of his chubby little fists he tried to fit them in his mouth at the same time. His fat rolls on his stocky thighs, had now developed rolls. Changing his diaper, then buttoning his onesie, realizing before long he would be as tall and handsome as his father. Picking up the baby, she braved the next altercation with her daughter. Guessing the source of her daughter's anger she quickly found her child staring at the walls of her old room.

Joe's memorabilia took up an entire wall. His desk, with computer in the corner. A small area for Natalee's crafts on the opposite corner.

"I don't understand. He is taking over our lives."

"Excuse me darling daughter. But you managed to change my life then leave me with the responsibility. You honestly believed that nothing else in this house would change? You have been jet setting around the globe with your new job. You have your life. The one that you chose, I might add." Natalee kissed her son's chubby cheeks. It dawned on her, she finally relaxed enough to realize he is her son. In every way. She had the legal paperwork to back it up. She has been the only mother he knew. Her spoiled daughter needed so much, a reality check should be first on the list.

Reaching out and touching her daughters arm. "Jenny, I love you. I will always love you. You will always be my daughter. But I have devoted every moment to you since your dad's death. I love Jake, and I will continue to raise him as my son. I cannot forsake his future happiness and security because it changes things for you. I am trying to make the best of the situation that you created." Jenny began to cry. Natalee followed her daughter to the kitchen."Jenny, you don't want to hold him?"

"No, he is nothing to me." Devastated by the hurtful words. Natalee made Jake a bottle and laid him down on the blanket in the living room with his toys.

"Jenny that was uncalled for. I do expect you to at least treat him like a brother."

"I don't know how to treat him. How I can even look at him or you. Knowing you are sleeping with Joe." Anger boiled inside of Natalee. Words threatened the tip of her tongue, worried if she let them escape she would never be able to take them back.

"Jenny. That's enough. I am still your mother. You will not talk to me like that. I love Joe."

"What you don't know and obviously Mary did not tell you, was that Joe and I hit it off from the first moment we met. He asked me out several times. I turned him down because of the age difference and life differences. He wanted a family. I felt like I was through."

Jenny flipped her hair around. Snarling. "It was you he got that from then. He said the same thing to me at the club that night. Something about the experiences that we have had, further separate our age."

Natalee continued. "So yes, that probably stemmed from our conversation. I fought my feelings for him. I did not want to hurt him. I wanted what was best for him."

"How can you have feelings for him. Don't you wonder if he is thinking of me when he touches you?" There were no words for the sharp pain that pierced Natalee with those parting words. She could not help but blame herself for the mess she had created.

"Oh Patrick. Why did you die and leave me to screw this all up like I did?" Realizing she had not said the words out loud. Natalee gripped the counter in front of her while her world spiraled out of control. She had nothing to respond. Nothing to say.

Tears ran in rivers down her cheeks. Hearing his truck pull in the drive, did not break her from the spell of anguish she felt.

»»

"Lee, babe where?" His words drowned out as he took in the situation. Natalee clinging to the counter. Jenny's eyes wild with anger. Her hair in disarray.

"What the hell is going on here?"

Jenny pointed a finger at Joe. "You. Lee, Lee that is what you said that night. I couldn't figure it out. Have wondered many times." Her words dripped with sarcasm and disdain.

"Yes Jenny. I was drunk. You took advantage of the situation."

Joe reached for his girl. "Lee are you okay?" She nodded. "Babe, where's Jake?"

Natalee responded softly. "Living room." Joe nodded. Directing his attention back to Jenny.

"Jenny, it is time for you to know the truth. I was crazy for your mom from the first moment I met her. I tried to convince her that we should date. The only reason I went to the club that night after Leo's party was because I thought she would go." Jenny listened, without an expression. Joe continued. "I tried to get her attention for weeks. Even showing up where I knew she was, even when she was on a date. I was at that Jazz club with friends, I had already been drinking when I saw your mom there on a date. She looked so beautiful in her red dress and she was in another man's arms."

He glanced at Natalee. Her grip on the counter loosened, relaxing her white knuckles. Natalee's tears slowed.

He looked back at Jenny and continued, "I went to the bar. I drank as much as I could as fast as I could to drown out my feelings. Then I walked home to the loft. When I first saw your legs on the landing I thought they were hers. I had no interest in you. I explained that to you many times. You took advantage of me and the situation. You don't get to come in here and criticize your mother and I for taking a bad situation and building a life together."

Wiping his hand over his face, his torment was interrupted by his crying son. Walking into the living room he picked up his baby. He took a few moments to focus on his beautiful face and breath in Jake's innocence.

When he looked at Jake, Joe only saw him and Natalee. He was now completely able to push that night out of his mind, instead seeing it as a surrogate situation. He only wished

Natalee could see it the same, he was happy with his family. Joe cradled Jake in his arms as he walked into the kitchen, concerned for the pain Natalee was going through.

Realizing in true Jenny form, she turned the situation around focusing back on her. "Well it looks like everything worked out for you both. So, glad I could be a baby oven for you both." Jenny slammed the door behind her. Joe worried as he heard the screech of her sports car peeling out of the drive, speeding down the street.

"Joe, I need to ask a favor."

"Anything babe."

Natalee reached up, taking the baby from him. "I need some time away from all of this." Holding Jake tight, she lightly kissed his small cheeks.

With tears in her eyes she handed the baby back to his father. "I am going to pack." His objection hovered on the tip of his tongue and yet he was not able to voice his fears. Following Natalee into the bathroom, watching in surprise as she packed her toiletries. Pulling a small suitcase from the closet, throwing in some clothes. Quickly she changed her clothes.

"Natalee. Can we talk about this?"

"No sorry, I can't talk about it. I just need time. There is plenty of baby food and formula to last the week. Jeanette, the babysitter's number is by the phone. Just call her and let her know when you need her. Everything else will be okay without me." Joe remained speechless as he watched the love of his life pick up her bags and take one last look at them, then walk away.

»»

With one last look at her son and the man she loved, she walked out of the door to her SUV. Starting her engine, she slowly backed out of the driveway. Turning up the radio. She did not recognize the song or the station, as she allowed the music to numb her heart as she drove. Stopping at the first traffic light, Natalee quickly text Mary letting her know she would be driving to the beach house for the weekend.

A simple reply. "Sure, no problem."

Natalee cried as she unloaded her small suitcase, putting on her swimsuit as the tears continued. Taking a bottle of water from the refrigerator. Picking up a beach towel, her hat and sunglasses she walked out onto the deck. Looking at her cell phone. A moment of guilt plagued her as she regretted walking out, leaving Joe to care for the baby. Pushing the thought from her mind as she walked down the steps onto the warm sand. With each step, her body felt the healing warmth of the sun. Walking towards the water, bending she spread out her towel. Lying down she immediately felt the warmth of the sand on her back, stinging of the sun burned against the pain of her body. Forcing herself to close her eyes and relax.

Surprised when she awoke a short time later feeling the effect of the sun. Leaning up, she looked at the redness to her skin, not caring that she would hurt later because she had not taken the time to apply sun block. Even with the amount of sun she had already this spring season expecting to feel the pain of this sunburn later. Rising from the towel, walking into the water, stretching before diving into the wave, swimming parallel to the shore. Looking up from the water, realizing how far she had swam. Changing her direction, swimming until she was even with the beach house once again. Rising from the water she walked towards the shore. Observing the families and groups of people on the beach. Fathers and sons, mothers and daughters enjoying time together. Fear gripped her heart wondering if she would ever get back the relationship with her daughter that she once had.

Picking up her towel and hat as two younger men approached her.

"Hi, we haven't seen you before." Natalee was surprised by the men talking to her.

"Yes, just got in today."

"We are down the beach. Four houses away. Come by tonight, we are having a party. And bring some friends." Smiling.

She declined. "Thank you for the invitation. But I am busy tonight. Thank you though."

"Oh, okay. Bye. Nice meeting you."

"You too." Natalee laughed, stepping into the outdoor shower washing off the salt and sand from her body.

Wrapping herself into a plush clean towel, as she slowly took the stairs up to the upstairs deck. Pausing for another look at the water before stepping into the kitchen. Looking at the blender wondering what Mary had left over from the last trip. Pulling some strawberries, blueberries and peaches from the freezer. Finding the bottle of Rum and lime juice. Adding some Rum to the blender, then tilting her head she added some more. A few pulses later, Natalee was pouring her concoction into a large margarita glass. Walking back onto the deck, she eyed her cell phone once more. Resisting the urge to pick it up and call Joe, instead she settled onto the deck with her drink.

Natalee lifted her head, looking around realizing where she was. Unsure of how she ended up on the couch in an over-sized t-shirt and underwear. Seeing the margarita glass on the coffee table, memories flooded back. Pushing up from the couch she attempted to sit, clutching her head.

"Ow." Having not felt like this in quite some time, holding onto the edge of the couch as she attempted to stand. Using the wall to balance she made her way to the bathroom. Cranking up the hot water on the shower, stepping into the hot spray, eyes half opened to block out the early morning light. By the time she had finished the shower and dressed she began to feel halfway human once again. Looking at herself in the mirror.

"Yikes," Pulling on a sun dress and pinning her hair into a pony tail, picking up her purse and sunglasses leaving the beach house in search of food.

Natalee left the market, driving through town towards the house watching families out this Saturday morning. Parents pushing strollers, others leading toddlers holding ice cream cones. Teenagers running down the street catching up to friends. Everyone appeared happy and together, she missed Jake. Missed holding him, rocking him. She missed Joe singing to him a Greek song he learned as a child. The guilt of choosing Joe meant losing a relationship with Jenny. Tears of indecision rolled down her face as she continued the drive back to the house. Putting up the few groceries she had bought, she changed into her black bikini. Looking at herself in the mirror, gone was the shine in her eyes that only Joe had brought out. Gone was the warm smile brought on by her son. Her fingers no longer itched to write. Gone was the passion of words, meant to become sentences. It was if the lit candle inside of her had been blown out.

"One day everything is perfect." Natalee spoke out loud. Twenty-four hours later her entire life changed. In one year, she had gone from finding her forever love, to having the son she never thought she would. And now to lose it all along with her daughter, the one thing she had before. Picking up her beach bag she walked onto the sand.

CHAPTER TWENTY-TWO

Joe pulled into Leo's driveway, opening the back door picking up his son from the car seat. He unloaded the stroller from the back of the truck one-handed. By the time he had his son belted into the stroller and all the baby's gear in the bottom compartment Mary met him in the drive. "Hi guys. There's my little man." Mary was instantly met with a toothless grin, and a slobbery fat little fist. "No toothie's in that mouth yet?"

Laughing. Joe shook his head. "You would think so the way he is knawing on anything he can get a hold of. But nothing yet."

"Come on around back."

Following her, Joe paused as they reached the gate. "Mary, please tell me she has been in touch." Mary nodded. "Do you know where she is?" Mary nodded again.

"What can I do?" Putting her arm around him, she led him to the patio.

An hour later Joe pulled out of Leo and Mary's driveway. Leaving Jake and enough supplies for the next two days he drove toward the beach house with determination to let her know how much he loved her. He just had to make one stop first.

»»

Walking into the waves, she cooled her body and cleared her head with a headache that lingered from the drinking the night before. A strictly out of character move for Natalee. Trying to numb the pain of the previous twenty-four hours was by best to be described as ridiculous. Her leaving and taking this time alone was strictly self- preservation. Feeling at a complete loss with her life at this moment drinking again today might be the answer.

Closing her eyes, she felt the rhythm of the Gulf pulling her pain from her body. Standing and walking across the beach to lay down on her blanket. The soft powdery Alabama sand warmed her body from beneath, the sun molded her from the top. She relished the cool spring breeze as it flowed over her body. She lifted her shoulders, arching her back. The breeze tingled up her arms to her shoulders as a lover would. The wind softly blew over her chest, teasing her nipples into taut nubs. Shivers ran down her sides, pulling her arms down beside her. The breeze continued its mission as lover's lips kissed up the inside of her legs pulling them apart. The breeze cooled her mound as it jumped across her flat stomach. Leaving her black bikini bottoms filled with moisture.

Desire raced through her body. Overwhelming urge to release almost had her running for the house.

Instead she turned slowly, moving the large beach bag next to her, sliding one hand beneath her. Using two fingers, pushing aside the material in search of the finish her body desired. Her left arm supported her hat covered head and dark sunglasses. Her right hand continued to tease the moisture covered nub. One last bit of pressure and Natalee bit off a moan into her hand, her body releasing spasm after spasm. Embarrassed, coming in public for the very first time in her life. Feeling the effects of release, she rolled over and relaxed. Her legs were warm and pliable with one knee slightly bent and the other straight.

Closing her eyes, she allowed the warmth to zing throughout her body. When she felt the light touch of fingertips caress the top of her leg she knew her imagination had to have gotten away from her. The caress moved higher. She opened her eyes to spy Joe sitting beside her. His chest bare and his eyes hidden by dark sunglasses. She looked around him in search of their son. Shaking his head, he gently took her hand and placed a finger over her opened lips as she started to speak. Picking up her belongings, Joe led her up to the beach house steps.

»»

Without words, they stepped into the outdoor shower, pulling the door closed after them. Turning on the water, Joe removed her hat and her glasses. Running his hands lightly over her sand covered body he noticed drank in the sight of her since she left home. Joe gently untied her bikini top, lowering his lips to her neck then down her chest.

Lifting her up, her back against the rough shower wall, taking a nipple in his mouth sucking gently at first.

"Mm." Hearing her moan, he took the taut bud deeper, sucking harder. Natalee bucked her hips, he pulled the tight nub from his mouth, looking her in the eye then claiming her mouth kissing her deeply. Joe reached down pulling the tie, dropping his swim trunks around his ankles. Lifting Natalee's legs around his hips, pushing the scrap of material aside uncovering her moist mound, shoving inside, sending Natalee in hundreds of tiny spasms as she continued to moan. "Oh, god Joe, don't stop, please don't stop."

Joe wrapped the towel around her shoulders. Pulling his swim trunks up and tying the string. Picking up her discarded swimsuit top and her beach bag, as he followed her up the stairs. No words were spoken as she led him to the bedroom. Slowly she lowered the towel stepping back until the back of her knees touched the bed. Dropping his swim trunks, he slowly lowered her to the bed. Kissing her lips, slipping inside of her finishing what they had began in the shower.

"I swear Joseph Costas if you do not stop laughing at me, I will." Joe continued to laugh, not afraid of her empty threat. Instead grabbing her he began to tickle. "Joe, really I hate to be tickled. Joe." She giggled as he continued to tickle up and down her sides, before she raced from the bed for the bathroom. He heard her yell from the partially closed door.
"It is not funny, do not make fun of me. There is not a woman on this planet over the age of thirty that can laugh that hard and not almost pee on herself." Joe continued to smile. He knew exactly what he was doing, by showing Natalee another side of life then she would realize what they have is worth fighting for. Walking naked back to bed she crawled in next to him in the late afternoon light. Joe ran his fingers down her back to her bottom resting his hand there.
"I still cannot believe what I saw from the porch." Natalee buried her face in her hands clearly embarrassed. "Babe its nothing to be embarrassed about. It was by far the hottest thing I have ever seen, pleasing yourself like that. I just hope it was me you were thinking about instead of any of those other young guys on the beach."

177

Natalee laughed. "You and only you. There is not chest, arms or abs anywhere on this beach as hot as you." Natalee leaned in for a kiss.

Joe suddenly pulled back. "Wait, you didn't say anything about my butt or my legs. You don't like them?"

She giggled. "Yes silly, I love your butt, and your legs and actually if you must know it was your feet in your flip flops that really turned me on the first time we met."

Joe dropped his mouth and raised his eyebrows. "You have a foot fetish and I am just finding this out?" Natalee rolled on top of him, sliding her bare breasts down his chest until they were hip to hip, leaning up she lifted her hips encouraging him inside of her. Just when he slid in he suddenly stopped her hips before she moved.

"What's wrong?" She asked.

"I just want to make sure that if you get the urge to do you know again outside you might want to remember our neighbors." He laughed as Natalee swatted him on the arm. Pushing down with her hips, she gyrated and started to buck.

"Future husband, it's time for you to fulfill your duties."

"Yes ma'am, with pleasure."

»»

Joe kissed her cheek, running his fingers through her hair, as she awoke from her very satisfied nap.

"Hey, what about we get dressed and go to dinner."

"Hmm, we have to get dressed?"

"Yes, not much food in the house. I will buy you a greasy burger or a shrimp dinner?"

"Hmm." Natalee considered the options, fluttering her eyes open, she responded. "The greasy burger with fries is very tempting but you do owe me a real night out. So, I say spring for the seafood." Natalee laughed as she walked to the shower. "Do we have time for you to join me in the shower?"

Joe checked his watch. "We do."

Natalee slipped on a pale pink dress and a light gray cardigan. She was bending over tightening the straps on her white wedge heels, looking up, seeing Joe wearing trademark flip flops, but instead of his cargo shorts, his legs were encased in khaki pants and topping it off with a white cotton button up shirt. His olive skin radiating against the stark white cotton, the sleeves rolled up to just below his elbows.

Reaching out she ran her fingers over the shirt. "You look like you just came off a tropical island."

"You like?"

"Yes, you look very handsome."

"Thank-you, ma'am this here is a top of the line Florida dress shirt."

Natalee snarked. "Oh, really does that mean bankers wear them."

"Only the most successful." Natalee giggled as he closed and locked the door, realizing they had played and joked together more in the past six hours then they had in the year since they had met. Suddenly saddened by the thought, she wondered how much she had taken for granted the good things in their lives instead of focusing on the bad.

Joe reached for her hand leading her down the steps. Joe hesitated, reaching down he removed her shoes one by one leaving them on the bottom step and led her to the sand instead of the truck as she had expected.

Without talking, Natalee followed him as he walked closer to the water, the sun low on the horizon, turning from pink to orange. Natalee pointed to the group of pelicans flying low over the water, returning her eyes to Joe, surprised to see him down on one knee in the sand. Immediately her hand went to her mouth, speechless as she heard the words she dreamed about. "Natalee, I love you with my whole heart. I have since the first time you shot me down, through the second and third and even the fourth time of you telling me no." Natalee playfully shook his hand. Joe continued. "Natalee, I kept trying because I love you, always have and always will. And I cannot imagine going through one day of this crazy thing called life without you beside me. Babe, please take a chance on love again, take a chance on me."

Natalee began to cry, biting her lip as she attempted to stop the tears. Joe continued.

"Will you marry me?"

Nodding. She finally whispered. "Yes. Yes." Joe stood, taking her in his arms, spinning her around then lowering her to her feet, he pulled out a small jewelers' box from his pocket. Natalee watched as he opened the box, revealing a beautiful diamond in a platinum setting.

Slipping the ring on her finger, she whispered. "So. Mr. Costas, whatever are you going to do with me now that you have me?"

She asked teasingly. Joe laughed. "I will spend the next sixty years showing you."

"Only sixty?" She questioned.

"Damn woman in sixty years I will ninety-one years old, do you think it will still work then?" She didn't respond as they started walking toward the truck.

Joe opened the truck door, concerned about her silence when she teased. "I hope it will still work, I'd hate to think I should have been looking for a younger man now so that I have one that satisfies me when I am older." Natalee giggled, before she could get into the truck Joe pulled her close.

"Joseph, you still owe me dinner. Do not tickle me and then we have to go back inside."

"Hmm, let me think about this. What about pizza in bed?" Natalee thought, then looked down to her ring on her finger, wondering if she wanted the romantic dinner in town.

Before he could answer his own question, she said. "You know, eating pizza while naked in bed is probably something we will not get another chance to do with a baby in the house. We can always use Mary as a babysitter for a couple hours to go to a restaurant but an all-night naked pizza dinner that is a opportunity of a lifetime." Joe took her hand, shutting the truck door and pushing the lock button as they grabbed her shoes and ran up the stairs. Joe had his phone out calling for pizza delivery while Natalee unlocked the door.

Natalee called Mary to check on Jake and to tell her about the proposal and letting her know they would be home the next afternoon. Natalee walked out onto the deck and slid into

Joe's lap on the deck chair, watching the moon and the stars while they waited for their food.

"You know, I appreciate that you wanted to take me out to a nice dinner. But I really could not imagine anything more romantic then this."

"I love you."

"And I love you." Hearing the car pull into the drive Joe went down the stairs to meet the delivery, Natalee walked into the house taking off her dress as she walked, ready for naked pizza dinner night.

CHAPTER TWENTY-THREE

"Oh Natalee, you look so beautiful." Mary smiled with tears in her eyes.

"That dress is you, it is perfect." The dress consultant agreed.

Mary insisted. "It fits you perfectly, this is definitely the perfect dress for you." Natalee pondered over her reflection, slowly running her fingers over the white chiffon sweet heart bodice, to the elaborate single shoulder strap to the tiny ruffled flower on her shoulder. Smiling, placing her hands on either side of the lightly jeweled empire waist, tilting her head while inspecting the full skirt of light and airy chiffon, poking her bare pink toes from under the material. Turning to admire the back of the dress in the three-way mirror, a smile came to her lips when she noticed the lace up back, a fond memory of Joe unlacing her from a dress during a rather wild weekend less than a year before.

Natalee pointed to the train, asking Mary. "Do you think it is too long with the sand?"

Mary was deep in thought as she contemplated the options, then responding. "I know what you are thinking, I think that the sand will dust off after the ceremony as long as it is not wet, so the dress should bustle fine for the reception."

The dress consultant added. "We can have the alterations specialist have a look and see if she can offer some suggestions." Both Natalee and Mary agreed. The consultant added. "I will see if she is available."

"Okay thank you." Directing her question to Mary. "What do you really think? Is this crazy. Joe and I have only known each other a year and here we are getting married in three weeks. Can we even pull off a wedding that fast? Should it even be a beach wedding at the beach house? Should we make his whole family come here? And Jake, he is just now four months old yet. He will be fussy and how will we do all of this."

Mary caught both of Natalee's arms before she swung them around her again. "Nat, breathe." Mary demonstrated big deep breaths. "Okay, first. You and Joe belong together, you love each other and you have a beautiful family. The rest will work itself out. And yes, we can have all this ready in time. You will have a beautiful beach wedding in front of the beach house. The dance floor is already reserved. I ordered the lights. We have a crew of volunteers for the day before, already arranged. There are so many of our friends who love you and Joe both, and are excited about making this day special for the both of you. And that is not even taking in to count Joe's huge family." Mary squeezed her hand then continued. "Alissa has already called and given me a list of things they are providing. It will work. I love you but you cannot turn into one of those bridezillas now. No time for it. Got it?"

"Yes, I get it. You know when he proposed, I guess I thought we would go to the judge or something I just took it for granted that he didn't care about the wedding. But I realize now this is as much for his family as it is for us." Natalee looked back in the mirror, her face softened. "It is the most beautiful dress."

"Yes honey, it is and it was made for you."

Natalee nodded, taking a deep breath. "Okay let's do this." Mary laughed. The alteration specialist showed the pair their options for the train. After thirty minutes of indecision, Natalee relaxed and purchased the wedding dress with reassurance the dress would be ready in two weeks in time for her bridal portraits.

Walking out of the store Natalee exclaimed. "I cannot believe you talked me into bridal portraits also, who am I kidding I have been married before, are you sure I should be wearing white?"

"My little scared duckling, let us get you some lunch before you have a nervous breakdown." Pulling Natalee into a cafe a few doors down, choosing an outdoor table. "Do you want wine?" Natalee nodded as she quickly responded to an email from her editor. "Is everything okay?" Mary inquired.

"Yes, just my editor having a few questions about my plans for a new book." Wine delivered. Mary picked up her glass saluting her best friend, taking a sip.

"Okay, back to your latest freak out." Natalee shook her head. Mary continued. "Yes, you should wear white, yes you need bridal portraits and the reception. All yes, because you did not get to do this the first time around. The justice of the peace with Patrick was a nice ceremony, even the dinner with all of us after. But don't you want the whole package this time?"

"Yes, I do. Just feels weird." Taking a sip of wine, Natalee suddenly gagged with a sudden urge to vomit. Mary asked.

"Are you okay?"

"Yes, that was weird I had this weird feeling I was going to lose it right there." Mary stared intently at her best friend.

"Maybe after you eat you will feel better."

Natalee arrived home two hours later, missing her son but agreed for Joe to pick him up from the babysitters on his way home from work so they could run an errand together. Exhausted she set the full bags of wedding supplies in the corner of her office, quickly kicking off her shoes sitting down on her chaise lounge. Looking around her office, wondering what she should do with the next three hours of freedom. She didn't have to wait long, leaning back, Natalee quickly fell asleep.

Awakening a short time later, realizing what she had done she could not believe she had napped during the day. Changing into shorts and a tank top, she decided to pack a picnic for a dinner boat ride once her boys got home. Natalee was sitting by the pool, excited when she heard the truck pull into the drive. Walking towards the driveway to meet her men.

"Hi honey, look at my little man." She took Jake from his arms.

"Oh, boy how quickly she forgets me I thought you were talking to me." Kissing her husband to be.

"So, what did you two do?"

"Well, we got you a present."

Surprised. "You did, why?"

"Let's go inside and we will tell you won't we son." Met with a slobbery fisted grin. "Son, how are you going to get a beautiful woman if you can't keep your hand out of your mouth."

Natalee interjected. "Jake don't you listen to your daddy, the only woman in your life until you get really, really big is me." Joe opened the door for his family as he motioned for Natalee to sit at the kitchen table. Taking Jake from her, he sat on the opposite chair. Pulling a gift wrapped, box from the bag, he motioned for Natalee to open it. Natalee untied the tiny ribbon, opening the small box.

Surprise registered on her face when she first saw the silver chain and charm. Gently removing the necklace from the small box mesmerized by the engraved heart charm. Tears filled her eyes as she read.

"Mother" turning the small heart over, seeing the engraved picture of Jake. "Oh, it's beautiful. But why?"

"Happy Mother's Day babe, it's late I know it. I am so sorry, but Jake here was the one that was keeping up with the calendar. Then I remembered he doesn't read yet." Natalee laughed. Looking at her son.

"Next year we will set the calendar on daddy's phone." Jake kicked his legs and giggled his baby giggle.

Joe added. "Seriously, I hesitated because of the Jenny situation. By the time I ordered the necklace it took a lot longer than I thought it would, that is why it is so late." Natalee stood and moved close to him and their son she kissed his lips.

"It's perfect and what day it happens doesn't matter, all of us is what matters."

Joe helped her with the clasp as Natalee let him in on the surprise boat picnic. A short time later, everything loaded on the boat Jake in his baby life jacket, sitting on Joe's lap as he directed the boat down the river for an evening river. Natalee dished the food as they moved into Mobile Bay then dropping anchor while they enjoyed their meal.

Natalee stowed the remnants of their meal when a larger boat passed them causing a wake, rocking their vessel. She heard Joe ask if she was ready to head back, before she could answer, she jumped up, running to the side of the boat, retching into the water.

Natalee's mind raced with possibilities while they continued their boat ride home. Jake clearly enjoying the ride attempting to help with the large steering wheel. Natalee sat to the front, breathing the fresh air in trying to avoid another bout of nausea, quickly realizing she had never experienced sickness while on the boat after growing up around boats her entire life. With dawning recognition, she remembered the last time she had been sick on a boat. Placing her head in her hands, talking to herself. "With Jenny." Quickly recalling her pregnancy with Jenny, she spent the entire nine months unable to be on the water. Looking back at Joe, fear built inside of her. "My nice little quiet life, it's gone. There's no way. It has got to be a fluke. Wait a minute I felt nauseous at the cafe. Maybe it's a virus. Yes, it has to be." Relaxed for the moment she enjoyed the view when another thought hit her. "My period was when?" Suddenly she started counting days. Thinking back. Then. "Oh crap."

By the time Joe docked the boat, Natalee took Jake from Joe and almost at a run raced for the house and her calendar. Quickly laying Jake down under his mobile on the floor as she ran into her office looking at her calendar. Flipping back to May, her mouth dropped as she looked at the dates, flipping then to April and back to May then she let out a low yowl.

"Yikes." Grabbing her purse just as Joe walked into the door. "Babe, I need to run to the drug store really quickly, can you bathe Jake I promise I will be right back." Yelling as she walked out of the door. "I have my phone."

»»

Natalee's hand shook as she accepted the bag from the clerk. Quickly she called Mary, speaking as soon as Mary said hello.

"Mare, I've got a problem I am on my way."

"Okay." Mary watched as her husband rinsed his dinner plate before setting it in the sink. Moving into his waiting arms, she whispered. "I am very fortunate to have found a wonderful man like you. Thank you for loving me." They swayed together to their own music, when she announced. "Natalee is having a girl's crisis and is on her way over here now."

"Thank you my dear for the heads up. I think I will go check on our neighbor Bill and see how the repair on his boat motor is coming. Give me a text when the coast is clear."

"Will do. Love you." One last look at his wife before he walked out the front door.

"Love you back." Leo closed the front door as the kitchen door burst open.

"Hey honey, what is going on." On the verge of tears when she sat her bag down on the table pulling out the two boxes.

"Oh boy."

"Oh boy is right and if these are positive I know a boy that will never get to touch me again."

Tears welled in Natalee's eyes as Mary led her to the bathroom. "So, can I ask what makes, you think you need to test? Surely not the wine today."

Mary began reading the directions while Natalee answered. "Nope not the wine, but we took the baby on a boat ride, and I brought a picnic. Joe anchored us in the bay. A large cabin cruiser went by sending us a small wake. And I promptly tossed my cookies over the side."

Clearly confused. "But you never get sick on a boat." Mary announced. "Unless." Natalee dropped her jaw and

186

waited. "Oh, crap unless your pregnant. Like when you were sick with Jenny."

"Yes, I could not go out on the boat the entire time."

"But when? And what about your birth control?"

Natalee thought a minute, trying to process. "Oh crap. Oh no, the beach house. I took off so fast I did not bring my pills with me. And I was extremely horny that weekend. I even you know on the beach."

Mary handed her the first stick then shook her head and stared at her best friend. "You did what on the beach?'

»»

"Will you just pee, then we can discuss the gory details of your sex filled weekend that once again you are the only one getting."

"Yes ma'am." Following directions, handing the first one to Mary and accepting the second. Mary carried both, to the kitchen counter laying them on a paper towel, then pouring herself a glass of wine.

"Okay while we wait tell me." Her friend snarked.

"I left in such a hurry, I did not think about my pills. I was on the beach right before Joe got there, I was tipsy and well extremely horny and I pleasured myself on the sand." Natalee promptly buried her face in her hands in embarrassment.

"And." Mary probed.

"Joe saw me, he ran his hand up my leg, and then well we were in the shower before we knew it." Natalee continued. "Basically, it was two days of very hot sex, and now I think I have a little problem."

Mary looked down at the results of not one, but two. "Honey, for a girl who did not want any more children. You have a big problem." Natalee's eyes opened wide as one stick showed pink and the other just said, yes.

"Oh my God." Natalee covered her face then opened, looking once again. "Oh crap." Taking a few steps from the counter, looking out the window, then turning back looking once more at the two plastic sticks. "What the hell am I, going to do now?" Mary bit her tongue, debating how to respond. Before she could answer any of the questions Natalee spoke. "This baby will be born in February." Mary nodded. "Jake and the baby will only be one year apart." Mary nodded again. "I will turn forty before this one is due." Mary nodded once again. "Mary damnit, aren't you going to say anything?'

"Nat, what do you want me to say?" Her friend pulled out a chair, leading Natalee to sit down and gave her a glass of juice. Mary sat next to her, waiting for her best friend to tell her what really scared her. Mary announced. "First thing I am going to do is text Joe and tell him you are here and safe, then we are going to figure this out." Sending the quick text. His response came quickly. Pouring herself a glass of wine. "Nat, we have to talk, you can't hold this in.

"I know, it's all his fault, don't you?'"

"What do you mean? You were the one who forgot to take your pills when you ran away like a teenager." Mary was quickly moving past irritated to full blown anger.

"Yes, that was clearly my fault. I am talking about Joe for coming into my life a year ago and weaseling his way in and completely changing everything." Natalee dramatically demonstrating a hand fish swimming. Mary fought the urge to laugh at the absurdity of the situation. Natalee continued. "I had a quiet, calm, orderly life with time for myself until he came in and mucked it all up." Mary laughed, then giggled, snorting, then a full belly laugh. Natalee quickly became angry. "Are you finished yet?" She asked her laughing, friend.

Mary replied. "Are you? Do you even hear yourself? What Joe did was fall in love with a sad lonely woman in a very clean and orderly house that was afraid to love again due to fear of loss. You now have love that you never knew and a family instead of a mother and child. Nat, you are happy even if you don't want to realize it."

"But I wasn't going to have another child, I told him that."

"Yes, we all remember quite well what you told him. But guess what, fate gave you Jake, and one to grow on. Sounds like you should have spent more time telling fate what you didn't want instead of Joe." Mary stood, clearly exhausted by the year long, conflict. "Nat, I love you but it is time for you to grow up, you finally have the life you wanted in the beginning, you are happy you just have to let yourself see it."

A short time later, armed with her baggie filled proof of the newest change to their already complicated life, she headed for home. Thankful for the support of her best friend and for the man she loves.

"Now all I have to do is tell him." Pulling into the drive, hearing soft strains of music coming from the direction of the backyard. Moving quietly toward her man relaxing in his chair, soft music and the baby monitor nearby as he stared at the water. Interrupting his thoughts. "Hi."

"Hi yourself." Sitting the baggie down next to her purse on the patio as she eased into her chair.

"Did Jake go down okay?"

"Yes, but I really think he likes your singing better than mine." Natalee smiled. Joe asked. "Are we okay?"

Without hesitation, she responded. "Yes."

Nodding as he could not help but still feeling unsure. "What happened tonight?"

"Sorry about that, I had a teensy weensy nervous breakdown." Holding up two fingers close together. "Mary straightened me out. But the source of the breakdown is something we need to talk about." Bending down, she opened the baggie pulling the first stick. "I have some news."

Clearly confused. Showing him the results in the early evening light. "Is that what I think it is?" Nodding. Natalee pulled the next stick, showing the "Yes." Joe read the words. "Lee, this is not funny if this is a joke."

"Nope, no joke."

"How did you know?"

"Throwing up on the boat. Never done that before except when I was pregnant with Jenny."

"When?" Natalee continued to respond to his one word questions.

"Beach house weekend, I forgot my birth control. And well we were not careful."

Nodding, taking a deep breath in when he asked. "What do you want to do? You didn't want another child, we already have one. Do you?" He paused, thinking the words, but could not say them out loud. Natalee stood, climbing into his lap as she laid the baggie on the table.

Taking Joe's hand and placing it on her now flat belly she said. "I want to have a baby with you. I love you. I was a fool to think I could place such restrictions on life, and love. I was afraid and I was a fool. Please forgive me for pushing you away for so long. At least our wedding is planned and I won't be huge by then." Kissing her, holding her tight.

He whispered. "We will make this work. Oh my gosh they will only be a year apart." His eyes open wide, his jaw dropped.

"Yes, it will be nuts."

Joe shook his head. Announcing his first thoughts. "We will never get to have sex again." Laughing.

"With all of my panic I completely forgot about that one." Natalee confessed.

"Well, future Mrs. Costas our son is asleep we should probably take advantage of this situation."

»»

"Oh honey, you look beautiful."

Natalee smiled accepting a hug from Alissa Costas. "Thank you. I am so nervous I really don't know why."

Alissa whispered in her ear. "It is the baby that has you stirred up, he is also responsible for the glow to your cheeks." Surprised Natalee leaned back.

"Did Joe tell you?"

"No, it was obvious when we arrived in town yesterday. I just wanted to make sure, you confirmed my suspicions when the waiter poured you ginger ale in your wine glass last night."

"I didn't want, anyone to notice."

Alissa reassured the nervous bride. "It is okay, no one else did. Your secret is safe with me until you are ready to announce. Everyone will be so pleased. Baby Jake is already the hit of the wedding outside, he is a charmer just like his daddy." Natalee enjoyed her conversation with Joe's proud mother.

"Are you ready, my dear?"

Taking a deep breath. "I think I am."

"Okay I will let them know." Natalee took one last look in the mirror, flashes of memories swam before her eyes, her parents wishing they were here. Thinking briefly to her sister she no longer had contact with, nor her daughter. A flash of pain created a void in her life where her daughter had always been.

"Patrick, I hope I have your blessing for moving on with Joe. And I hope and pray you forgive me for failing our daughter. Please watch out for her. I just want you to know, you are my past and a part of me will always love you. Thank you for loving me and everything you did. It is time for me to move on now." Natalee swiped a lone tear from her cheek, checking her make up one last time when she heard a knock on the door.

"I am ready." The door opened as Natalee turned to see Jenny, beautiful as always in a pale yellow flowing dress, barefoot and holding a matching bouquet to Mary's. "Oh honey, I am so happy to see you."

"Momma, you look so beautiful. I know it's time, I should have gotten here earlier, but I." Natalee interjected. "It's okay. You are here and that is what matters now."

Jenny gave her Mother a hug. "I am going to say one thing then we are going to get you down that aisle. I was wrong, about you and Joe and the baby. I was searching for something that I did not have the maturity to find. I've learned a lot about myself these last few months. I just hope you can forgive me and we can move on." Natalee nodded. "Momma, do not cry it will mess up your makeup. Let's go okay?" Nodding. Jenny stepped onto the porch, looking over her shoulder with parting words. "I would like to know if I could get to know my baby brother?"

Smiling, Natalee whispered. "I would love that."

Epilogue

"What is it with this winter weather? Two years of unrelenting cold winters. We live in the south damn it." Joe laughed at his grouchy, with her wide girth yet still beautiful wife as she propped her feet up on the pillows. "Joseph this is not funny I cannot sit in this bed with nothing to do. Do you hear me? I will go silently insane. I can't do it."

Using his firm, serious tone. "Lee, I love you with all of my heart, and I will do everything in my power to protect you. When the doctor said, bed rest he meant bed rest. You could die. I cannot lose you. Jake needs his momma, and it is not time for baby Alex to make an appearance. My parents are on their way, the bad weather is slowing them down but they will be here. She will help me cook, and dad will help keep an extra eye on your son, that five minutes ago while you were calling for me was trying to do flips off your treadmill. So, for my sanity please, please do something that involves lying in this bed." Joe ran his fingers through his hair. His exhaustion beginning to show.

"Yes sir. I get it you have your hands full and I am just being a baby."

"Yes. You are. So. I have a project for you, that will keep your mind busy and your itchy fingers from anything other than the assignment. Okay."

"I told you I can't write right now it is like my brain is fried. Everything I have written in the past month has been pure junk."

Reassuring her. "I promise it is not writing." Joe walked out of the room returning five minutes later. "Sorry it took me a minute. I was making sure our son had not escaped from his bed when I assumed he was taking a nap. I swear I am going to put a monitor bracelet on that kid yet."

Natalee giggled. "You will not, you will just have to get faster at finding him."

Joe lifted the large bag onto the bed. "This is a project that I thought we could do together and I will be in here with you as much as I can." He slowly opened the large bag and pulled out a beautiful scrap book with an opening on the front for a photo, and the words *"Our Life."* Before his eyes, her face softened, eyes became dewy and a smile came to her lips. Joe continued unloading the bag. Packs of photos, new and old along with mementos of their time together. Lastly, he pulled out their wedding photos. "Natalee, you were such a beautiful bride. That day when you walked down those steps, the breeze softly blowing through your hair in the amazing dress and then I saw your bare pink toes wiggle out at me. All it did was reassure me you are it for me." Tearing up as they went through each photograph together.

"Look at Jake, he was so little. Oh, your grandmother holding him, I am so thankful she is still healthy to meet Alex."

"Are you kidding YaYa, is going nowhere, she is a tough old bird." Natalee pinched him, then kissed his cheek. Joe laid back beside her as they stared longingly at the photograph of their first dance.

"You know you were a pretty hot groom."

"Yes, I was." Laughing and remembering the memories he could not help but wonder what would have happened if he had not gone to the party at Leo's two years ago.

She interrupted his thoughts with, "Do you think February will ever get here?"

Laughing. "Yes, my beautiful bride. Ten more days then they will pull baby Alex into this world kicking and a screaming and then we will never get to sit down and eat, watch tv or have to have a babysitter so that we can get alone time."

"Ha, I knew it, you are already feeling sorry for yourself because the doc said no sex."

"You know what you do have pregnancy brain, because you miss it as much as I do. And now I have a sink full of dirty dishes and a son that will awaken at any minute. So, you do your assignment. Bye."

He gently kissed her lips, touching her expanded belly then walked towards the door, hearing behind him. "I will love you forever, my pain."

Throwing it back over his shoulder. "Ditto."

www.ingramcontent.com/pod-product-compliance
Lightning Source LLC
Chambersburg PA
CBHW032138170626
46808CB00006B/2291